FORTUNES OF FATE

Jean Walker

1

Cover photograph by courtesy of
LYNDA WILSON
Taken in the lanes around her
beautiful home in North Wales
during the Covid pandemic of 2020

Only an amateur photographer
but a very talented one

Thank you for giving me
permission to use your images

CHAPTER 1

Frank and Alison Lacey dozed in their armchairs either side of the fireplace, Frank's newspaper having slid to the floor long ago, where it lay half in and half out of the fireplace. The fire had burned low, but the room was warm, and they'd both slept for some considerable time. Outside, the light was beginning to fade as evening drew near, and the remains of the sunset could still faintly be seen receding into the encroaching darkness.

The air raids over Liverpool had come thick and fast during the past week, fortunately not over their particular area, but over the town centre and the docks, causing a considerable amount of damage, and disrupting businesses badly; but there was every chance that the next one could drop bombs anywhere on or around the city.

They'd hardly had any sleep at all during the week, what with the noise and rushing for the shelter when the sirens sounded, usually just after they'd gone to bed, or just as they were getting ready to. Alison had taken to leaving warm blankets, packets of sandwiches, and a flask of tea near the front door before they went up, just in case they were woken again after retiring; but even as they waited in the shelter, they were still unable to catch more than the odd few minutes of sleep due to the constant noise of aircraft, and the constant bombardment of the bombs exploding near the docks and the town centre.

Frank had tried to enlist at the beginning of the war, but had been turned down due to a heart condition, much to Alison's relief. He'd known nothing about it until he went for the medical, and it had come as a complete surprise. They'd assured him that the condition wasn't life threatening, and his doctor gave him tablets, which he had to keep taking for the rest of his life, but it was enough to preclude him from joining the army, or any of the other armed forces.

Mitigating his disappointment, he'd enlisted his services as an air raid warden, but that too had been curtailed for the moment when he'd cut his leg badly on a piece of jagged timber, and the cut had become infected. Now wrapped in bandages, he had hobbled around for days waiting for it to heal, but it seemed to be taking far too long for his liking, and he was beginning to get fed up with his enforced idleness. Even tending to the vegetable patch which had replaced the small lawn in their tiny back garden was beginning to pall. He'd enjoyed the feeling of satisfaction he'd got when their first crop of potatoes and carrots was ready to eat, and later on felt even more satisfied with the peas and runner beans, interspersed with salad vegetables, when they too were ready for eating, but now he longed to be doing something more useful.

Alison had also asked him build a small hen coop alongside the outdoor lavvy, which had taken up his interest for a while, and where she now kept half a dozen hens. They were able to enjoy an egg for their breakfast most mornings, but the toast that they ate with it had become most unpalatable just lately. He'd heard that the government had instigated the addition of other things into the making of bread to conserve what little flour they had, and although it had made it go further, the taste, and more so, the texture, seemed to be getting worse as the weeks went by. It wasn't made any better by the meagre amount of margarine they had to spread on it; butter being almost unobtainable now, except on the black market.

As they continued to doze, they were suddenly both startled awake by a loud bang, followed by the living room door crashing open against the side of the Welsh dresser.

"Dad! Dad!," the imperious voice of their son Callum filled the air. "That factory where you work – it's goin' up in flames!"

"What?" Frank couldn't believe his ears, too sleepy to do much more than look at his son in surprise.

"What's happened? It wasn't a bomb was it? I didn't hear anything?" he continued, trying to clear the sleep from his head.

"Don't know! We was playing football on the playing field, and all of a sudden somebody spotted the flames. They're right up over the roof now!"

Frank was already getting to his feet, gingerly putting the weight on his injured leg as he walked towards the door, ready to follow his son.

Standing on the back doorstep, he looked across the surrounding rooftops and saw the smoke billowing into the air. It certainly looked like Hensons; the factory where he worked as a maintenance man. Callum had already taken off once more through the back gate he'd carelessly left open, calling to his father to follow him.

"Come on, dad, you've got to see it! It's brill! The flames are right up in the air!"

Not so sure that 'brill' was a word he would have used, he edged his way down the path to the back gate and followed him. If it was too bad and the whole factory went up, he'd have no job any more.

The back gate opened onto a small lane at the back of the row of terraced houses, and by turning to the left, they reached the field where the boys had been playing.

Callum joined the small knot of boys who were looking across the field and down onto the dock road long before his father, eagerly waiting for him to catch up.

"Look dad, look!" he cried as Frank reached the group. "It's massive!"

Two fire engines were already standing in the factory grounds, but some way from the actual blaze, and another was just making its way towards it, the clang of its bell seeming loud in the hushed evening air.

With a sinking feeling in his heart, he did indeed see that the fire was massive, with flames reaching way up into the air, and seemed to be engulfing all in front of them. Would there be anything left after this? Would he have a job to go back to? He very much doubted it!

They stood watching for a while as people came and went from all round the site, before a couple of ambulances arrived, and they saw stretchers being carried in and out, a couple of them covered completely by grey blankets.

So there'd been fatalities as well!

He hoped it wasn't anybody he knew or worked with!

Soon afterwards, he saw the factory owners' car arrive and park near the fire engines, where he hopped out and went over to talk to the crew. They didn't have much time for his questions at that moment, and he was left standing watching the flames take away everything he'd worked so hard to build up. Although Frank had never had much to do with the man, and held no opinions about him, at that moment, he felt very sorry for him.

As if it wasn't bad enough to have the war to contend with, this would be an even harder blow for him.

Eventually, his leg beginning to ache after having stood on it for so long, he had to admit defeat and hobble home.

"Come on, Callum, time to go home," he said, "it's too dark to play football now, and I'm sure your mates will want to be going home too," looking towards them with a commanding eye.

They all grinned and began to drift off home as he and Callum made their way back together.

"What's going to happen to your job now, dad?" Callum asked.

"I've no idea," Frank said. "I have to see the doctor next week, and he'll tell me if I can go back to work – that's if I still have a job to go back to!"

Then more brightly he continued.

"There's one good thing though. I'm a qualified engineer, and if the factory can be saved, I'll be one of the ones needed to get it back on its feet again."

Callum, no longer so excited, was now matching the much slower steps of his father, and they walked back together, opening the kitchen door just as Alison was putting the kettle on the stove.

"You timed that well!" she greeted them. "I was just going to make a drink – and I'm sure you won't say no to a biscuit to go with it!"

"A biscuit?" they both chorused.

"Yes," she laughed, "a biscuit! Mrs. Holmes, the old lady at number 4, has just had to have all the rest of her teeth out, and she can't eat them until she can manage to get some false ones. She doesn't know how long that'll take, so she's given me the last of her biscuits. There's just one each!"

"Wow!" Callum whooped. "I haven't had a biscuit in ages. What sort are they?"

"Only plain ones, I'm afraid," his mother answered, "but you'll have to count yourself lucky you've got that! There haven't been any biscuits for sale in the shops for weeks."

Later that evening, just as they were getting ready for bed, the air raid warning sounded again, and with a disgruntled sigh, they had to shrug their way back into their clothes and hurriedly make their way to the shelter once more. Luckily, it was only a short distance away at the end of the street, but once more they'd have to spend another cramped night wedged in with their neighbours and strangers alike.

Unlike previous nights though, bombs rained down much nearer to them; nearer than they'd ever been before.

Realising what was happening; Frank leaned over and spoke conspiratorially to Alison.

"The factory must still be burning – they're probably using that as a beacon to aim their bombs at!"

She nodded.

"Yes, you're probably right. Let's hope it doesn't take a direct hit, otherwise your job will really have gone up in smoke!"

"Not only that," he continued in a much quieter voice. "There's an oil storage depot only a couple of hundred yards away from it. If they hit that ... !!"

More subdued by this thought, they both settled down to listen and try to ascertain where the bombs were landing, but in the cacophony of sound all around, they were unable to ascertain very much.

After a couple more hours of furious bombardment, the sound of planes overhead eased off, and they began to think the raid was coming to an end, but all of a sudden they heard the sound of a single plane overhead. It seemed very low, almost skimming the rooftops, and as it passed overhead, they heard a loud whistling sound near at hand, getting louder as it drew nearer. The sound of the plane passed over, but the sound of the descending bomb became louder.

A hushed murmur began to ripple through the gathered throng. Everybody knew what this meant, all looking upwards and holding their breath in fearful anticipation. Suddenly there was silence; everyone wondering if their last hour had come, before, seconds later, an almighty bang split the air around them.

The whole building shook with the impact, and dust fell from the roof, covering everyone in a fine layer, causing them to cough and splutter, as people began jumping up in sheer panic. No bombs had yet landed anywhere near this area before!

Someone ran to the door, anxious to get out in case the shelter was about to collapse as others rose to their feet, clinging onto their children, and ready to get out of there as soon as they could; but before the panicked rush could begin, the door was thrust open. The shelter, being a few feet below street level, had five steps leading upwards to the entrance, so the ARP wardens were clearly visible in the doorway.

They wore their heavy greatcoats, tin helmets on their heads, and gas mask bags slung over their shoulders. They were covered from head to foot in a thick layer of dust and debris.

"Everybody ok?" they called. "Don't panic – you're safe enough here. It landed lower down the street, but we're not sure if it's over yet. Stay here and wait for the all clear, we're just on our way to see if anybody's been hurt."

Of those nearest to the door, some peered out after them, not sure if they were being told the truth, but eventually came back in, confirming that everything was as they'd been told.

A man by the door stood up and assumed control.

"Everybody sit back down and stay calm until the all clear sounds. It's almost five minutes since a plane went over, so it's probably all finished now. I reckon the one that just hit here was a Luftwaffe pilot getting rid of the one he had left. He didn't want to go back to Old Man Hitler and say he hadn't dropped one!"

A titter of laughter rippled around, but most were far too anxious about whether it might have been their house that had been hit to feel any kind of humour about the situation.

The scene of chaos that greeted them after the 'all clear' had sounded was utterly pitiful, and reduced many of them, even those not directly affected by the bomb, to tears.

Further down from the shelter, one house had taken a direct hit, the bomb landing fair and square in the centre of the roof, the subsequent collapse and explosion blowing away most of the houses on either side, and rendering the adjoining walls to their neighbours in a precarious condition.

One bomb had, by the way it had landed, rendered three houses to rubble, and the adjoining two unstable.

Bricks, slates, smashed bits of furniture, and items of clothing littered almost the whole street, and the remnants of a child's tattered dress was fluttering forlornly from the cross members at the top of a lamp post, almost fifty yards from where the bomb had landed. The frayed remains of the local children's rope swing hung idly below it.

A water main had taken some of the blast, and a fountain of water was spurting many feet up into the air immediately in front of the demolished house, beneath which a dead cat lay sprawled out on the pavement, nearly all its fur singed off. The water was running sideways now, filling up the gaps between the piles of debris, and beginning to form a stream running down the road.

Two air raid wardens were carrying a canvas stretcher up the pavement; covered by a tattered eiderdown with the filling hanging out; the only thing they'd been able to find to cover the bloody mangled corpse beneath it.

Frank, knowing both men, stopped to ask them if they knew who it was as they passed. Their reply was none too savoury!

"Looks like an old woman, but we can't tell for sure as her face and most of her head have been blown off. We picked her up outside number four if that's any help – the one next door to the direct hit."

Frank returned to where Alison was waiting with Callum.

"Did you see Mrs. Holmes in the shelter?" he asked.

"No, I don't remember seeing her," she mused, thinking back, and then suddenly turning to him once more as she realised what he was implying. "That wasn't her on the stretcher was it?"

He shifted his eyes towards his son, who seemed to be busy taking in the scene in front of him and not paying

11

any attention to them, before lifting them back to her, and giving a slight nod.

"It could have been," he answered more quietly now, not wanting his son to hear. "It was an old woman and they found her outside number four."

Alison gasped.

"She mustn't have been able to get to the shelter in time! I remember her saying she was having trouble with her arthritis when she gave me the biscuits. She must have been caught out before she could get there!"

Frank nodded gravely.

"Nothing we can do for her now! At least she won't have any more trouble with her arthritis, and she won't be needing those new teeth anymore either!"

It wasn't meant to be funny, but it did manage to lighten the atmosphere surrounding her death.

The stretchers containing the dead were laid out on the pavement and covered with whatever was to hand, awaiting identification. The makeshift ambulances, of which there were only two available, were being used to treat the injured, and to whisk the more seriously injured of them away to hospital.

Luckily, there'd been plenty of warning beforehand, and most people had been in the shelter when the bomb landed, so there were only a few casualties, none of them seriously injured.

The most serious of those was a lady who had fallen when leaving the shelter and gashed her arm on a piece of jagged timber, the rest were just minor cuts and bruises.

'Old Bob', as everybody called him, had been making his way home from the pub, in a somewhat inebriated state, having just turned the corner of the road on his way to the shelter, when the bomb landed. He'd managed to throw himself flat on the ground just before the blast, somewhat aided by his intoxicated state, but had been unable to get up unaided from the amount of debris that had landed on him, spluttering and coughing his way up into the fresh air as everything was lifted from around him.

Another warden arrived shortly afterwards.

"Quiet please!" he shouted at the top of his voice, stilling the voices all around him, continuing only when a modicum of silence had been achieved.

"I only want to have to say this once, so please, everyone listen! My throat is hoarse enough as it is!"

All eyes were now turned on him, waiting to hear what he was about to say.

"St. Andrews church hall is being opened, where you can all spend the night until we've assessed what damage has been done, and which homes can safely be occupied once more. The ladies from the WVS will be here in the morning to provide you with some food, so please remain in the hall until you are told it's safe for you to return to your homes. We'll try to get back to you as soon as we can and thank you for your patience.

So please, make your way to the church hall now," and he stood aside, showing with a wave of his arm the way to the hall; most already knowing where it was.

Blankets and possessions were retrieved from the shelter and they hurried up the road, where the vicar met them.

"Welcome everyone," he said. "I'm glad to see you've all come through the ordeal unharmed, and I hope you all manage to get some sleep. I and my helpers will be on hand if you need anything, so please feel free to ask if you're in need.

The toilets are through there, although there are only four, so please be patient and give way to someone who's more desperate than yourself."

There was a titter of laughter, not appropriate under the circumstances, but more productive than crying, as they all found a place for themselves and prepared to bed down for what was left of the night.

CHAPTER 2

The night was an uncomfortable one, as they had to snatch what little sleep they were able to on the hard wooden floor, conversation taking up most of the night. Few managed any sleep, wondering if they'd have a home to go back to next morning.

At least when the ladies from the WVS arrived next morning, they brought with them some good-sized helpings of porridge for everyone, and plenty of hot tea, although they could only offer saccharine for those with a sweet tooth; there was no sugar, and only a tiny amount of powdered milk available. They also brought with them a good-hearted cheerful banter, which lifted everybody's spirits for the time being.

It was nearly lunchtime before the man they had seen the previous night arrived back once again, with the ubiquitous clip-board in his hand, and began to reel off the house numbers which could safely be occupied again, although he issued a warning to be careful approaching their homes as the street hadn't been fully cleared of debris at this stage. He also warned of broken glass, as the windows facing the street had been blown in by the blast and there may be lots of glass inside their homes.

Luckily, Frank and Alison's house was one of those listed, as they were further down and on the opposite side of the street, but it was a sorry sight that greeted them as they arrived back.

Groups of men were busy clearing debris into whatever means of transport they had, and carrying it to an open backed lorry, which took away as much as it could carry on each trip.

The water main was still flowing, and the pool in the road had become a lot bigger, although being on a slight incline, it was beginning to flow slowly away. A lot of sandbags had also split open, and if it hadn't been in the middle of a street of houses, it could have looked as if they were at the seaside.

The pavements had also been cleared to a certain extent, and it was now possible to walk along them safely, although the front of three houses almost opposite the bomb damaged one had been cordoned off, their roofs in imminent danger of collapse. A space had been cleared in the roadway for people to walk around, but unfortunately, it hadn't been possible to clear all the water away yet, and sandbags had been strategically placed, through which water still seeped and their feet were still getting very wet as they walked through it.

As they stood watching, a man in a long sacking apron and pushing a handcart turned into the street, and stopped near a pile of rubble. He began rummaging through, but they noticed that he wasn't just helping to remove rubble; he was sorting through and loading only items that could be of further use.

"What's he doing?" Alison voiced her suspicious thoughts out loud.

"I hope he's not looting," Frank said, "but I rather think he might be."

Just as he spoke, the warden in charge also noticed what the man was doing, and stood up from where he was working. He stretched his aching back for a few moments while he watched the man, before he walked over to him.

"Oi!" he said. "I 'ope you're not looting 'ere. It's against the law y'know."

By this time, some of the other workers had heard what was going on, and they too stopped to watch the scene.

The man stopped what he was doing and laughed in a good natured way.

"No mate, not me," he replied. "These 'ouses all belong to Liverpool Corporation. I'm just collecting any useful bits and pieces that we can use to fix other damaged 'ouses. 'Ere, 'ere's me authority," he continued, handing over a grubby piece of paper. "I'm just gonna' take these bits back to the yard when I've finished and let them sort froo' it for anythin' they need."

The warden seemed satisfied with this explanation as he folded the piece of paper and gave it back to him.

"Okay," he replied, "I'll tell the others and if they find anything useful, we'll 'and it over! Anythin' to 'elp out the Corpy!"

"Thanks mate!" the man replied. "Just stick it in the cart and I'll take it away."

Alison, losing interest in the shouted conversations going on around her, and eager to see their own house, had already made it to the front gate, and was surveying the damage.

Although the windows at the front had all been criss-crossed with sticky tape, most of the glass had been shattered by the blast, and that that wasn't still stuck to the tape was lying in the small area at the front. The side windows of the small downstairs bay hadn't fallen out, being a little more sheltered, but were completely crazed and cracked.

The two upstairs sash windows were also devoid of glass, and both of their stone ledges had broken away from the brickwork, looking ready to crash down at the slightest tremor.

Opening the front door, whose six smaller stained glass panels had luckily eluded breakage, they let themselves into the tiled vestibule.

The inner door with its stained glass panels to the upper half had also come through the blast unscathed, partly due perhaps to it having been left open during their rush to get to the shelter. Alison had always admired this door, and the workmanship that had created it, glad that it had weathered the ordeal, as had the hallway and the staircase.

The front room, however, was a different matter!

It had always been used as a dining room, the table now having been thrown against the opposite wall, and losing two of its legs. Some of the four chairs which stood around it had also been damaged, and two of them were missing legs. It hadn't been a very expensive piece of furniture, so she wasn't too bothered about its loss. They'd bought it when they married, and always intended to replace it with a better one when they could afford to.

The wooden fire screen with its central glass panel which had once contained a picture of tulips and daffodils lay in pieces in the hearth, surrounded by paper, sticks and coal which had been laid ready to light the fire.

Broken glass littered everywhere – some of it from the broken bay window, and some of it from the mirror which had hung above.

"I'm too tired to bother with that now," she sighed, as she peeped into the living room and kitchen at the back of the house, both comparatively unscathed. "Let's all try and get some sleep first."

Their bedroom, also at the front of the house, was a mess of broken glass and debris, and so they both slept in Callum's bed at the back, bringing in the mattress from the single bed in the front room for him to sleep on.

Not being used very often, this bed had been covered in a dust sheet, and it was only the work of a moment to lift all four corners, enclosing the glass within, and lifting the whole thing onto the floor.

The clearing up still continued in the road outside, but being in the back of the house, they were far enough away for it not to disturb them, and so all managed a good few hours sleep.

It was already early evening when Alison awoke, still drowsy from so much lack of sleep, and wondering for a moment where she was; Frank and Callum still sleeping soundly.

She put on her dressing gown and wandered downstairs, peering round the dining room door once more to assess the amount of work that needed doing, and seeing the men outside still clearing away the rubble.

Then she wandered into the tiny little kitchen and made herself a cup of tea and some toast, which she took into the living room to eat, glancing out of the window to see how things had fared out there.

The vegetables were still intact, as was her small chicken coop and all the hens, which seemed none the worse for wear, although rushing around and clucking wildly as they saw her at the window. She usually fed them after breakfast each morning, and realised that she hadn't done so that day. During all that had happened, she'd completely forgotten them.

19

Finishing her tea and toast, she picked up their feed and filled the small bucket she used for water, before making her way down the yard to see to them.

"You all right?" she heard a voice say, seemingly from nowhere.

Looking up she saw her neighbour, Lena, peering over the high wall which marked the boundary between each garden.

"Hello, Lena," she said. "We're fine – just some broken windows at the front. How about you?"

"We're all fine too. Tom was down the pub last night, so he was in a different shelter to me. We wuz both worried about the 'uvver, but he made it home long before me and 'eed done some of the clearing up before I got back."

"We've got it still to do! We just went straight to bed this morning – we've hardly had any sleep this week!"

Lena sympathised.

"I'll give you an 'and if you like. Tom had done most of ours before I got back, so I don't 'ave much more to do."

"Thanks, but I'm not doing anything today – it's too late now. I'll try and get down to it tomorrow. Just now I need to give them something to eat," she said, inclining her head towards the back door where Frank had just appeared in the doorway.

Lena greeted him, and with a cheery wave and a shouted "tarr'ar lad," she disappeared, climbing down from where she'd been standing cursing loudly as the bucket clattered down the yard.

Alison had collected some eggs from the hens while they were busy eating and there were enough for two each, so she made them all poached eggs, glad to find that they still had a gas supply, together with some peas which Frank had found whilst checking his vegetables. There were only enough for a tablespoon each, but together with the eggs, it was enough to suffice, and she'd also found a tin of peaches which they finished off with.

While she washed up, Frank, standing at the back door and surveying the vegetable situation, turned back to her.

"It's just starting to rain," he observed. "The heavens are completely clouded over, so there might not be a raid tonight."

"Thank heavens for that," she said. "We might as well get back to bed and catch some more sleep while we can."

At the end of a week of wet and miserable weather there'd been no more raids, and they managed to make the house more habitable, although all the front windows were still boarded over, and Frank took Callum with him to check on the factory.

He'd seen the doctor, who'd declared him fit to go back to work once more, and he was anxious to see if there was any job for him to go back to.

He found fencing all around the site, with two padlocked gates at the front, and there appeared to be no sign of anyone in attendance. The factory itself, being of brick construction, although blackened on the outside, and with its roof having collapsed, seemed to be still standing and fairly well intact.

He called out to see if there might be anyone inside, but his calls went unanswered, and having walked as far as he could down another of its sides, he finally gave up and returned to the road.

He stood at the gates and called again, but still received no answer. Turning to go home, he almost bumped into someone coming towards him.

"'Ullo Frank," the voice said. "You ready to come back to work then, are you?"

It was Ted Freeman, another fitter that he'd worked with for some years.

"I'm ready – but are they ready for me?" he quipped good-naturedly, gesturing with his head back to the factory.

"I doubt it'll ever be ready again," Ted replied. "Looks like you and me's wiv'out a job for the foreseeable."

"It doesn't look too bad," Frank said, glancing back towards the building.

"No, the outside doesn't," Ted said, "but I believe the inside's shot at. All the machinery inside's ei'ver burnt or melted, and no chance of replacing it at any time soon while this war's on. Looks like we're all gonna' 'ave to look for 'uvver jobs – and that's gonna' be a job and an 'alf in itself. I been the job centre meself, and there's nuttin' doin'."

Sadly, Frank returned home to give Alison the news, while Callum decided to call on his mates and go down to the town centre to see what was happening there.

"How are we going to pay the rent with no money coming in?" Alison said, almost in tears when she heard the news, but he could only shrug his shoulders.

"I can't answer that," he said. "We've little in savings, so I'll have to ask around and see if there are any more jobs going.

If not, I'll have to go down the Labour Exchange and see if there's any dole money to be had."

Glumly, he knew there wasn't much chance of either in the immediate future!

In the meantime, Callum and his friend Ian had gone into the town alone, not finding any of their other mates around.

They were both astounded by the amount of devastation they came across, and it was almost impossible to make progress anywhere, spending most of their time standing and staring.

The shops in the major shopping centre were devastated; windows blown out, walls collapsed, roofs missing, and what was left of their stock littered the road. Fires burned everywhere, and nobody seemed to be doing anything about them, but there weren't enough workers around to cope with everything, most of them still busy elsewhere, although everyone was working flat out.

Many buildings had collapsed altogether under the bombardment, and their debris filled the wide roads from one side to the other.

Workmen clambered precariously over timbers, bricks, and other detritus, trying to reach burst water and gas mains, whilst volunteers from the medical profession, as well as those less qualified, helped the injured during the course of the work – mainly cuts and grazes, but occasionally the odd broken limb; and the piles of dead and dying found under the rubble kept growing all around. The living mattered more – the dead would just have to wait!

Luckily, the Infirmary wasn't too far away and the more seriously injured were conveyed there by whatever means possible, but there were so many that a lot died before they were able to reach it, or before the staff found time to treat them.

Callum and Ian tried to make their way through the debris in order to stand and watch what was going on, but they were shouted at so many times to 'get away home before you get hurt', that they eventually decided to do just that.

Tram lines had been ripped up throughout the city, and there were none running, so they had to walk once again, although by this time becoming tired.

Just outside the town centre, they found some small stalls set up alongside the road selling mainly garden produce, but some also selling bric-a-brac and trinkets. They both stopped to take a look, and Callum noticed one stall near the back on which stood a fire screen.

It was very like the one his mum had that had been smashed in the bomb blast, and he went over to take a closer look.

Seeing his interest, and having no other customers, the woman behind the makeshift stall came forward and hovered nearby.

"How much is that?" he eventually asked, making up his mind to buy it for her if he had enough money.

"You can 'ave it for sixpence," she said.

She had intended to try and get ninepence, or even a shilling for it, but seeing that nobody else had shown any interest in it during the day, she decided she might as well let him have it a bit cheaper to get rid of it.

He turned out his pockets, but all he found were four penny pieces.

"Ian," he said, "have you got two pennies I can borrow?"

"No," Ian replied, "I got no money."

Sadly, Callum began to turn away.

"Sorry, I've only got fourpence," he said.

Seeing a sale evaporating before her eyes as they walked away, she called out to him.

"'Ere, luv', it's nearly the end of me day, and I don't wanna' 'ave to cart it 'ome again. Give us your fourpence and yer can 'ave it."

Overjoyed at how happy his mother would be when she saw it, he quickly whipped the money out of his pocket and handed it to her, not having given a thought to how he was going to get it home.

He was never to know that his mother had always hated that firescreen and was glad to see the back of it. It had been a wedding present from Frank's parents, and he'd insisted that they keep it on display in case they called on them at any time.

It was quite large and cumbersome, and heavier than he'd expected, and although he was able to tuck it under his arm at first, it was so heavy that he had to keep changing arms every so often.

Remembering his manners, he turned to thank her for letting him have it so cheaply; just at the same moment as a man emerged from a cart behind her.

The man looked familiar as he stood and looked at the boys, and for a moment Callum couldn't place him, but just as he turned away, he remembered where he'd seen him before. It was the man who'd been collecting things after the bomb had been dropped in their street - it was the man who'd said he was collecting things for the 'Corpy' so they could repair other properties!

So he hadn't been collecting for them at all – he **had** been looting!

CHAPTER 3

Twelve months later found them living in a large wooden shed in the fertile farmlands north of Liverpool.

Frank hadn't been able to find a job, and Alison, not having worked since her marriage, had also had to seek employment, but neither had had much success, other than temporary jobs which had lasted just a few short days, or perhaps a week if they were lucky. Unable to pay the rent any more, they had had to move out of the house.

Luckily, he remembered Uncle Ben, and wrote to ask if he needed help on the farm, and if so, did he have any accommodation they could use. He remembered on previous visits Uncle Ben saying it was always hard to find enough help during the picking and harvesting time, and crossed his fingers for a favourable reply.

Both were from farming backgrounds. Ben Lacey, his fathers' brother, had eventually written back and offered them use of the shed on his farm, in return for a small wage and their labour.

Having been used previously during the summer months by itinerant workers digging and picking the crops, it was cold and draughty during the winter months, but Frank's skills as an engineer soon brought them some comfort and a bit more warmth from an old wood stove he'd found in one of the barns. His uncle said he'd forgotten it was there, so agreed that they could have it.

It was a bit smoky at first, but Frank soon found a way of conducting the smoke outside, and left them with just the warmth it produced.

There was always plenty of wood to be collected from the nearby woodland, which his uncle also owned, and they were never short of fuel for it. Ben was glad of someone to maintain the area, and they also provided him with wood for his own fire, by way of recompense for the greater amount they used.

Callum also became adept at snaring rabbits, and they were always a ready supply of food for their table.

Their days were often long, and the work hard, but at least they had food and a little money in their pockets now, and best of all, no rent to find.

Uncle Ben kept livestock on the farm, and when animals were slaughtered, he often gave them small quantities of meat, or the odd chicken, which he only killed when they were past laying and were often tough. Alison overcame this by making a stew in a pan which she left cooking for hours on top of the little stove. Together with the vegetables he was allowed to take home, this made a tasty meal, and they never went hungry.

Frank had eventually installed another chicken coop at the side of the shed, and they now had twelve chickens, courtesy of Uncle Ben, who'd reared several broods of chicks. They now had an endless supply of eggs; Alison sometimes having some to sell at the farm gate.

She left an honesty box when she couldn't be there, and it never seemed to be abused.

Soon after they'd moved in, some prefabricated buildings began to be erected on open land on the opposite side of the road to the farm entrance, and they found that they were to house the displaced residents of the

Liverpool area. Ben soon began to find them a ready-made source of income for the vegetables he produced.

He built a proper stall at the entrance to the farm, putting Alison in charge of it, where she managed to sell everything most days; sales increasing as more and more pre-fabs were finished and became occupied. He still allowed her to sell her own eggs, but topped them up with his own once hers were all sold.

Alison enjoyed it immensely. She had regular customers who came to see her every day, not just to buy produce, but to enjoy a lengthy chat, and her days flew by.

Callum, now having turned fourteen, had left school, and spent his days helping out on the farm with his father and the other labourers, becoming well-muscled and tanned, as did his father.

One day, as they were digging up potatoes and hefting them into the waiting horse and cart alongside, they heard the sound of an aircraft overhead.

The sound grew louder, and they, along with the half dozen other workers, stopped to look up into the sky.

It seemed the plane was getting lower, and it skimmed the field barely fifty feet above their heads. Soon the cry went up "it's a Jerry – everybody down!" upon which they all threw themselves to the ground as the plane circled and turned back towards them.

Wearing brown overalls, they all hoped the pilot wouldn't be able to see them against the brown and sandy soil, but they were too late, he'd already picked out where they were all working.

As he came closer, and much lower than before, the roar became deafening in their ears, and he opened up with his guns, strafing the ground all around the area they'd been working.

After he'd passed over, Frank ventured to look up, just in time to see him turning and coming back for another pass.

"Keep down," he shouted. "He's coming back!"

This time the plane passed even lower still, but after a short burst, the guns cut out and he seemed to be out of ammunition, turning at the end of the next field and disappearing from sight.

Frank stood up and shook the dirt off him.

"You all right son?" he inquired of Callum, who was also shaking himself down alongside him.

"Yes dad, I'm okay," he replied.

Turning towards the rest of the workers, already picking themselves up, he asked the same question, to which most replied in the affirmative.

One lady had a nasty cut on her cheek, but it hadn't been caused by a bullet, just by a stray stone that had been thrown up and had caught her a glancing blow.

Suddenly, a shout came up from the far side of the field, near the hedgerow, and they turned to look.

"Marion's caught it! I think she's dead."

Hurrying over they found that Marion was indeed dead! The bullet had caught her fair and square in the middle of her back and passed right through her body. She'd probably died instantly!

Knowing they had to get her back to the farm somehow, and unable to find anything more suitable, they had to resort to lifting her lifeless body onto the potato cart. Not a very reverent way to carry her, but the only one available at the present moment. Whilst he and the other workers returned to the potato picking, Frank and Callum trotted the horse back to the house in order for Ben to inform the authorities.

"I don't know about you," Frank said, "but my heart's gone out of doing anything more today. Shall we go back to the shed and see if we can have a meal ready for your mum when she gets back."

"Yes, ok," Callum agreed, and they walked back together in silence, both thinking how quickly and easily a life could be lost. Marion was only 25.

It was later found that Marion's husband, a soldier serving with the armed forces in France, had been killed just two days before, and in his pocket was a letter from her. It informed him that she was pregnant, and she hoped he would be as happy as she was about the imminent birth of their first child.

Frank had caught a rabbit yesterday and cleaned it ready for their dinner that night, so he jointed it and made a stock with the bones, before removing them and setting the meat to boil with some vegetables.

When half past five arrived and Alison still hadn't come back, they began to wonder where she could be. She had usually sold all her stock by four o'clock and was already back and had a meal prepared when they arrived, which could be anything between six and eight o'clock.

When another hour had passed with still no sign of her, Callum volunteered to walk down to the gate and see why she was so late. When he arrived, the stall had the shutters pulled down over the front of it and there was no sign of her.

Thinking she might have gone up to the farm to speak to Ben, he walked back up the track, but when he got there, Ben said she hadn't been there at all that day, and the last he'd seen of her was when he took some more vegetables and eggs down to her around midday.

Wondering where she could be, Callum called her name across the fields as he walked back to the shed, but there was no answering call, and she still hadn't returned when he arrived back.

By this time, Frank had also become anxious, and as the sun was now beginning to set, they decided to walk the fields, each taking a different one and calling her name as they went.

After fifteen minutes had elapsed, Frank eventually entered the farthest side of the potato field from where they'd been working that day, still calling her name, and still receiving no answer.

This side of the field, having been planted later than the other, still contained potato plants less than knee high, and it was amongst these that he finally came across her, sprawled face down amongst the plants.

Another of the German pilot's bullets had found its target in the back of her head! Perhaps she'd been coming to speak to him for some reason, but he was never to find out why.

The German plane was found the next day in a field twenty miles south east of them, the young pilot still in his seat. It appeared that not only had he run out of bullets on that fateful day, but he'd also run out of fuel. And his luck, as well!

His mistake was put down to a faulty fuel gauge, but many wondered if it hadn't just been that, but his youthful exuberance in trying to take as many lives as he could before returning to base in order to brag about his exploits.

CHAPTER 4

All the life seemed to go out of Frank after Alison's death and he was morose and moody, not seeming to find anything worthwhile any more. He carried on with his daily tasks like an automaton, but the spark had gone out of his life, and he took no real interest in anyone or anything.

Callum, also feeling her death badly, felt his disinterest, not only in what was going on around him, but also in himself. He often ignored him, and left many of the chores to him, letting him become his fathers' carer, and not the other way round.

When they returned from their days' work, he was left to find something to put together for a meal, his dad often just sitting outside and brooding, either whittling away at a stick, or just staring into space, not caring whether they ate or not.

Ben, seeing the way things were with them, provided them with more pieces of meat, and the occasional strips of bacon, together with the odd loaf of bread his wife made, but he was unwilling to do any more. It was time Frank began to pull himself together. Although his wife was gone, he still had a child to care for!

It was just as the last days of summer were upon them that a band of gypsies arrived and camped in some nearby woods.

Ben wasn't pleased at first with their presence, fearing trouble from them, but as they soon offered cheap labour to bring in the last of the summer produce in exchange for food for themselves, he agreed to give them a chance.

Although a bit come-day, go-day, in their attitude to work, arriving when they felt it, and going in the same manner, there were enough strong hands to complete the work in the days before winter arrived.

He also noticed the odd chicken disappearing from his coop, but as he had plenty of them now, he didn't make too much fuss as they also caught plenty of rabbits, helping to make that ongoing problem more manageable. Rabbits often decimated sizeable areas of his crop, particularly in digging up his carrots, and nibbling the leaves of his cabbages. The digs and scrapes they made in the fields were often a hazard to the horses pulling wagons or the plough.

Frank seemed to get on well with their leader, a big swarthy, dark-skinned man called Giovani, wearing an earring in one ear, and with long black hair. He was very Italian looking, and in the fullness of time, he discovered that he was descended from an Italian family.

For a short while, Callum was glad to see him beginning to come out of his shell, but that was short-lived when he visited the gypsy encampment with him one evening at his father's insistence.

Although fiercely loyal to their families, and to other members of their clan, they were intolerant of newcomers and regarded everyone with suspicion.

Truth be told, Callum was rather afraid of them!

His fathers' apparent friendship with Giovani broke the ice however, and they found themselves being accepted more and more as time went on, although Callum declined his father's offers to take him with him on more than one occasion. He found their way of life unacceptable to him, and preferred the company of his own kind, having become friendly with Tommy, Ben's son.

The gypsies never stayed in one place long enough for the children to go to school and most of them were completely illiterate. Likewise with washing! They never had any running water, mostly washing in a stream or lake when there was one available, or just making do with a quick swill in whatever water was to hand, several people often using the same bucket of water.

They never had any compunction about stealing either, and seemed to live by the rule of 'what's yours is mine'. If they found an unlocked door or an open shed, they'd take whatever they could find, and flog it to whoever was willing to buy from them. The children, right from being knee high, followed their example, and so they never knew right from wrong.

One day, completely out of the blue, and without warning, his father told him they were leaving the farm and going out on the road with the gypsies.

"Their life is so uncomplicated!" he announced. "Go where you want, do what you want, and whenever you want; nobody telling you what to do and when to do it. No hard work every day of your life, and plenty of food for the taking! If you want something, you just take it when nobody's looking."

Callum was appalled.

"No dad! I don't want to live like that! You've always taught me to be honest; I can't just steal from other people like that!"

"Do unto others before they do unto you!" was his father's wry comment. "I've always worked hard all my

34

life – and look where it's got me! I've lost my home, and I live in a shed on a farm, working from morning 'til night for a pittance – and now I've lost my wife as well! Why shouldn't I take something back from what life's doled out to me? I want to take back control of my life again, and do what I want to do for a change; not be at somebody else's beck and call all the time."

"I'm not going with you," Callum cried vehemently.

"Oh yes you are," Frank said, standing his ground. "You're only fourteen and you're too young to be left on your own."

"But I don't want to live with them," he tried again, finding himself near to tears. "I like living here."

"Tough!" was Frank's only reply as he marched over to the stove and opened the door to put another log inside. "You're going with me, and that's all there is to it!"

Callum knew it was no use arguing, he knew his father meant what he said.

Maybe he could run away – but where would he go? He worked all day on the farm, and he had no friends or acquaintances away from there. He wondered about prevailing on Uncle Ben to give him a home here with them, but he knew he'd never go against his fathers' wishes. There seemed to be no alternative except to go with him, but he hated the idea of living amongst the gypsies.

They left the farm one evening after work. They packed up their clothes and personal belongings and just walked out of the door with not a word to Uncle Ben or anyone else. His father would never have done that before. He'd always had respect for other people and their feelings.

They were greeted at the encampment with friendship and camaraderie, Giovani clapping Frank on the back and welcoming him, glad to have him join them.

"We leave here tomorrow morning at first light, so you won't be missed for a while," he enthused, showing them to the caravan they'd be occupying.

"This van belonged to my mother, but she died last year, so it's yours if you want it. It hasn't been lived in since she died. The horse, Archie, has pulled it for years, so he'll just follow the rest of us. All you need to do is hold the reins, he'll do the rest."

Opening the back doors, he took down the steps for them and they climbed up into the interior.

There wasn't much room inside.

There were two long bench seats on either side which were covered in cushions, with a small stove tucked into the space at the end, and a frying pan and a saucepan hanging on a couple of hooks alongside. A kettle was balanced on a metal plate attached to the top of the stove.

He showed how the seats lifted, and their belongings could be stowed beneath, but as they'd only brought a haversack and a small suitcase with all the belongings they had, there was just enough room for everything, although it would cause a lot of disruption when trying to get things out. The bunks also contained a pillow and blankets for each bed, and Frank wondered if they'd ever been washed since Giovani's mother had used them. He doubted if they would have been! But at least it was something – they'd never even given a thought as to what they'd use as bedding when they left the farm.

A folding table was stowed alongside one of the bench seats, with a small cupboard above. This turned out to contain one knife, one fork, one spoon, one plate and one tin cup for each person.

When he asked if there were any more, Giovani guffawed loudly.

"Why do you want any more? You can only eat off one plate at a time, and only drink from one cup," and with that, he left them to get acquainted with their surroundings.

Next morning, true to their word, it was just beginning to get light when they heard people beginning to move about.

They hadn't yet found any water for washing, and Frank said it wouldn't hurt to go without for one day, although Callum did insist on cleaning his teeth, using some of the precious water from the kettle which had been filled for them to make tea. Giovani had already told them he couldn't guarantee the waters' purity, and to boil it well before drinking. They gathered it had probably come from a stream, and they would learn later to put it straight onto the stove first thing when they got up so that it would have boiled properly before they made their tea.

Giovani brought them a jug of milk while they were dressing, laughingly saying, "Straight from the udder to your table," and they knew he wasn't joking!

Frank had brought a packet of porridge with them, so they had that for breakfast, together with some ripe rose hips and some blackberries which Frank picked from the hedge next to the van.

"This is the way to live!" Frank declared, wiping the ripe blackberry juice from his chin. "Mother nature will always provide!"

Callum knew that would be true for the summer months, but she wasn't always so ready to provide in the winter!

And winter would be very depressing in this little caravan, with the two of them huddled together round the stove in this small space with no form of entertainment, apart from reading; and what about relieving oneself? It would be cold and icy outside when they needed to go, and every time the door was opened, it would drain out whatever heat they'd accumulated inside.

The prospect was daunting!

Having harnessed the horse for them, showing Frank how to do it as he went along, they moved out two hours later, the little convoy of brightly coloured vans moving slowly in single file along the lanes.

Some of the children ran alongside for a little way, bowling along hoops and shouting loudly; but eventually, becoming tired, they hopped up onto their own caravan wherever they could find a wide enough ledge, and sat dangling their legs as they trundled along.

Several hours later, they stopped and hauled their vans off the road and onto a patch of open ground, where they unharnessed the horses and tethered them to stakes while they grazed. Tea was made over an open fire, and slices of cake were handed round, as they all sat or lay around enjoying the afternoon sunshine, before they once again harnessed the horses and continued their journey.

"Now isn't this the life?" Frank crowed. "Better than hoeing weeds or digging potatoes, isn't it?"

Callum agreed, but wondered how nice it would have been if it had been pouring with rain, which it surely would be a lot of the time.

Eventually, after several more hours of travelling, they seemed to have reached their destination, and they pulled the caravans off the road and onto another patch of flat land in front of some woodland, standing them in a semi-circle facing the road.

"Where are we?" Callum asked Giovani, when he came past the caravan.

"Does it matter?" he laughed. "We've arrived safe and sound, and this is our home until somebody decides it's time to move us on again. If you must know, we're just near Delamere Forest, and there's a nice little village just down the road. We should be able to find work there and earn a bit of money."

True to his word, Giovanni rapped on the door next morning, just as they were finishing breakfast, bringing with him his eldest son, Paolo, a tall eighteen year old, well-muscled and looking very like his father.

"Paolo will go with us today. He is my son, and good and strong. We should easily do a day's work and earn plenty of money with his help."

Frank had noticed an open backed cart trailing behind the caravans, the reins held by different people during the course of their journey, and wondered what its purpose was; now seeing it was this they were to use for forays away from the camp.

Giovani hopped up onto the driver's seat and the big, placid horse trotted patiently towards the village with them all sitting in the back.

When they arrived at the village green, they stopped outside the shop; not yet open. Outside was a small churn of milk left by the local farmer, and Paolo quickly hopped down from the cart and hefted it into the back before anybody saw them. Without a word, Giovani quickly moved the horse on down a small lane alongside the shop to where it crossed a river, and Paolo jumped down once again with the churn, going down the bank and bedding it deep into the water below the bridge, before they returned once more to the village.

By now the shop was just opening up, and the bewildered shopkeeper was standing outside. He knew the farmer always left his milk in the doorway out of the sun, but although he looked around to see if it had been left anywhere else, he could see no sign of it.

"Morning," Giovani called out cheekily as they trundled past. "Nice morning isn't it?"

Thinking they'd just arrived in the village, he didn't suspect them of having taken his milk, and looked up at them.

"You haven't seen a farm cart with milk churns on it, have you?" he asked.

"No," Giovani called back, a picture of surprised innocence. "Perhaps he's a bit late today."

"I've never known him be late before!" the shopkeeper called back, still perplexed.

Giovani chuckled as they moved on.

"They fall for it every time!" he announced. "They never learn!"

By this time, the rest of the village was stirring, and he pulled the cart up outside a large house with a very overgrown hedge, assessing how much work they could get away with, he and Paolo nodding at each other, "Now that looks like our first job of the day," he said, indicating for Paolo to knock at the door, as he hopped down off the back and started to walk up the path.

Knocking loudly on the front door, Paolo pointed out the hedge to the surprised occupant, and asked if he wanted it cut, promising to do a good job for him. Having agreed a price, he went round to the shed and brought out a couple of pairs of shears, and while he was watching, Giovani and Paolo set to on the hedge.

Frank and Callum watched for a bit before Giovani called for them to give a hand clearing up the cuttings.

"Where do we put them?" Callum asked, his arms full.

Checking to see that the house owner had now disappeared inside, Giovanni grinned and indicated a gap at the end of the hedge.

"Just dump them over the wall round the side," was the laughing reply, "he'll never notice until after we've gone."

"But they'll be in the lane," Callum protested.

"That's not our problem, is it?" Paolo said, and both of them laughed. "We only said we'd cut his hedge. We never said anything about clearing the cuttings away!"

Frank merely laughed and told him to get on with it, beginning to carry out the instruction himself, much to Callum's surprise.

When they'd finished and knocked at the door for payment, Callum strolled round the side to see how badly the lane was obstructed while he waited for them, and noticed that the outer side of the hedge hadn't been cut at all, only the inner side and the top.

The owner came out and looked at the job they'd done from the front path, and seeming well satisfied, handed over payment, as Giovani, now sitting back on the cart, prepared to drive off.

"You haven't done the outside," Callum protested as they moved away.

"No, we haven't, have we?" Giovani laughed, eliciting a sly chuckle from his son. "And he won't miss his shears for a bit either!"

All day these botched jobs continued.

One lady had a partly completed rockery in her front garden. Paolo told her they had some stones in their cart left over from another job, and they'd finish it off for her, to which she agreed.

She told them that her husband had started the job a few weeks ago and had pulled a muscle in his back, so wasn't able to continue. She was grateful for their help, as she wanted to get it finished.

Little did she know that they had no stones, and those they used were taken from the top of a neighbouring wall; likewise the plants they planted it with were taken from other neighbouring gardens. This time they took a trowel and a spade with them when they left.

An elderly man gave them some money to collect his order from the village shop. Thinking the shopkeeper might now be suspecting them of taking his milk, they stopped the cart round the corner and sent Callum to collect it on foot, but the man's shopping was never returned to him. Instead they added it to their own little horde of treasures, along with the nice wicker basket he provided to carry it in, and his change.

When they arrived back at the camp in mid-afternoon, they'd amassed quite a haul of items, including an almost brand new child's bicycle which some unwary youngster had left propped against a wall outside his house.

"What are you going to do with all this stuff?" Frank asked. "Most of it's no use to you."

42

"We clean it up and sell it," Giovani replied. "We take it to local markets and sell it to the stall holders, or sell it ourselves at the side of the road. How else do you think we make money?"

Callum found their lack of morality very distasteful. His father had always taught him to be open and honest with his fellow folk, and always to work for his own living. This went totally against the grain, and he couldn't understand why his father was now condoning it.

Unfortunately, as they had no other form of income, he had to go along with the way of life he was now caught up in, but resolved to get away from them as soon as he could.

The next day, they repeated their excursion, this time to a different village, where there were different people to con. They never went back to the same village twice, until all their possibilities were exhausted, and Giovani decided it was time to move on.

This time they moved deeper into the Cheshire countryside, where there was still some fruit and vegetable picking to be done, as autumn was fast creeping up on them

He soon found their idle ways extended to their fellow workers as well, and when a box of apples or pears was left for a few minutes, most of its contents were emptied into their own baskets, with little effort on their part to do any of the picking. Vegetables were also treated in the same manner, and when it was noticed what they were doing, or suspected of doing, they just moved on to the next farm.

Callum noticed that there was also a glut of food on offer in the camp at the same time, probably from the same sources, although he noticed it seemed to be share and share alike amongst their compatriots.

His father also seemed to be accepting their ways more and more, the morality he'd always taught Callum waning as time went by, and he was just as ready to lie and steal as the others these days.

Nor was he averse to stealing into the woods with some of the unattached women, although taking up with another man's wife was strictly outlawed within the community.

Callum's distaste for this way of life was increasing as time went by!

Winter in the camp was as hard and cold as Callum had expected. They had a site in the south of Cheshire where several of the gypsy clans met up and stayed for most of the winter months. The site was a flat meadow, surrounded by trees and bushes, affording plenty of shelter during the worst months of the year, with a clear, clean stream running alongside.

This had been their meeting place since time immemorial; and the only time they paid a farmer for the use of his land.

This was the time when he met Jess!

She was a beautiful girl, dark and swarthy, with long black hair, high cheekbones, a full mouth, and a strong aquiline nose. He was just sixteen, she the same age, and he was smitten for the first time in his life!

The small band of only four caravans arrived whilst they were on their fifth day at the camp, and he noticed her almost immediately. He knew she'd noticed him too as she smiled at him immediately their eyes met.

During his time with the gypsies, he himself had grown taller and filled out, gaining the look of the young adult he was becoming, and he knew he looked older than he actually was.

She seemed to spot him at almost the exact same time and they exchanged a tentative smile, before he met her once again while they were collecting water at the stream in the late afternoon.

Seeing him a little further down, with no one else in sight, she filled her bucket and came towards him.

"Hello," she said. "I'm Jess. I haven't seen you before. Have you joined Giovani since last winter?"

He nodded, his mouth feeling dry, and words failing him.

Seeing his awkwardness, she tried again.

"What's your name?"

"Er . . . Callum," he managed to croak.

"Well, er . . . Callum," she laughed. "I'm only an ordinary human being! I won't bite, you know! That is – unless you want me to!"

And that was the ice broken!

Standing up, he laughed with her at his own comical inability to communicate, and they walked back to the camp together.

They spent a lot of time in each others' company after that. Her mother had miscarried just a week before they arrived, and she had to spend time helping her out, but as he was out early most mornings, just he and his father working together now, he managed to spend most afternoons with her. They had no place to be alone in the evenings, and it was too cold to be outdoors, so they both stayed in their own vans with their families.

One winters' afternoon, there was uproar in the camp.

A small boy had given cheek to his mother, and had received a resounding slap for his troubles. He ran from the van in a fit of temper and humiliation, and by late afternoon, as darkness had begun to fall, he still hadn't returned.

The camp was turned upside down looking for him, but he wasn't to be found, initiating a wider search of the surrounding area, and an hour later, panic grew as he still hadn't been found.

It was by now almost completely dark; cloudy, and no hint of light from moon or stars, and everyone was becoming frantic.

Having searched the surrounding trees and bushes, their thoughts turned to the stream. If he'd fallen into that, he would surely have perished after all the time he'd been missing, and the men turned their attention to walking along its banks.

They carried a couple of railway workers lanterns – consisting of a metal framework with glass panels in the side and holding a candle burning brightly within, which they somehow seemed to have 'acquired' during their travels.

The first place they'd searched was the camp site, but as a couple of hours had passed since that first search, Callum was given the task of searching around it again, in case he'd returned and was hiding somewhere. He could well be thinking he'd be in for a good hiding for the trouble he'd caused.

Several of the women had also joined him in the search, and it was as he walked round the side of one of the vans, peering underneath and not paying attention to where he was going, that he walked into something warm, soft, and unyielding. Unable to stop himself, he pitched forward, realising as he regained his balance, that it was far too large to be a child.

Suddenly, he felt a movement alongside him. In what little light that shone from the lantern hanging at the back of the caravan next to him, he could dimly make out a white face and nose, as the horse looked at him and whickered softly; just as a small sleepy voice came out of the darkness.

"Go to sleep Sandor, it's not time to get up yet."

Picking himself up, Callum patted the horse and called, "Is that you, Billy?"

Someone had now heard the noise and appeared from the back of the van, lifting down the lantern and holding it out towards them.

It threw enough light to see the child curled up between the great shaggy chest and forelegs of the animal – enormous compared to the size of the eight year old child.

Sandor, completely impervious to what was going on around him, continued to chew away contentedly at the nosebag hanging from the side of the van.

The cry that he'd been found reverberated around the camp, and soon Billy's mother arrived, their previous altercation all but forgotten as she scooped him into her arms and whisked him away, encasing them both in the warm shawl she wore around her shoulders. The other searchers, alerted by the noise, also returned to their own vans, an older boy being sent down to the stream to bring back the men, who returned cold, but in good spirits.

Sandor, unperturbed by the noise around him, put his huge shaggy head down onto the ground, his job of protecting the child at an end, and he slept himself.

CHAPTER 5

Spring arrived at last, and blossom began to spring forth on the wild sloes around the field.

Giovani announced one fine, but still rather chilly morning, that he had some business to deal with back on the Lancashire coast, and they would be setting off for there in two days time.

Most of the other groups had already left, and there was only theirs and one other left, that to which Jess belonged.

Callum was pleased to be heading back towards his old haunts, and wondered how far away they'd be from Uncle Ben's farm. He couldn't ask his father, as he might guess what he had in mind, but he did ask Jess to see if she could find out. Her answer surprised him when he found out they'd only be about ten miles to the west of there, an easy walk, one which he should manage well within a day.

That evening, he confided to Jess what he had in mind.

"My father and I lived in a converted shed on Uncle Ben's farm. I want to go back there and see if he'll let me live in the shed again, and go back to working for him. I know my father loves the life of your people, and he won't go with me, but I wondered if you'd be minded to join me, then we could stay together, and you could work on the farm too, and perhaps we could get married when we're old enough."

She was shocked by this sudden outpouring, and then her face fell.

"I can't Callum," she answered sadly. "Our people believe in arranged marriages, and I've been pledged to another since I was two years old."

"What?" he was incredulous. "Do you love him?"

"No," she answered. "I've never even met him!"

More than incredulous, he was now outraged.

"But you can't mean to go through with it! I love you and I want to be with you forever. Don't you love me?"

She looked down at the ground before she nodded.

"Yes," she managed, "I do – very much, but you don't understand the ways of our people. I could never go against my father's wishes or I'd be an outcast from the gypsy community, and I've never lived any other way of life. I probably wouldn't fit in to your ways!"

"Now hang on a minute! If we love each other, wouldn't you be willing to give it a try?"

"And then what?" she answered. "If it didn't work out, my people would never take me back again. You've no idea how traditional their ways are!"

He tried wheedling, and then cajoling, but she was adamant, shaking her head with tears rolling down her cheeks.

"I was born in a caravan and I've lived in one all my life. I've never been in a house more than once or twice in all my life; I think I'd go crazy living in the same place all the time. Please don't keep asking me."

When he got up the next morning she was gone, and enquiries from Giovani found that they'd gone in exactly the opposite direction to the one which they were taking. Her family were going into Shropshire and then on into Worcestershire, where they intended to spend the summer months, and she was to marry her intended, as he put it, at the end of August, on her eighteenth birthday.

Callum was almost frantic when he heard this, but both Shropshire and Worcestershire were big counties, and he had no idea where to start looking for her.

Enquiries around the rest of the families brought no help either. The group he was with had always kept to the northern part of the country, and never ventured further south than Cheshire, so weren't familiar with any more southerly locations.

Next morning, they too started out on their journey to Lancashire, and he knew there wasn't much chance he'd ever see her again.

Now that the weather was better, and the days were longer, they took almost two months to reach the outskirts of Southport, where they were to stay for most of the summer months.

On the second day after their arrival, Giovani took one of the horses, and rode away from the camp, telling Paolo he'd be away for about a week until his business was concluded, and leaving him in charge of the group. His wife, Rosita, he told nothing about his intentions, as was traditional among the gypsy bands.

CHAPTER 6

Jess, dreading the thought of her forthcoming marriage, had agonised long and hard about going with Callum and leaving it all behind. She desperately wanted to be with him, but their lifestyles and upbringings had been so different, she didn't know whether she'd be able to cope with such a change.

Eventually, they reached Worcestershire, her thoughts still going back to what might have been with Callum, and the daunting meeting with Silas.

Her father, Brendan, told her Silas and his father were to arrive at the beginning of July, giving them time to get to know one another properly before the wedding, but it wasn't something she was looking forward to.

It seemed that his mother had died in childbirth some years ago, and Silas was the only child left, his elder brother having died from a kick in the head by an unbroken horse some years earlier.

She spoke to her mother on the subject, but her mother was of no help either; she herself had been the subject of an arranged marriage, and it had worked well for her.

"Callum asked me to marry him before we left. Do you think father would agree. I love him very much and I've never even met Silas."

Her mother was shocked.

"This marriage was arranged many years ago, you can't back out now, your father would never agree. Silas is the

51

son of his cousin, and he promised his parents the two of you would be married when he considered you were ready. It's a good match. Silas will be head of their band of gypsies one day when his father dies. You should count yourself lucky he's willing to marry you. You will produce many fine children to carry on the tradition."

"But I don't want to be a baby machine," she protested. "I want to marry the man I love, not somebody I've never even met before!"

"Tosh!" her mother almost shouted at her. "You should count yourself lucky to have such an opportunity. You'll soon grow to love him. I was promised to your father when I was just a child, and we've managed all right."

She'd never heard this from her mother before, and never knew theirs had also been an arranged marriage.

"And do you love my father now?" she asked.

"Love isn't all that's important," her mother said, somehow evading the question. "He's been good to me, and always provided for you and your sister. If he has occasion to hit out at me in chastisement, it's usually been through some fault of my own."

Jess was speechless, remembering the black eye she'd seen her mother with a few months ago. She said she'd walked into one of the shafts of the caravan when unharnessing the horse. Was that true – or had her father given it to her?

But even before she could ask the question, her mother, realising she'd said too much, changed the subject.

"No more of this nonsense now. It's time to get something on for the men's dinners. Go and pick me some nettle tops to put in the rabbit stew – and mind you put some gloves on. Don't forget that terrible itchy rash you had for days when you forgot to take them last time."

Walking towards the edge of the field, she thought back on what her mother had said.

Thoughts of Callum had gone from her head for the moment.

Had her mother lived all these years with a man she really didn't love – or even known before her marriage?

They'd had five children, two of them, both boys, having died in infancy, and the last being the latest miscarriage, but they'd raised her and her sister, she being the elder.

Had she also just been a baby machine? And did her father really hit her? Apart from the obvious black eye, she'd never seen any other marks on her, or heard any serious altercation between them.

Her mind busy thinking all this through, she bent to the task of picking the nettle tops, remembering to pull on the long gloves first, and didn't notice the two men watching her from the next field.

They'd absconded several weeks ago from the nearby army base and been hiding out in the woods across the road from the gypsy camp. Their platoon was soon to be shipped out to France, and they had no wish to go with it.

Becoming bored with being 'on the run', but not wanting to go back, they'd been glad of the distraction of some pretty faces to look at.

They'd been watching the gypsy encampment for some time, noticing how lovely some of the girls were, and sometimes watching them undressing to wash in the pond away from the camp. Unfortunately for them, the girls all seemed to go there in a group and they hadn't had the opportunity to find one or two on their own, which would have made them fair game for what they had in mind.

Now the perfect opportunity had presented itself, and they watched her intently as she wandered along the line of the hedge.

Eventually, she reached the gateway where they were waiting and as she came within reach, one quickly pulled open the gate, while the other ran through and grabbed her by the arms; pinning them behind her with one hand, and clamping the other over her mouth to stop her screaming.

Completely taken by surprise, she struggled and kicked out, but the other had her feet by now, and they lifted her off the ground and carried her into the screen of some nearby bushes, where the one holding her arms knelt against her shoulders and held her down, whilst the other pulled up her skirt.

Realising she wore no underwear inflamed him even more, and he licked his lips in anticipation. He tore at his own trousers to open them, but she was not to be an easy target. She was used to heavy and usually hard work, and she was strong, fighting and clawing like a wildcat, and it was hard work; trying to open his trousers with one hand, and at the same time hold down her flailing legs.

"Get a grip on her," he shouted to the other man, who leaned over and tried to pin her arms as they both struggled with her.

Suddenly she became still, her eyes wide and staring, and he took the opportunity to rear back and pull his trousers down over his buttocks, before leaning down towards her once again.

But this time, he was to get the shock of his life! As he knelt down and took hold of one of her legs to push them apart, still fumbling inside his trousers with the other, the awaited moment came, and she brought up her other knee in a hard jab towards his groin. She connected hard with her intended target!

He fell back, clutching at himself, and rolling around in agony on the ground.

The other man, surprised by this sudden happening, swiped hard at the side of her head in an attempt to subdue her, making her senses reel, followed by another blow to the other side of her head, and she felt herself beginning to black out. If she lost consciousness now, they'd both be able to have their way with her, and that was the last thing she wanted to allow, as she vainly tried to stay conscious.

All of a sudden, mayhem erupted all around!

A group of soldiers appeared as if from nowhere, rifles pointing at the two soldiers on the ground, forming a semi-circle around them.

"Okay lads, game's over!" one of them shouted, as he pulled the man at her head to his feet, knowing it was going to be some time before the other would be able to stand again.

As she felt herself released, Jess's senses began to return, and she quickly pulled down her skirt and tried to rise to her feet, but she was still too dizzy and fell back.

"It's okay, lass," a strong Lancashire accent spoke kindly. "You're safe now! Take your time!"

Opening her eyes and trying to focus, she saw the kindly face of a man, perhaps in his mid forties, and wearing a military police uniform leaning over her. His face swam before her unfocused eyes for a moment, before becoming clearer, as he pulled down her skirt and helped her to sit up.

"Are you okay?" he asked quietly, as he held out a hand to help her up.

She nodded and took the proffered hand, feeling a strong arm pulling her to her feet.

"Th . . . thank you!" she stammered, her head reeling once more as she tried to stand upright, swaying as his other arm took her elbow to hold her steady.

"You'll be all right in a minute," he said, "just take a few deep breaths."

Within a few minutes, she was feeling better as he offered to walk her back to her caravan, but she refused. She knew her father would be furious when he found out what had happened, and she'd much rather she told her mother first. She could then relay the news to Brendan well after the soldiers had gone.

She was still intact, even if she was beginning to have a headache, and all she wanted to do was to get back and lie down for a bit.

Picking up the basket of nettles she'd dropped by the gate, she slowly made her way back across the field and sat down on the steps at the back of the caravan; her mothers' face appearing at the open half door above her.

"You took your time, didn't you," she cried in annoyance, before she suddenly realised something was very wrong.

Opening the bottom half of the door, she took one step down and nimbly jumped the rest of the way, coming to rest alongside her daughter.

"What's happened?" she cried in consternation, seeing the darkening bruise on her daughters' cheek.

That was enough to open the floodgates, and Jess put her head in her hands and began to sob violently as her mother gathered her into her arms and waited for it to pass, before guiding her up into the caravan.

She put the kettle over the stove and made her some calming herb tea, before sitting alongside her and waiting to hear her story. It wasn't long before Jess, sipping at the hot tea in between sentences and sobs, had told her mother the full story.

"Your father will be furious!" she declared. "He'll go after them!"

Jess shook her head, telling her mother they'd been taken back to the army camp, but her mother still worried about what Brendan might do. He was a fair man, but was sometimes inclined to be hot-headed, and she knew he'd want justice for his daughter. The gypsies had their own idea of extracting punishment, and that would not be through the law!

"Did they do anything?" her mother finally ventured to ask. "You are still intact, aren't you?"

She nodded. She knew if she hadn't been it would have affected her forthcoming marriage to Silas, and although it would have pleased her, it certainly wouldn't have pleased her father.

He was furious, as expected, when he found out about the attack, but his mood was greatly appeased when he heard that they had been taken away by the military police. He knew the ultimate punishment for desertion during wartime could be a firing squad, but at the least, it would be a lengthy jail sentence.

July finally arrived, bringing with it the arrival of Silas and his father. They were trailed by the rest of the group of around six caravans during the following week, and they all met together that same evening after they'd settled in.

The evening was warm after a hot day, and a large camp fire was built, around which several families were gathered, much food being cooked and consumed during the evening's festivities. Many tales were exchanged of their exploits since they'd last met together, and families caught up with long-lost counterparts.

Silas was polite and friendly enough, but she knew he just wasn't somebody she could ever come to love, even if she hadn't still been in love with Callum.

She was fairly tall, as were all her family, and he was two inches shorter than her, and at least ten years older. His hair was very dark, as was that of most of the gypsy families, being of Italian descent, but there the resemblance ended. His complexion wasn't swarthy, and although he had the long aquiline nose of his compatriots, he was paler skinned and of a more rosy complexion, having blue-grey eyes and a thicker lipped mouth. She later learned that his father had married a native English girl, and he seemed to have acquired more of her features than his father's.

After the meal, they were encouraged by both their fathers to get to know one another, a rough wooden bench having been set up further from the assembled group, where they could talk without being overheard, but still remained within sight of the others.

Knowing they were being watched, although covertly, she sat down alongside him.

"You are very beautiful," was the first thing he said to her.

It was a surprise opening gambit, and she didn't quite know how to reply at first.

"Thank you," she finally mumbled, and looked up to make sure he wasn't mocking her.

She was finding it hard to look at him, knowing how she felt about him, but his next words almost took her breath away.

"Yes, you certainly are!" he verified, "But I really don't want to marry you any more than you want to marry me."

Her head came up at once and her eyes swivelled towards his face, this time causing him to look away, his eyes travelling towards the far horizon.

"I must tell you now, before things go any further," he managed wistfully.

She hesitated, waiting for him to go on, and presently his eyes turned towards her.

"Can I trust you with a secret? Will you promise me that if I tell you, you won't tell anyone else?"

"Of course I won't," she said, touching his arm with the tips of her fingers.

"I am already in love with another woman. She lost her husband two years ago in a knife fight, and we've been seeing each other in secret whenever we can. Knowing our fathers had already arranged my marriage to you, we have to be very careful how we meet."

She smiled, a weight being lifted from her mind immediately, deciding to trust him with her own secret.

"I'm also in love with somebody else," she confided, "but he's not a gypsy and he's far away from me now – I don't know when, or if, I'll ever see him again. I certainly hope we'll meet again, as I know now that I should have put my fears aside and gone with him. If I get the chance again, I will do."

He smiled and took her hand.

"Thank God for that!" he said, "I was hoping we'd be able to sort it out between us somehow. I was in two minds whether to trust you with my secret, but I'm glad now that I did."

"But how are we going to get out of the marriage? They're probably sitting over there discussing it even while we're talking."

"Kyla hasn't arrived yet. She had someone she wanted to see before she followed us, so she'll be here tomorrow. I'd like you to meet her."

"I'd like to," she said, warming to his friendly open nature.

"Kyla has her own caravan that she and her husband lived in when he was alive, with their two boys, ten and twelve years old. We planned to leave the group and go off on our own just before the wedding, which is why she decided to arrive late and park on the edge, away from the other vans. We can then get away, hopefully without anyone knowing.

"You seem to have planned it all well," she said, still smiling. "Good luck to you both. I'll help in any way I can."

"Thank you," he replied, smiling in return. "You seem a good person. Perhaps if circumstances had been different, we two could have made a go of it."

She very much doubted it, but agreed with him in any case!

Kyla arrived in mid morning two days later, and they exchanged brief shy smiles, but she kept her distance in case she spoiled any plans they had, and Kyla might have been a complete stranger to Silas for all the notice he took of her.

She turned out to be a typical gypsy woman: long dark hair, aquiline nose and swarthy features.

Her two boys also bore her looks, being extremely polite, and always kept in good order. It was no wonder Silas had fallen for her!

Jess spoke to Silas often, as would be expected of them, which pleased their parents, as they thought they must be discussing the forthcoming wedding, but little did they know that they were often discussing his escape.

On the second day after Kyla arrived, Silas asked if he might take Jess for a walk as it was a nice day, and with a beaming smile on his face, Brendan agreed.

"Those two seem to be getting on well," he remarked, standing on the top step and sipping his tea as he watched them walk away together.

Rosita joined him and she too watched them until they reached the trees and disappeared from sight.

She wasn't too sure he was right. They certainly seemed to have become friendly, but she'd never seen any sign of love or affection between them, and Jess certainly wasn't acting like a girl in love normally would have done.

When they were well out of sight amongst the trees, Silas gave a low grunting sound like the alarm call of a deer, and Kyla appeared from behind some bushes. The two greeted each other like long lost friends, but not wanting to embarrass Jess, they showed only minor affection towards each other.

"I thought it was time you two met properly," he said, his arm around Kyla's shoulders as he turned towards Jess.

Kyla shrugged off his arm and came towards her.

"I am so glad to meet you," she said, in a calm and self-assured way, "and I'm so glad Silas has been able to trust in your silence. We knew your fathers would be angry when we left, but I worried more about you, and whether you would be upset by his desertion."

Jess laughed.

"Not me! I didn't want to marry a man I'd never met before, although I'm glad he's turned out to be such a nice person. I've been worrying about it for a long time, so this is the perfect solution for me."

The three of them walked on into the woods for some distance to be a safe way from the camp, Silas between the two women, before sitting on a fallen tree and having a good long talk about the situation.

"You do realise our father's will search for you, don't you?" Jess said. "They won't be willing to let you get away with things that easily."

"We've thought about that," Kyla replied. "I've already let it be known that I have a lover and I will be leaving the camp before your wedding to join him, when I intend to live amongst his people after our marriage.

I have no kith or kin among Silas's people, they were my husband's kith, and I joined from a band which originated in the south of England, so there will be nobody looking for me."

"But that won't stop them looking for Silas," Jess interjected. "They may even make a connection between your two disappearances."

Here Silas joined in the conversation.

"Jess has already made it known that she will be continuing southwards to join her lover. She will leave in her caravan a few days before our wedding. I will leave the night before, as soon as my father goes to bed, and ride through the night to join her, although we won't be going south, we're going to make our way west into Wales, eventually hoping to make our winter camp somewhere in the south west of England; well away from where she's told them she'd be going."

"Will you stay on your own then, or will you join up with another band?" she asked.

"We will eventually, perhaps even back with Kylas's people, but for the time being, we'll stay alone," Silas replied. "Her people never come north, and my people never go further south than they are now, so the two groups have never met, and hopefully, never will in the future."

Just then, they heard the sound of some of the gypsy children playing in the trees, and beginning to move nearer.

Kyla stood immediately, reached over and gave Jess a brief hug and smiled at her.

"Who knows – we could have turned out to be good friends given different circumstances," and without a further word, she disappeared like a wraith into the nearby trees. Silas helped Jess to her feet and turned back towards the encampment.

"I'm so glad to have found such a good friend in you. I just know that I can trust you to keep our secret," he said.

"Of course you can," she replied, "and I just hope we'll meet up again sometime in the future, but I doubt if we ever will. We move north again into Cheshire after this, into our winter camp, and by that time you should be far away to the south. Our paths may never cross again, so the best of luck to you both."

One morning, when she awoke, her father was just returning after his morning wash in the nearby pond. She heard the door open and snuggled down under the blankets when she felt the chill air from outside.

Her mother, already up and having washed in the big bowl behind the caravan, now had a large pan of porridge cooking on the stove, as her father handed her a jug of milk.

"Nice and fresh . . . and still warm! And there are some nice juicy plums to sweeten it," he said, tipping the handful into one of the bowls ready for serving. "There's some mushrooms just coming through in the field too. They should be ready to pick by tomorrow."

Jess's sister stirred alongside her, mumbling as she came awake.

"Time to get up, sleepy-heads," their mother said, as the two of them scrambled out of bed.

At this point, their father made a hasty retreat outside and shut the door to spare their blushes as he sat on the top step and lit his old clay pipe.

He'd once had an old briar pipe that his father had fashioned with his own hand, but his wife, finding its gelatinous spit-filled interior obnoxious, had banned him from using it. It had finally disappeared from where he hid it, but he suspected that she'd found it and it had gone into one of the many rubbish piles which they left buried in a corner of the fields when they moved on.

He had taken then to using a clay one, easily discarded, and easily replaceable for just a few pence, or even less if the shopkeeper were preoccupied. It wasn't as enjoyable as the briar pipe, it would suffice for now.

The girls soon tumbled from the caravan and raced round the back to have their own wash, giggling and laughing over some little unknown joke, as Brendan was called for his breakfast. Rosita had cooked the plums and mixed them into the porridge, making it sweet and delicious; and there was plenty of it, as she spooned him out another helping.

Smacking his lips after he'd finished, he threw the door open wide and breathed in the fresh morning air, as the girls took the dishes round the back to wash, whilst Rosita tidied up the caravan, and he savoured the herb tea she had given him to drink outside.

"Mornin' Brendan," broke in the Irish brogue of Cormack, another distant cousin from over the water, who had joined their band many years ago now. "And a grand mornin' it is, too!" he continued, taking in a deep breath.

"Aye, it is that!" he agreed.

"We're all off to say goodbye to Kyla this mornin'. She's after goin' to join her family today," Cormack continued.

"Is she going alone?" Brendan queried.

"Aye, she is that, along with her two boys. A long way to go on her own, but I'm after thinkin' she's used to that since Owen's death."

Brendan nodded, and continued sipping his tea as Cormack walked away.

He wanted to check his rabbit snares first, and then he'd take a walk over to Kylas's caravan and wish her a safe journey, as was customary. A nice rabbit stew for his dinner was something to get his juices flowing; then he'd a mind to speak to Jacob, Silas's father, and continue their plans for the wedding. It was less than a week away now, and would need some careful planning of the festivities that were to take place.

As he reached the tree line, he heard a rustling sound over to his right, and glanced around, expecting to see another of their band carrying some sort of forage for a meal, but was surprised to see Silas emerging somewhat furtively.

He hadn't seen Brendan, and was standing under the overhanging branches of an ash tree, glancing around the field as if making sure he wasn't being observed.

Brendan pulled closer into the hedge line and watched him, and after a few seconds of checking the field was clear, Silas stepped out and strode off across it back towards the camp.

Wondering why he was acting so furtively, but supposing he'd never know, Brendan continued on into the trees and began inspecting his traps. He found a rabbit in both of his first two; quickly disposing of both by snapping their necks, but the third one contained a badger which was very much alive, and extremely ferocious.

Knowing it was badly hurt by the amount of blood around, he knew he had to dispose of it, and searched for a heavy branch with which to deliver the fatal blow. Finding one within easy reach, he delivered the blow, and while it was still groggy, he quickly dispatched it as he had the rabbits, and threw the lifeless body into some undergrowth.

Going deeper into the trees, he checked the other two snares, but they'd caught nothing; however, the two plump rabbits he already had were plenty for a stew that evening, and if enough water was added, and a good few tasty herbs, a soup could be forthcoming for the next day.

Emerging from the darkness beneath the trees, he came across Kyla, and his suspicions were aroused at once. Could there be a possibility that she'd been meeting with Silas? They'd never shown any interest in each other around the camp since she'd arrived, and he'd never seen them in each other's company before – but all the same, Silas had seemed very shifty when he'd left the woods.

She was carrying a woven reed basket, and when she noticed him, she dropped it as if his presence had surprised her; several large mushrooms rolling out onto the ground.

"Sorry, I didn't mean to give you a fright," he said. "Here, let me help you!"

She stepped back as he jumped down the bank to land near her feet, picking up the mushrooms and putting them back in the basket before handing it to her.

She still appeared flustered, and her attitude seemed very suspicious to him.

Maybe she had been meeting Silas! Maybe something had been going on between them! After all, a young man was allowed to sow his wild oats, and she'd be gone that day, so maybe they'd just been saying their last goodbyes. After all, they'd be at almost opposite ends of the country, and it was unlikely they would ever see each other again.

Seeming to rally from her fright, she thanked him and said she would continue to try and find some more mushrooms before she returned, and so he walked back alone carrying the two rabbits.

He found Jacob just over an hour later, having skinned and gutted the rabbits ready for Rosita to cook for their dinner.

They talked over some home-made nettle beer; becoming not a little inebriated in the process.

Soon the cry went up that Kyla was ready to leave, and they all trooped out to wish her well, as the caravan, pulled by a big piebald horse with large white shaggy hoofs, pulled away from the outside of the group.

She was smiling and happy and her two boys waved excitedly from the back door until they disappeared from sight round a bend in the road.

She had told everyone she was heading south, but not very far to the south, she veered off onto another road heading west and towards Wales, marking her direction of travel with a coloured piece of cord tied to a tree branch. Silas was to follow these signs a few days later until he caught up with her.

On the day before the wedding, Jacob woke to find Silas was not in his bed. They'd retired at the same time after an evening of drinking and talking with some of the others, and as the drink had been flowing rather copiously, he was surprised Silas was up so early. His bed was turned down, but it didn't look very rumpled.

After dressing, he went outside for his morning wash, and noticed Silas's big bay horse was also missing. It was usually tethered with the others at the far end of the field, but today it was gone, and when he arrived back, a quick search of his belongings showed that most of them had gone too.

It began to dawn on him that Silas might have gone for good, but he had no notion in his head as to why. Could it possibly be to do with the forthcoming wedding? He'd never shown any objection to marrying Jess, but then, they weren't that close since his mother had died, and perhaps he'd decided to just disappear instead of making his feelings known. He was a grown man, and maybe he'd decided he didn't want to be told what to do any more and this was his way of making it clear.

He felt angry with him for not telling him he intended to leave, but even more worried about what Brendan was going to say.

Preparations for the wedding had been underway all week, everybody in the camp joining in with some kind of activity, and it probably wouldn't only be Brendan who would be angry with Silas.

But more than angry himself, he realised he would now be totally alone in the world without him by his side!

CHAPTER 7

By now, Giovani's group had reached their destination near the seaside town of Southport, on the west coast of Lancashire, and were camped on a flat, sandy meadow.

They had used this site previously, and for a fee, the farmer had agreed to let them use it once again. He made as much money from their use of it as he did from the crops he could have grown, and with far less effort on his part, still leaving him time to plant a winter crop when they departed later in the year.

It was propitious for both parties as a hosepipe fed a horse trough in one corner of the field which the travelling folk could use for washing in, and the water itself was also fresh drinking water.

For toilet facilities, they erected a few planks behind the midden heap for privacy, and used the outer edges of it for their defecation purposes. Crude and smelly, but then, they didn't spend much time there anyway and it saved digging pits.

Callum had already formulated his plan to return to Uncle Ben's, but his conscience was getting the better of him, and he eventually decided to tell his father what he intended to do; but he was upstaged by Frank before he had made his mind up when to approach him.

"Callum, I think I'm getting a bit fed up with this trailing all over the country and not having a permanent home. I wasn't born to this life, and it's beginning to feel unnatural to me."

Taken by surprise at his father's words, he could only nod in agreement. That was exactly how he felt.

"How do you feel about returning to Uncle Ben's farm and living in the shed again?" Frank asked.

"Yes," Callum agreed, "I've been thinking about that myself."

It wasn't a total surprise to Frank. He'd been thinking for some time now that Callum wasn't totally enjoying the life they'd been leading.

After Alison's death, he'd wanted to get away from the place where memories of her were all around, but just lately, the rawness had worn off. He felt he wanted to return to the place where they'd all once been happy together, and go on leading that life again, even if it wasn't with her. Memories of her would still be all around him, but he thought he'd be able to live with that now.

"I don't think it can be too far from here. How about you and I leave here and try to find our way back there?" Frank said, putting his hand on Callum's shoulder and looking seriously into his eyes.

"Yes, I'd like to do that," he agreed.

"We know the name of the village, and we've tramped around the area enough times to know when we're near, so all we've got to do is ask for directions on the way there."

Callum agreed he was all for it, so they spent the rest of the day getting together their small amount of clothes and belongings, intending to leave the camp the next morning before first light. Nobody would notice they were missing until they were far away. That's if anybody cared!

Although having been accepted into the community, they'd always been on the fringes of their society, being alien incomers and not of their own stock, and sometimes they'd been treated as such. The gypsies had always been friendly enough, but they were excluded from many of their dealings.

Mid morning found them several miles away, heading due east as Callum had been directed, and they sat down at the edge of the road to eat the last of the honey and wild strawberry cake they'd been given by one of the women back at the encampment. It was delicious but very sweet, and Frank milked a cow in the nearby field to give them something to drink.

She was suspicious of being milked so soon after the last early morning milking, but they managed to pen her in the corner of a field, and Callum held her head, while Frank bent to the task. At least she was fairly docile!

They passed a cottage further on where a man was busy weeding his vegetable patch, telling them they were going too far west, and needed to turn left and northwards at the next turning.

Having followed his instructions for some way, they finally reached a fork in the road, and were undecided which way to turn. As they stood deliberating, they heard the whine of approaching aircraft engines.

Shading his eyes, Frank looked up to see where they were, but they were coming from out of the sun, and although he could hear the noise of their engines, he couldn't see them. Suddenly they were upon them: six German fighter planes, zooming in very low, and very fast, seeming to skim their heads.

This was the first they'd seen of any of this type of activity since they'd left the farm, and they'd almost begun to forget about the war, although this was a sharp reminder that it was still going on.

Before they had time to react, the planes had passed overhead and carried on, before circling once more and coming back from the same direction.

Frank grabbed Callum and pulled him into the ditch on the opposite side of the road. Luckily it was dry and full of tall grasses and some ivy, which they were able to hide beneath.

"They saw us on the other side of the road, so if they intend to use us for target practice, they probably won't expect us to be on this side now," Frank hissed, as the planes once more roared towards them.

But they weren't the targets!

They passed straight overhead and flew up the road veering away towards their right.

After a few more seconds had elapsed, the planes began to open fire, twisting and turning in the air, rising up after each pass and into the sun, before returning once again, passing over them again and again, constantly firing at some unseen target ahead.

The cacophony of sound was terrorising, as they kept their heads down and waited for it all to be over.

Suddenly, silence reigned once more, as the planes re-formed into a group in the air and roared off once again into the distance.

They waited a while before venturing from the ditch, peeling the vegetation from their clothes and brushing themselves down, before turning and looking over the hedgerows into the distance.

Up ahead, all was silence, deafeningly quiet after what had just taken place, and then they began to notice spirals of smoke rising up into the air, followed by flames many feet high. Whatever it was, they'd found their target!

Gathering their belongings, they began to run towards the leaping flames, but they were heavy and it took them a little while before they finally arrived.

What greeted them was a sight of utter devastation!

Rounding a bend in the road, they saw that the target had been a convoy of army vehicles – whether they'd chanced upon them whilst returning from another mission, or whether they'd been the intended target, they'd never know, but their mission seemed to have been eminently successful, having exacted the maximum amount of destruction.

The lead vehicle, catching the first onslaught head on, had veered off the road to the left, its front end buried deep in a ditch, its windscreen shattered, and both the driver and his companion fatally wounded. The back end, carrying a great many ordinary uniformed soldiers, was canted high into the air. They had been thrown forward by the initial impact, but, in the act of trying to scramble towards the open back end of the vehicle and escape to safety, they had been an easy target for the aircraft as they returned for a second pass; the machine gun bullets angling directly inside and easily picking them off.

The second vehicle, in an attempt not to run into the back of the first, had veered to the other side of the road, taking with it an accompanying Land Rover alongside. Its right front wheel rolling into the ditch on the opposite side, it had pushed the other vehicle into the ditch and rolled sideways on top of it.

The canvas sides of the lorry were no protection from the impact, and many of the soldiers it was carrying were injured before the third aircraft sprayed that too with a volley of bullets, killing most of those inside.

The next vehicle had stopped in time, but before more than one or two soldiers had managed to scramble out, they too were fired upon, a lucky, or perhaps unlucky bullet for them, had hit the fuel tank, and they and the vehicle were quickly consumed by the ensuing flames.

Of the two vehicles behind them, they had managed to escape more lightly. Whilst the attack seemed to have been concentrated on the lead vehicles, there were still quite a number of dead or seriously injured casualties as they fled the scene, scrambling through hedges and trying to find cover in the surrounding fields.

Having been an air-raid warden previously, Frank had thought himself immune to the sight of the dead or dying, but today he found himself not knowing where to begin. The shouts and screams of the injured and dying eventually brought him to his senses, and he was galvanised into action.

Callum too knew he needed to help, and without thinking, followed his father.

Many of the soldiers were beyond help, and Frank urged him to look for the more seriously injured; a lot of whom were also beyond any help they were able to give at the present time, and Frank knew they would ultimately die before any help could reach them.

One man, completely unconscious, had lost both legs at the knee, but the gaping wound in his stomach, from which blood ran copiously and Frank was unable to stem, would mercifully die within the next few minutes, or so he hoped. It seemed bad to feel that way, but he really didn't want him to regain consciousness and be aware of the dreadful pain he would be suffering. Thankfully, even as he tried to staunch the bleeding, Frank felt his whole body relax, and a final loud sigh escaped from him as the man mercifully died.

Without giving him another thought, Frank moved on to the next soldier. This man was lying in the road, having broken both legs when he jumped from the back of a lorry. He was in pain, but urged Frank to see if he could be of more use to those more seriously injured.

"I'll be okay, go and see to the others," he said, trying to push Frank away. "I'll manage until help arrives."

Frank took the webbing belts from two of the dead and tied them tightly around where he thought the breaks to be. They weren't open, or obviously misplaced fractures, so hoping there wasn't any internal bleeding, he left him to wait for help.

Luckily there turned out to be a medic amongst the surviving soldiers. They found each other a few minutes later, and he helped him out as best he could, having had basic first aid instruction himself, but his training had in no way prepared him for the horrific injuries he was faced with today.

Callum too tried his best to help out, but he was unable to do much more than clean and roughly bandage cuts and grazes and give what comfort he could, but few had got off as lightly as that.

They never knew how long they'd spent treating the injured before help arrived, but arrive it did, in the form of army personnel: doctors, nurses, ambulances, and a few top brass, who were there just to watch and officiate.

Not being far from the army base, who were awaiting the arrival of the convoy, the attack had been witnessed, and a rescue mission had been mounted immediately, searching the lanes until they came across the site.

The main job they were given after that was to help put the dead into the backs of the flat bed lorries which had been sent to take them back to the camp, and who had to make several journeys to accommodate them all.

Talking to one of the drivers as he waited for instructions after the final bodies had been loaded, he elicited the information that the camp was only within a couple of miles of their destination, and as evening was beginning to draw on, he asked if they might have a lift.

"We aren't allowed to give lifts, especially to civilians," he said loudly through puffs on his cigarette, exhaling loudly into the still evening air. Then looking around to make sure no-one was within hearing distance, he continued conspiratorially, "but if you get off now, I'll pick you up on my way. I'll have to drop you off some way from the camp though, just in case anybody sees us." This was followed by a meaningful wink.

By now, most of the remaining casualties had been ferried away, and so Frank and Callum told the officiating sergeant that they'd be on their way. He thanked them for their help, and said they'd all be returning to camp shortly. The road was to remain closed overnight, and the damaged lorries would be returned to camp the next day.

As they moved off, the driver they'd been speaking to gave another wink and indicated the direction they were to go in, before puffing away on yet another cigarette.

It was almost completely dark by the time he dropped them off, and they didn't recognise any of their surroundings.

"The main road's just a couple of hundred yards further on, but I'll have to drop you here in case we're seen.

Once you get there you might recognise the area," and with that he drove off, even before they could thank him.

It was too dark, and they were too tired by now to even walk that extra couple of hundred yards to the next junction, but luckily spotted a roofed bus shelter just a few yards further back along the lane.

When they reached it, there was a rough wooden bench seat inside, and although there was only enough room on the bench for one, Callum reckoned he'd be just as comfortable on the ground beneath it. He was so heavy eyed and weary after their long journey, he felt he could sleep anywhere.

They'd also had no time to think about food since they'd stopped to eat their cake that morning, their bellies rumbling with the lack of it, but there was nothing to be done about it for the time being.

Next morning, when Callum awoke, his father was asleep on the ground alongside him.

"That wooden bench was far too hard to sleep on for long," he explained when he was woken. "The ground was much more comfortable," making them both laugh.

There was a large meadow behind them and Frank reckoned there might be a chance of some mushrooms growing there, as there were piles of horse dung everywhere, but no sign of a horse. Mushrooms often found horse dung a favourable place to grow, and there was also a stand of trees nearer to hand. It might be possible there were mushrooms growing there as well.

The horse trough near the gate was, however, almost full to the brim, so they were able to make a small fire from dry and dead twigs under the hawthorn hedge, and boil up some water in a discarded tin can they found near the shelter, making some nettle tea to slake their thirst. As the sun was well up, Frank's glasses, together with some dry grass clinging to the bottom of the hedge made an excellent aid to lighting the fire, and they managed to dig up some tasty roots to make use of for breakfast, not having found any mushrooms. Slightly unripe beech nuts that the squirrels hadn't yet managed to find rounded off their meal, breaking them open on a flat stone, and they were ready to make a start, finding some sweet and ripe rose hips and plenty of blackberries to chew on the way.

Their gypsy way of living had at least taught them to make the most of foraging in the countryside!

On reaching the main road, they still didn't recognise any of their surroundings, but the smell of the sea was strong, so they hoped they weren't too far away, although whether to go left or right was another problem.

As they were deliberating, a farm cart came along. The elderly man stopped to pass the time of day, and they were able to ask him if he knew of Beech Tree Farm.

"Cain't say I do," he said, taking off his old battered hat and scratching his head through his wispy white hair. "One thing I do know though is that it ain't that way," he said, pointing to the left. "That's the way I'm going, and I ain't heard of it around there in all my seventy odd years, so you'd best go t'other way," he said, pointing to the right.

They stifled their smiles, and laughed once he'd gone.

"Real old country bumpkin, ain't he?" Callum joked.

"Bain't he!" Frank contradicted, as they prepared to go towards the right.

"We've got nothing to lose by going this way, and as we're supposed to be quite close, we can always retrace our steps and go back the other way if he's wrong," he continued more seriously.

They continued along the road, and even though it was a main thoroughfare, they passed few vehicles or people. Petrol was scarce now during wartime, and there was only enough for really necessary journeys.

One vehicle that passed them was a motorised lorry carrying some sheep, and an army staff car hurried past, carrying a driver and his more senior passenger, but of people there was very little sign, the only one near enough to speak to being a woman collecting berries in a hedgerow. They exchanged a few words with her, and she offered them a few of her berries, with which she said she was going to make some jam – if she could manage to get enough sugar – but apart from her, the only sign of life were two men clearing a ditch in a field, but they were too far away to communicate. They asked the woman about the farm, but she'd never heard of it, saying she left her little cottage very rarely.

They'd been walking for perhaps half an hour, before Frank suddenly stopped and peered across a field on the opposite side of the road.

"What's up?" Callum, some yards ahead of him, stopped and looked back.

"That Dutch barn opposite - I'm sure I recognise it! I delivered some sacks of carrots and potatoes to a farm while we were working for Ben, and I remember putting them in a barn like that. I remember the corrugated iron was loose at one end and it was flapping in the breeze. It made an awful grinding sound, and we wondered how they'd manage to sleep through it on a windy night."

As they watched, the end flapped upwards, caught in a gust of wind, making a resounding screech as it landed back on the metal framework from which it had become detached.

They could hear the sound it made from where they were standing, fully two fields away.

"I'm sure that's it!" Frank said. "I'm sure we're heading the right way!"

They continued once more in the direction they'd been going, and soon both began to notice familiar landmarks, eventually spotting the stall at the gate from which Alison had once sold her eggs and vegetables.

A wave of nostalgia gripped them both at the same time, making them stop and gaze at it.

Frank was the first one to pull himself together.

"Well, looks like we have come the right way after all," he said, clapping Callum on the shoulder. "Come on, we'll carry on and have a long rest when we get there."

They reached the stall quickly enough with renewed energy, knowing they were nearing their destination, and passed it with hardly a glance, trying to keep their eyes averted. It evoked too many memories for both of them!

It didn't look as if it had been used since her death, and the paint was blistered and peeling. Obviously nobody had ever taken over her job!

Continuing along the track, the hawthorn hedges were higher and more unkempt than they remembered them, and Callum was the first to remark on this, Frank agreeing with him.

"Must be finding himself short of labour with the war still on," Frank remarked. "Still, we're back now, and we'll soon have them whipped into shape again."

But turning a slight bend in the track was to bring them the shock of their lives!

The field on their right, in which usually potatoes, cabbages and Brussels sprouts grew, was nothing more than a crater in the ground, soil and stones heaped all around the depression, and the hedges on either side were completely flattened.

"Looks like they've caught a bomb!" Frank gasped. "Wonder if everywhere else is all right!"

But they were soon to find out it wasn't!

When they hurried on towards the farm, skirting the mounds of earth lying on the track, they found a scene of devastation here also.

The once solid, stone-built farmhouse was nothing more than a shell, with just a few bits of its walls still standing, surrounded by heaps of rubble and a few scattered possessions.

Part of an old cast iron bed frame lay in the yard, the singed remains of its flocked mattress lying in tattered bits around it. A cast iron frying pan was wedged amongst the branches of a blackened old oak tree standing alongside a collapsed wall, and an upturned and burned armchair was sitting in the middle of the yard, surrounded by slates and a myriad of other detritus. Bits of paper and pages of books blew about amongst the debris.

They were both upset by the sight, and Frank put his arm around Callum's shoulders as they stood trying to take it all in.

"Wonder if they got away!" he eventually said, at last voicing the thought in both their minds.

Suddenly, the light breeze seemed to have turned into a cold wind blowing through them, the thought in both their hearts – now what? Their last chance of having a home once again was gone, and they were now completely and utterly destitute.

Were his aunt and uncle still alive or not? Were they still inside when the bomb landed? That seemed to be quite likely. They'd have had no reason to believe a solitary farmhouse so far from the docks or factories of Liverpool would be a target for a bomb!

"Come on, let's see if the shed's still standing," Frank said, eventually pulling himself together and trying to lighten the mood. "At least we might have some shelter for tonight."

But here their hopes were to be dashed once again!

Crossing from the farmyard to the smaller track leading towards the shed, they smelt burnt wood before they even reached it.

It was nothing but a blackened shell, the corrugated iron roof having collapsed inwards once the walls and roof timbers had begun to burn and warp.

Callum, despite his age and sense of bravado, felt himself ready to cry, and Frank had the same feelings as they sat on the remains of a dry stone wall, staring at the shed, and wondering what they could do next.

Their home in Liverpool was long gone, and they had no money to rent another one anyway. His beloved wife was gone too, and all he had left in the world was himself and his son! If it hadn't been for Callum, he might have thought of doing away with himself.

Callum too seemed to be in a dazed state as he eventually turned and said to his father, "What are we going to do now?"

This raised Frank from his forlorn state. What was he thinking of! He still had to provide for his son – he wasn't old enough yet to make his own way in the world, and it was up to him to think of something.

"Come on, me old son," he said. "There must be tools lying about somewhere – they'll have survived, wherever they are! We've plenty of materials, so we'll have to try and build a shelter for ourselves while we think of what we can do. There's plenty of corrugated iron around, so at least we'll keep dry if it decides to rain."

The wooden shed where the tools had been kept hadn't survived, but they hunted around and eventually found the big metal tool box that usually stood on the bench. It was dented and battered, but after a bit of careful prizing of the lid, it finally came open, and there were most of the things they needed inside.

By the time evening was beginning to arrive, they'd sawed, hammered, and nailed together a very passable shelter, with a large sheet of corrugated iron providing an adequate roof - if it didn't become too windy!

"Food is the next consideration," Frank stated, as they stood back to examine their handiwork. "Let's go out into the field and see if we can find any veggies to make a meal. We've plenty of water in the stream in the woods and it should be okay to drink if we boil it first."

Callum offered to go and get the water, finding a galvanised bucket in the yard which hadn't received any damage, apart from a few dents, whilst Frank searched the field, arriving back carrying two large potatoes, a cabbage, and a couple of carrots, which he scrubbed clean of earth with water from the trough.

They roasted the potatoes and carrots over the fire between two sheets of corrugated iron, and boiled the cabbage, from which they made a sustaining, and surprisingly palatable, meal. At least it filled their bellies!

Bits of the ripped flock mattress they pushed together, and with the aid of a roll of sticky tape, managed to make a couple of separate, and soft, surfaces to sleep on, covering the ground first with an old tarpaulin they found, dirty but surprisingly unscathed. It was a fairly warm night, and they were able to get a good amount of sleep.

They'd covered themselves with their coats, which had kept off the pre-dawn chill.

Next morning they were awoken by the sound of a female voice.

"Cooee," she called. "Are you awake?"

The both awoke simultaneously, and turned to look at each other in surprise.

"Hello? Are you in there?" it continued.

Wrapping his coat around him, Frank went to the entrance and lifted away the wooden door.

"Hello," she smiled brightly. "I heard you hammering and banging yesterday, and I came up to see if you'd stayed. I thought you might like this for your breakfast," and she held out a basket.

He looked at her askance, and then recognition dawned. Having been bombed out, she was living in the refugee accommodation across the road from the farm, and had come up to clean at the farm a couple of times a week. She'd also bought produce at the gate from Alison, and they'd become quite friendly.

He took the basket from her and beamed his appreciation.

It contained four large brown eggs, with a small pat of lard to cook them in, a small loaf of homemade bread, thoughtfully sliced beforehand, and a jar of rhubarb jam.

"I would have brought bacon, but I haven't been able to get any this week," she continued.

Callum had by this time joined him, and they both thanked her appreciatively.

Things were beginning to look rosier the more he thought about it! What was to stop them building a better shelter, perhaps even a small shed of their own in time, if they could find enough materials, and working the land

85

themselves; perhaps selling their own produce at the gate to earn money as Alison had once done?

Who knows, there might even be enough materials left to rebuild the house itself given time – if not two stories high, at least enough to turn it into a single storey dwelling. Two rooms would be all they'd need – a living room cum kitchen, and a large partitioned bedroom.

After she'd gone, they set about building up the fire again and cooking the eggs, dipping the bread into the lard afterwards and making fried bread. They were so hungry they ate the whole pot of jam using up the rest of the loaf, before sitting back, hunger satiated, and contemplating their plans for the day.

Frank's plan was to look around the house and see if the idea of re-building could be possible, and at the same time picking up what materials he could find to make their temporary dwelling more habitable. At the moment it was only big enough for them both to sleep in, and if they were to live in it during the winter, he would have to make it bigger and more weatherproof, as well as finding some means of heating it. There was still time, and there were plenty of good long days ahead; plenty of time to plan, and plenty of time to carry out those plans.

In the meantime, Callum had found Ben's old shotgun in the remains of the shed, together with a box of ammunition.

"I'll go into the woods and see if I can pick off some game for a meal," he told his father, as he saw him preparing to go back to the farmhouse.

"Great idea!" Frank told him. "Vegetables are all very well, but we need a bit of tasty meat to go with them."

Callum was lucky enough to come across an unwary pheasant just after he entered the woods. It was pecking away at the ground and didn't notice his presence at first, which was its downfall, as he quickly lifted the gun and took a clean shot at its head, almost severing it from its body.

Involuntary nerve reactions sent it running forward for a couple of steps before it sprawled on the ground, and Callum was well pleased with having found a meal so quickly.

At one time he wouldn't have known what to do with the bird after having killed it, but spending time with the gypsies had taught him valuable lessons, and when his father returned at lunchtime, there was a tasty pheasant stew cooking over the fire. He'd found a couple of runner bean plants still standing, with plenty of beans still on them; having been sheltered from the blast by the remains of a wall. Together with those, and some more potatoes and carrots he'd also found, as well as some wild thyme for flavouring, they enjoyed a hearty meal.

They spent the afternoon hauling the useful items that Frank had found that morning back to their camp, their labours being interrupted in mid-afternoon by the lady they'd met this morning.

"I've baked you a cake," she said, holding out her offering wrapped in a tea towel. "I'm afraid it's only plain – you can't get the ingredients for anything else - but I've filled it with some of my strawberry jam; and there's a bit more lard if you need to cook anything."

Sociably they offered her some herb tea they'd made, which she found she enjoyed, never having tasted anything like it before, but declined a slice of the cake they offered her.

"I made it for you, so I won't take any of it. I have another at home for myself," she explained. "I had just enough ingredients for two, so I might as well make two at the same time and conserve the gas. It's not cheap, you know, and you never know when they might bomb a gasworks, and then there'd be none for days or even weeks."

Having told them her name was Maura, and learned their names as well, she left them to get on with their labours, knowing they wanted to get it finished before nightfall. Following the large midday meal they eaten, they were so full they only ate half the cake, and left it inside the shelter for the next day.

Callum had sliced up some of the pheasant breast with the pocket knife he'd taken to carrying, and had put it inside the tin can, covering it with some large leaves and holding them down with a flat stone. He immersed the can in a bucket of water and well out of the sun during the afternoon to keep it fresh.

That evening, two more large potatoes were wrapped in mud from the stream and baked in the fire, being enjoyed with the fried pheasant breast for their evening meal, which they cooked in the frying pan they'd retrieved from its resting place in the oak tree.

Sitting down and leaning his back against the shelter afterwards, Frank thought that life wasn't turning out too badly after all, and maybe they would be able to survive on their own means after all.

If only he could have foretold what the future held for them at that moment in time!

CHAPTER 8

Brendan and Jacob were furious at the disappearance of Silas, but Jess was only too glad that he'd managed to get away without being caught – sad to lose the company of both he and Kyla, but glad not to have been forced to marry against her will. She was glad nobody had linked his disappearance with Kyla's departure.

A search party was sent out to try and find Silas, but Jacob already knew that if he didn't want to return, nothing on earth would make him do so, even if he was threatened with being ostracised from the group. He was stubborn as a mule, and if he'd decided on another way of life, nothing would make him change his mind. After a couple of hours searching, they returned with no news, and plans for the wedding were called off.

They had no idea where he'd gone, or why, but Brendan had his suspicions and voiced them one night to his wife; Jess overhearing their conversation.

When Brendan had asked her if she knew where Silas might have gone, she'd feigned as much surprise as him, and knew she'd have to go on playing the part of jilted sweetheart so as not to arouse their suspicions, but her heart was much lighter.

She was only young yet, and didn't want to become a baby machine before she'd had time to live and experience life.

Silas was so much older than her, and his father would surely want them to start a new dynasty as soon as possible after the wedding, but that was the last thing she wanted.

Two weeks later, still with no sign of Silas's return, they decided to break camp and make their slow journey towards their winter quarters, hoping to arrive before the end of October; but meeting up with, and renewing old acquaintanceships, on the way.

In the meantime, Silas had caught up with Kyla. He had followed the markers she'd left, untying them before carrying on; hoping to throw any followers off the trail. For the time being at least, they seemed to have done so.

She was camped on the edge of a forest glade a short way off the road when he found her, sitting on the steps of her caravan and tending a cooking pot, whilst the children played amongst the trees.

She was delighted to see him, and they hugged wildly, pleased to be together as a couple for the first time in their lives, and not having to look over their shoulders every time they met in case somebody might be watching them.

He slaked his thirst with some rather potent cider she'd made, and he ate some of the food she'd cooked, while the children played amongst the trees. Afterwards, he proposed they move further away from the road.

"They'll probably send out a search party for me. This is somewhere we can easily be seen, and they'll smell the smoke from the wood fire, even if they can't see us. We should move further away and see if we can find a track deeper into the trees where we won't be seen."

She agreed and they called in the children, who were also pleased to have some company, and scampered madly around collecting their belongings, before they left their present camp.

They found no more suitable tracks into the trees, but returning to the road, they soon came to an area of open moorland some way past the woods. A rutted track wound into the distance towards a farmhouse set on a distant hillside. Whilst Silas went off to explore the possibilities of finding a suitable place to camp for the night, Kyla stayed vigilante for signs of pursuit, but all remained silent. The only sound the noisy cawing of a colony of crows on the edge of the woodland.

Perhaps they'd managed to give them the slip. Nobody apart from the two of them and Jess had known their real destination, and as Silas had untied the coloured markers as he'd passed them, there was nothing to show where they'd gone.

Her only worry now was Jess. Might she unwarily let something slip? Although she'd not had much to do with the girl, Silas seemed to have every confidence in her, but she was only young. Would her father sense she knew something and badger the truth out of her? If that did happen, both she and Silas could be in danger from his anger, and they needed to get off the road as soon as they possibly could.

Silas was back within half an hour. He'd followed the track towards the farm and found another smaller one leading off towards the right, which led into what had once been a small quarry. It was a bit overgrown in places, but her sturdy horse should be able to pull the caravan through, provided it stood up to the rough ground, and it would provide them with shelter from the weather.

There was also a small waterfall cascading down one of the sides, which should provide them with fresh water. It hadn't tasted at all brackish when he'd tried it.

It was almost dusk by the time they managed to get the caravan into the clearing at the bottom of the quarry, and after a quick look around, they decided it would be a safe place for them to stay for a while.

The sides were at least twice the height of the caravan, and the entrance hidden from the track they'd followed to reach it, so they couldn't be seen unless someone actually came into the quarry, which it didn't look as if anybody had for a very long time.

Having saved some rabbit from the afternoon meal, she sliced and fried it, wrapping it in some sort of flat bread she'd also made in the pan, and together with some edible leaves she'd found, it turned out to be quite tasty and filling.

That night they were able to sleep together for the first time ever, a foretaste of the unfolding future before them.

CHAPTER 9

Several weeks had passed and Frank, with Callum's help, had made a reasonable job of their new shed. It was made of wooden planks, most of them retrieved from the barn, and the remains of the old shed. There was plenty of corrugated iron for roofing, although they had to make the walls fit the roof, as it wasn't possible to cut the metal. Still, with a bit of ingenuity and holding smaller pieces together with cross members, it made a reasonable sized shelter, and they'd found a roll of roofing felt, which they nailed around the sides facing the prevailing wind to keep out the worst of the draughts. The roof kept the rain off them, which was the most important thing; however, it definitely wouldn't stand up to the winter weather, and he turned his attention to the house.

It took them a week of hard work to clear all the rubbish and debris from just the kitchen area alone, before they were able to stand back and consider what could be done with it, but Frank was more than pleased with what he saw.

The stone flagged floor was intact, perhaps sporting a few more cracks than it had before, and the cast iron range had survived. The one problem was whether they would be able to get it going, as there was plenty of coal in the stone building across the yard, which was undamaged, and which also contained a good supply of kindling, matches and candles.

Most of the house walls, being of solid stone construction, still stood to above head height, so he had to figure out how to get them all to the same level, and how to put a roof on it.

Another thing in their favour was that the tap still worked when they turned it on, and they both let out a cheer. Fresh water had been one of their main concerns.

The larder too, on the outer side of the kitchen, had mostly been undamaged, which on inspection they discovered contained a good store of tinned goods and bottled fruit, along with some very mouldy bread and cake, and some rancid butter. The only thing they lacked was a tin opener, but a chisel and a hammer managed the job for the time being.

Luckily the bomb hadn't scored a direct hit on the house, but had landed in the field where they'd found the crater, so they were left with a good amount of materials to work with. Being of strong stone construction the structure had weathered the blast better than one made of brick would have done.

During the course of their labours, the lady from across the road, Maura, visited quite often, always bringing some sort of goodies with her, and they were glad of the time to stop and have a break and a chat while they ate them.

During the course of conversation, she mentioned Alison quite often, and her sad death, something they themselves never spoke about; rarely speaking about her at all these days, although she would always remain in both their hearts.

He often wondered whether Callum thought about her. He never spoke her name. Perhaps he wanted to try and forget that sad part of his life, and just look to the future.

One day, when they'd been talking about other things, she suddenly mentioned her husband. Frank had noticed she wore a wedding ring, but being in refugee accommodation, he'd never liked to ask what had happened to her and why she was alone.

"My Alf would have given you a hand if he'd still been here. He'd have loved to get his teeth into something like this. Always tinkering with something, he was."

Frank looked at her enquiringly.

"What happened to him?" he asked, not knowing if he might have gone too far.

"Our house copped a bomb! Got a direct hit, it did, and with him still inside it. You might say I was lucky to get away with it, but I'm completely on my own now, and it doesn't always feel that way."

"Weren't you with him then?" he asked.

"Naw!" she answered. "Went to see a friend a few streets away and we had to go in the shelter. The house was gone when I got back. Blown to kingdom come! Nothing left of it! Don't know why he wasn't in a shelter too."

"Have you no relatives? No children?" It was out before he'd meant to say it. He'd definitely gone too far this time?

"I did have!" she looked down at her hands for a few moments before continuing. "Colin was my eldest, he was just 24 when he copped a bullet in the second month of the war, and then our George. In the navy he was. His ship was torpedoed and went down with all hands – no-one survived. That was only a year after Colin and he was just 22."

There was a pause, and just as he was about to commiserate, she continued speaking.

95

"We had a daughter too. Never see her now. I doubt she'd even know where I'm living. She was the eldest. Took off with a gypsy before the war started and I've never seen her since."

"I'm so sorry," he started. "That must be very hard for you."

She sighed, and then suddenly seemed to pull herself together.

"Can't complain! I'm getting back on my feet again. I've made some good friends since I moved here, and at least I've got a roof over my head. I've also got myself another little cleaning job as well at a farm, and I often stay on to help with other jobs as well, such as butter and bread making. They've got six children, so there're plenty of mouths to feed."

"Callum and I have been living with some gypsies since we left here. What's your daughter's name, we might know her?" Frank said.

"Her name is Katherine, but everybody called her Kath, or Kathy," she brightened. "Have you come across her?"

"No," he shook his head. "Sorry, I don't know anybody of that name. Most of the gypsies have hereditary names, handed down through the generations, and I think Kath's a bit too Anglicised. She may possibly have changed it to fit in."

"Possibly," Maura replied, seeming somewhat demoralised again.

"What was the name of the gypsy she left with?" he asked, wondering if he might at least know him.

"No idea," she replied. "We never met him. All we found was a note after she'd gone. We knew she'd been seeing someone, but that was a complete surprise to us both. One day she was there, the next she was gone."

He was finding himself liking Maura more and more as time went by. She was open and friendly, and very easy to get along with, and he found himself looking forward to her visits and their long chats. He wasn't sure that it wasn't just that he was feeling sorry for her: but then again, she had as much reason to feel sorry for him. Apart from still having his only son, he'd lost his partner and his home the same as she had.

A week later, he heard a vehicle come up the track and turn towards the farmyard.

He was having a well earned break after working on the kitchen all morning, deciding what to do about building the roof. He knew it needed to slope, so he was considering the best way to go about it.

Making his way to the farmyard, he found a military Land Rover parked in the entrance way; a lance corporal standing by the driver's door, accompanied by a captain just stepping down from the passenger side.

"Can I help you?" he asked.

He was feeling responsible for the farm now.

The captain turned and looked at him, seeming surprised to find anyone else here, before regaining his composure and saying peremptorily, "And who might you be?"

"I'm the owners' nephew!" he said, pulling himself up to his full height, feeling himself to be in charge of his surroundings. "My uncle isn't here at present, and I'm taking care of the place until he returns. Might I ask what you're doing here on his property?"

The captain's attitude mellowed a little, feeling sympathy for what he had to tell him, although still retaining a formal attitude, as befitted his rank.

"I'm afraid to tell you that your uncle is dead, as are the rest of the people who were here when the bomb exploded, and the property now belongs to his son, Captain Peter Lacey, who is serving with the armed forces abroad. He has agreed to the army making use of the property until he is in a position to return. From now on, the farm and its surrounding land have been requisitioned by the army."

Frank stood rooted to the spot with shock. He'd never imagined anything like this might happen. He hadn't even known where Uncle Ben and his wife were, let alone that they were dead - and as for his son Peter - he'd never even known that his uncle had a son called Peter! He'd always thought Tommy was their only child. Ben had never mentioned him while he was working there, and neither had his wife Priscilla, on the odd occasions he'd had the chance to speak to her.

Seeing he had the advantage, and knowing Frank didn't know what to say, the captain dropped his officious stance.

"I have to ask you to leave straight away," he continued in a softer voice. "Military vehicles will be arriving within the hour, and we will be setting up a temporary camp in the fields for the duration of the war."

They stood looking at one another for several moments: he trying to take it all in; and the captain waiting for him to start collecting his belongings. Gathering himself once more, he retraced his steps to the shelter, where he slumped on the ground trying to piece his thoughts together.

Where could they go now? It wasn't just him who he had to look after, but there was also Callum to consider. The lad had a sensible head on his shoulders, and had learned a lot during the time since they'd left Liverpool, but he was still only seventeen, and still needed a fathers' guiding hand.

While he was thinking this over, Callum returned from the woods, where he'd been checking their snares for rabbits. He'd found nothing that morning, and was surprised at his fathers' slumped attitude as he sat gazing into space.

"What's up, dad?" he asked, thinking his father was trying to solve a snag he'd hit with the rebuilding work.

Frank looked up, taken by surprise at his reappearance, before finally patting the ground alongside him.

"Sit down son, I've something to tell you," he said, trying to sound as matter-of-fact as he could, and as Callum sat, he told him the story he'd just heard from the Captain.

Callum too was stunned by the news.

"Where do we go now?" he eventually asked of his father after a few moments silence between them.

"I've no idea son. The only other option we've got is to throw ourselves on the mercy of my brother in Liverpool. We've never got on, and I haven't seen him in years – but we haven't any other choice. I know, or I did know, his address, but that was about five years ago. I only hope he's still there."

And so, two hours later, found them on their long walk towards Liverpool.

CHAPTER 10

Two days later found them entering Liverpool and making their way along Scotland Road towards the West Derby area where his brother lived, but it wasn't the Liverpool Frank remembered. He'd lived here all his life, but everything was so changed that he found it hard to find his way, let alone find any landmarks from which to check their progress. The face of Liverpool had changed completely after the 1940 blitz, with the demolished rubble of familiar landmarks lying all around.

The ground underfoot was also treacherous and hard to traverse, with huge holes many feet deep lining the road. Ripped up tram lines, broken paving stones, and the remains of bombed buildings, their bricks and broken glass heaped high in the streets, made progress hazardous. They had to stop every few yards to try and negotiate their way around ever increasing obstacles in their path.

Planks of wood, criss-crossed against each other, stood many feet in the air, some falling noisily as they became dislodged by falling debris, and due to the rest of the rubbish, it wasn't always easy to dodge them. Callum had to side-step quickly at one point as two huge roof trusses fell towards him, only missing him by inches. He would surely have been killed if they'd landed on him.

Where streets of cramped little terraced houses had once stood, their front doors opening straight onto the pavement at the front and tiny little backyards backing onto narrow alleyways at the rear, all that now remained of their presence were heaps of bricks and other detritus. Here and there the sad relics of the home life they'd once housed littered the streets, or what was left of them.

There was an old copper boiler lying on its side next to the remnants of a kitchen wall; a tap clinging to the remains of the brickwork the only other reminder of its past use.

A dolly tub lay on its side in the middle of the road, where its progress from the narrow little side street had been halted by an uprooted tramline. Lots of pots, pans and broken dishes littered the cracked and broken pavements all around.

Even more poignantly, a child's doll, still inside its miraculously intact pram gave out the sound of 'mama, mama', as the chill wind rocked the upturned pram against a broken lamp post.

Nowhere was it possible to walk more than a couple of yards before having to climb over or around an obstacle or heap of rubble, and their progress became even slower because of it.

A group of workers finally pointed out the turning for Everton Valley, the start of their uphill climb towards the suburbs, once so well known, and now almost unrecognisable.

They sat down on the remains of a wall to rest before tackling the long steep hill, their arduous walk and the hard work of climbing over rubble and traversing obstacles making them weary. One of the workers handed them a tin mug of water to share between them, asking them not to drink too much.

"Sorry, mate, that's all I've got for now. I'm gonna' be 'ere clearing for the rest of the day, so I need the rest meself!"

They were grateful even for that, and told him so before moving off.

Never having had to climb the hill before, Frank hadn't realised how steep it actually was, and they both had to rest after the strenuous uphill slog which seemed to go on forever. Even Callum seemed to have had all the spirit knocked out of him by the time they reached the top, and they both sat on the remains of a wall to recuperate.

"Could have done with some more of that water now," Frank gasped, and Callum nodded his agreement.

It was quarter of an hour later before Frank got to his feet.

"Come on," he said. "We've still a long way to go, and we need to make sure we find it before nightfall. Don't want to be finding our way through this debris in the dark."

Callum would have liked to sit there for longer, but realised his father was right; besides, he was becoming hungry now as well as thirsty.

Two hours later they reached the street they were looking for. As they'd left the city centre, things had become easier, as there seemed to have been less bombing further out into the suburbs, and they moved along looking for the number he seemed to remember.

"I think this is it," Frank said finally, looking at a row of terraced houses built at the end of the Victorian era, with bay windows on both upper and lower floors. "I seem to remember that shop on the corner, although I've only been here once or twice."

"No harm in knocking and asking, is there?" Callum supplied, marching up the short path and knocking loudly.

After two or three repeated knocks, there was still no answer.

"Let's try round the back," Frank suggested.

The house was at the end of the terrace, with another road cutting through alongside, and it was only the work of a moment to walk round the back and enter the alleyway to try the back door, but that too was locked, and their loud banging went unanswered.

Returning to the front once more, they sat on the low wall and waited to see if he'd come back.

Eventually, tired of waiting, Callum stood up.

"I'm going to knock next door and see if we've got the right house. We could be waiting for nothing if it's not!"

It was opened almost as soon as he knocked.

"Sorry to bother you," Callum said in his politest voice, "but do you know if George Lacey lives next door?"

The woman was rotund, although quite well dressed, with a pinafore over her clothes, and her hair in curlers, covered by a brightly coloured head scarf.

"'E did!" she answered his query, "but 'e don't no more. 'E was an air raid warden and 'e got killed about three month ago in the bombing."

"And what about his wife, Flora?" Frank asked, anxious to be under cover before dark.

"Oh, she died about twelve month ago. Fell down the stairs and broke her neck in the rush to get to the shelter. Proper cut up about it 'e was too!"

Frank sat heavily down on the wall and put his head in his hands.

"Come far, 'ave you?" she asked.

"All the way from Southport," Callum said, wearily

103

Seeing how tired and weary they were, she walked down to the front gate and joined them.

"Tha's a long way!" she stated. "Come inside and I'll make yez' a cuppa."

They trudged inside and dropped their packs in the hallway as she ushered them into the front room and busied herself making some tea. They were glad to see a few slices of cake on the tray as well.

"Cake's not up to much, but it's all I've bin able to get," she said. "Tuck in!"

They needed no second bidding!

"Now, tell me about yer'selves," she urged when they'd finished eating, and between them they told her everything, right from being bombed out, through working on the farm, and ended up with their stay with the gypsies and their disappointment when they returned once more to the farm.

By the time they were finished, it was completely dark, and it was now raining heavily outside. They'd no idea where they'd spend the night. Frank had thought about trying to find a shelter in Newsham Park where they could bed down for the night. It wasn't far, but it seemed an insurmountable hurdle when they'd already come so far, and they'd be soaked to the skin by the time they reached there – but then what? Where could they go after that? He knew of no other relative they could call upon for shelter until they could find something more permanent – if they were ever able to.

Suddenly, Imelda Middleton, for that was the name she gave them, stood up.

"Cheer up, lads," she said. "I wuz' good friends with Flora, George's wife, and he give me a key to let meself in. I've still gor' it in the kitchen.'

When she returned, she was brandishing the key.

"I used ter' cook the odd meal for George and leave it in the 'ouse for 'im after she died," she explained, "but before I 'and it over, ave youse got yer' identity cards? I don't wanna' seem suspicious, but yez' can't be too careful these days. I just wanna' make sure yer' 'oo ye' say yer' are."

Frank produced them both immediately, and after studying them she let them into next door, handing him the key as they went inside, where she left them and went back to her own home.

As they were about to close the door, she poked her head round and said, "I'll bring yez' some breakfast in in the mornin'. Won't be nothing fancy, but it'll give yer' a start. Ger' a good nights' sleep now, yer' look as if yer' need it."

Gratefully they thanked her and went inside, finding the house clean and tidy, if a little dusty, and the double bed in the main bedroom already made up. It looked just as George had left it.

While Frank was putting his things away in the wardrobe, an excited cry from Callum came floating up the stairs.

"Dad, there's some food in the cupboards. I've found some tins of soup, and some tinned fruit as well as some conny-onny to go with it! We can eat tonight, yippee!"

It was after they'd eaten and were sitting back in the luxury of an armchair each that a sudden thought struck Frank – something that he couldn't quite believe for the moment. He decided not to say anything to Callum for the time being as he needed to think it through, but he rather thought he might be right.

105

Both his parents were dead. George and he were their only children. George's wife was dead too, and they'd never had any children, so did that mean that the house belonged to him now?

Unless George had left a Will leaving it to anybody else, it must surely be his!

There seemed no reason why they shouldn't be here for some time, so he'd look around and see whether there was a Will to be found before saying anything to Callum.

It was also a niggling thought in the back of his mind that if he did find a Will, he could destroy it if it wasn't in his favour and the house and possessions had been left to anybody else. That would leave only the problem of there still being a solicitor somewhere in the city with a copy tucked away. If he didn't know of George's death, then nothing more would come of that for some considerable time and they'd be able to go on living in the house.

He spent many days after that searching cupboards and drawers throughout the house, even venturing into the attic to look for anything that looked like a Will – but he found nothing, and it seemed as if their fortunes had turned at last.

CHAPTER 11

They both settled down well to their new life. Living in a proper house once again was pure luxury after the nomadic life they've been leading for so long, and the neighbours were wonderful. Imelda must have spread the word about their plight, and offerings of food and supplies were soon forthcoming – everybody around seemed so generous and helpful, although money was soon going to become a problem, and they both knew they'd need to start earning as soon as possible.

The houses opposite were larger and had good sized back gardens, so Frank returned favours done by tending to the gardens and showing them how to grow their own vegetables, whilst Callum did some of the harder work like digging and hoeing, but as they were returning favours, it brought them in no money.

Neighbours in the smaller houses with little or no gardens were rewarded with small repair and painting jobs.

One day, Imelda knocked at the back door while they were having a much needed rest after a mornings' clearing of a weed filled garden.

"Cooee!" she called, popping her head round the door. "Are yez' busy?"

"No, come in," Frank called back. "It's always a pleasure to see such a trusted friend. What can we do for you?"

"I know you've been looking round for a job," she began as she entered the room, "but how would you feel about working down the Corpy yard?"

"I'll do anything to earn a crust," Frank replied, Callum nodding in agreement.

"Me son Donny works there; in the office like, and he's said they're looking round for more workers. A lot of their 'ouses have been damaged, and they want workmen to help with the repairs. They don't have to be tradesmen either, there's jobs for unskilled as well."

Frank laughed, making her look at him in surprise.

"But I am a tradesman," he answered when he finished laughing. "I'm a fully trained mechanical engineer! I used to work in a factory down on the dock road before it burnt down."

He thought her mouth would never shut when he told her that.

"Callum isn't trained, but he'd be only too willing to do unskilled work, wouldn't you?" he said, turning to his son, who nodded his agreement.

"Anything to get some money in our pockets," he replied.

A couple of days later, they were asked to report to the Corporation Yard, Frank taking his professional qualifications along to show them, where he and Callum were given work immediately, and over the next few weeks they worked extremely hard. They were re-building bombed out remnants of buildings, doing standard repairs, and even working on the building of some new properties.

The war was nearing its end, and air raids over the city had practically stopped altogether, although a lot more were still going on in the south of the country, and around the eastern coasts.

Frank and Callum were being kept extremely busy every day now. There was so much work that needed doing that the days went by in a flash, but Frank found himself thinking more and more about Maura.

They'd got on so well together and he couldn't help wishing she'd been able to come with them. It would be so nice to have a woman by his side once more, and she'd probably appreciate living in a proper house again.

In the end, he decided he'd go and visit her one weekend when he had the time off, and the perfect opportunity presented itself one Saturday when Callum had been asked to work the whole weekend on a job they were behind with.

A mate he worked with down at the Yard had a car. It had been laid up during the war years, but as petrol was becoming easier to buy now, Frank decided to ask him if he'd take him there and pick him up later in the day if he paid him for his services and the fuel. The man agreed immediately when a sum of money was offered, always glad to earn some extra over and above his weekly wage, and he wrote to Maura immediately, who replied that she'd be delighted to see him.

He arrived around mid morning and they had a really enjoyable day. She managed to produce a nice roast meal, a chicken having been procured from a neighbour who kept some laying hens in the garden, together with roast potatoes, vegetables and a thick tasty gravy. She even managed to make a rhubarb crumble and custard. He felt a prince indeed, never having eaten so well for a long time, and she gave him the rest of the chicken to take home and share with Callum for their supper.

After their lunch, they walked across the road and looked towards Uncle Ben's farm. It had never been possible to see the house from the road, but they wouldn't have been able to anyway now.

All the fields they were able to see from the road were filled with tents, and the hedges either side of the track had been removed, being replaced by prefabricated huts, with a command post and sentry on guard duty at the entrance. The little hut where Alison sold her eggs and vegetables had gone completely.

A wave of nostalgia overwhelmed him for a while and he was filled with emotion, Maura noticing immediately and taking his hand.

"This was a bad idea," she said seriously, "come on, let's take a little walk and get away from all this."

Sadly he agreed, and they walked a little way along the road before crossing over once again and turning down a lane which she said would eventually take them round in a circle and back to her home. It was a good long walk, and he was glad to see that she didn't feel the need to let go of his hand again.

They didn't have much time when they arrived back, just enough time for a cup of tea, as his mate was to pick him up again at five o'clock, but they both felt the time they'd spent together had been worthwhile, and both felt they wanted to repeat the experience.

Frank realised he needed to buy a small car of his own if he were to continue his visits. He'd already learnt to drive during the course of his Corporation employment, as it was necessary to get from one job to another when not working with a team. He soon sourced a small second hand Austin, which he realised he was now able to pay for with the amount of cash he'd been putting to one side each week, not realising how much his savings had grown over the weeks.

Callum too, now a tanned and strapping lad, had also learned to drive, and agreed to share the running costs, provided he was able to use the car as well, and if they were able to get enough petrol.

They were both away from home all day, and as there was plenty of work available, they also worked overtime in the evenings and at weekends, although Frank always tried to keep his Sundays free in order to visit Maura.

Their relationship was blossoming, and Frank was beginning to think it might be time to ask her to become his wife. He didn't think of the word 'love', and his feelings certainly weren't the same as those he'd felt towards Alison, but they got on well together, and a woman around the place was exactly what he and Callum needed. A nice warm body to be able to cuddle up to every night would be heaven, as well as being able to claim his conjugal rights once again.

Callum had met her on quite a few occasions while they were at the farm, and seemed to like her, so he decided to speak to him about it one evening when they both returned from work at the same time.

After they'd eaten a fish and chip supper from the shop he passed every night on his way home, he sat down and placed a mug of tea in front of Callum.

"How would you feel if Maura and I got married?"

He felt that if he were to come straight out with it, Callum might show his true feelings about the idea without having time to think, but was surprised by the answer he received.

"Well, it's about time too!" Callum said, grinning. "It's taken you long enough!"

Perplexed, Frank just looked at him across the table, not knowing what to say.

"How long have you been visiting her now? Six months? Nine months? Or is it even longer? How come it's taken you so long to make up your mind?"

Frank smiled, glad that things had gone so well, and that Callum wasn't averse to the idea. Now that the first obstacle was out of the way, he began to have doubts of his own. Was he making the right decision? Would Maura be an asset to their household, or would she come between the relationship of him and his son? Then Callum knocked all those thoughts straight out of his head!

"As a matter of fact, I've been seeing a girl myself for some time now, but you've been too busy with your own life to notice!"

Frank gaped at him – but what did he expect? Suddenly he realised that Callum was no longer a child! He was a grown man now! He'd grown into that man without Frank really noticing. He'd been so busy thinking about his own life and his own needs that he hadn't really thought about those of his son.

"Close your mouth – you look as if you're catching flies dad!" Callum laughed. "Did you think I'd stay a little boy all my life?"

Frank was too full of emotion to speak and hurriedly cleared the dishes off the table and carried them through to the back kitchen, where he put them in to soak.

"Your turn for the dishes tonight," he called back over his shoulder when he'd finally been able to control his emotions. "I'm going out the back yard for a smoke."

Their little back yard had also been transformed.

Once it had been just a yard, containing nothing but a wash house. The floor surface was tiled in red and navy; its' only other feature a washing line. Now it had had the walls painted in white, and a seat they'd made from some wooden palings he'd bought from the council.

Once sanded and treated with a wood preservative, also bought from the Council, they'd made a rather rustic looking seat

Being the end of the terrace meant that nothing overlooked them on one side, and the sun shone into it from late morning until sunset. A trellis had also been fixed to that wall, and it was now adorned with a couple of clematis growing right across, one flowering just as the other finished. They seemed to like their position and grew vigorously, eventually covering a most of the wall.

It made a peaceful place to sit and contemplate ones thoughts, and that's what Frank did that evening.

Eventually, as it grew chilly, he went inside. His mind was made up! He'd ask Maura to become his wife!

CHAPTER 12

Three months later, Frank and Maura were married at the Liverpool Registry Office.

They both agreed they just wanted a small affair with no fuss or frills, but Frank had purchased a new suit for the occasion, albeit an 'off the peg' one, which seemed to fit well enough, and Maura wore a wool mix dress as it was now the end of October and the weather was much chillier.

A neighbour of hers in one of the pre-fabs had turned out to be a dressmaker, and had made the dress for her from a roll of cloth she'd already had from before the war. She'd always intended to make it into a dress for herself, but had never got around to it, and Maura was pleased when she saw the finished garment.

The material was in a mid-blue with flecks of purple running through. It had long tight-fitting sleeves, a fitted bodice with a v-neck and a slightly flared skirt which swayed as she walked. The neckline and cuffs were adorned simply with little pearl buttons the woman had also found stored. The blue shoes she wore had come from Paddy's Market; the only place she'd been able to find a pair in near enough the same shade of blue. Luckily they'd been in her size – or near enough. They pinched a little, but she realised she wouldn't have to wear them for very long.

She wore a wide-brimmed straw hat in a cream colour, one she already had from a day spent at the races when her husband was alive, which, together with a corsage of artificial cream coloured roses that she admitted started life as a cake decoration, offset the whole outfit well.

Frank presented her with a necklace as a wedding gift, which sported a sapphire pendant, admitting many years later that he'd bought it from a pawn shop, but it matched perfectly with her outfit.

Callum was his best man, insisting that he would buy a suit himself. He'd never owned one before, and Frank was noticing the signs of him showing some maturity at last.

The ceremony went off without a hitch and a lot of their workmates and neighbours crowded into the house later for a 'knees-up' which went on into the early hours, Frank and Maura meeting Callum's girlfriend for the first time.

She was a pretty girl; quite tall and with very dark hair cut in layers, accentuating the shape of her head, but the dark eyes and Italianate features bothered Frank. They were very like those of the gypsy families they'd travelled with before, and he had the distinct impression that she looked very like someone, but he wasn't able to place who that person was. She was introduced to them both as Gina.

She was pleasant and friendly, and declared that she was pleased to meet them both in a polite manner, and he couldn't help glancing in her direction during the evening, trying to place the resemblance. There definitely was something distinctly familiar about her.

"Seems you're more interested in your son's girlfriend than in me," a voice beside him spoke, startling him.

He glanced around to find Maura standing alongside him.

"Sorry!" he apologised. "It's just that she reminds me of someone I once knew, but I can't for the life of me remember who!"

"Someone from your murky past? Someone you might have had a fling with?" she teased.

"No, definitely not!" he was outraged. "There was never anyone but Alison in my life – I never wanted anyone but her!" suddenly becoming conscious of what he'd said and wishing he could have taken it back.

She looked hurt, before turning on her heel and walking away, to be lost amongst the milling crowd of people.

It was too late to take it back! It had been said in the heat of the moment, and could never be taken back. It would be better to leave things as they were until they could be alone, where they could talk quietly and perhaps he could try to explain his words to her.

But what was there to explain? He knew their relationship could never compare with that he'd shared with Alison. Truth be told, if he could have had Alison back, he'd have shrugged Maura away without a second thought.

The party broke up about two o'clock and the tired and inebriated revellers returned to their own homes; those unable to do so made the best of a sofa or a couple of chairs pushed together, and one or two even bedded down on the floor.

When Frank went up to the bedroom, Maura was already in bed, and said nothing about their previous conversation, but she welcomed him in as if nothing had ever been said, and was willing to make love with him several times during the night. She seemed to have missed the act of sex as much as he had!

Next morning they awoke late, and when Maura went downstairs to make them some tea, everybody had gone. She looked around at the amount of mess that needed to be cleared up, but then realised that were three of them in the house now, and as far as she was concerned, the clearing up wasn't all going to be down to her. The men could lend a hand as well. Start as you mean to go on, she thought. She hadn't married Frank just to become their housekeeper and skivvy!

As it was Sunday, both Frank and Callum were home, although Callum had arranged to meet Gina that afternoon, so she set them both to work immediately breakfast had finished. By the time lunchtime arrived the place looked spick and span once more and she opened some soup and made them a sandwich for afters, declaring she'd do a proper roast dinner in the evening. She was glad when Callum said that he wouldn't be back in time, and that he might not be back until late. That meant they could enjoy some time alone together.

After Callum had left, and their dinner was cooking in the oven, having 'acquired' a small piece of pork from the butcher, she sat Frank down in the living room with a mug of tea to sort things out between them.

"I was upset by what you said to me about your wife last night . . ." she started, before Frank, anxious himself to clear up any misunderstandings, interrupted her.

"I'm so sorry," he said, "it came out without me thinking!"

She held up her hand.

"Please, let me finish before you say any more," she continued. "When I thought about it, I realised you were

117

right. I loved my husband too. He was my first true love, and I don't think I'll ever love anyone again like I loved him, but they're both gone forever and they're never coming back. We'll have to come to terms with that if we're to make a go of this marriage."

He nodded, feeling tears stinging the back of his eyes, and noticing them shining in hers also.

"Yes, you're right," he said. "We need to move on – both of us – and not keep looking back. It won't help."

She took his hands in hers.

"This is the first day of a new life! Let's look forwards and not backwards, for both our sakes, and for the sake of our marriage."

CHAPTER 13

Jess tumbled out of her camp bed amongst the hubbub of noise and excited chatter all around her. It wasn't a very comfortable bed, but when you tumbled into it as tired as she was every night; you slept the sleep of the dead in spite of everything.

She, along with two other young girls from the gypsy camp, had joined the Women's Land Army. Her father hadn't been pleased at what he called her 'desertion', but her mother eventually talked him into letting her go, saying that if they were to oppose it, there could be a row, and she may feel unable to return if she finally decided that life outside the camp wasn't for her.

He had long since realised that there was no chance of Silas returning for their marriage, being certain now that he had gone with Kyla and they'd never see either of them again.

This was also contributed to three months ago by her sister having run off with a boy from the local farm where they'd all been fruit picking. He'd also been one of the fruit pickers, some said of foreign extraction, but nobody seemed to know from which country, and after extensive questioning of their co-workers, of which there were many, nobody seemed to be even aware that they'd gone, never mind where. People appeared and disappeared on a daily basis amongst the fruit pickers.

After extensive searching, they decided that they'd stay where they were for the winter months instead of going on to their normal wintering ground with the rest of the families, to see whether she returned – but she didn't! A long lonely winter it was with just the three of them, which is what eventually decided Jess that she needed to get away.

When the rest of the group joined them again the following spring, she heard the other girls talking about the Land Army, and decided that would be a perfect way to leave the family without causing too much bad feeling. She loved her mother and father dearly, but after a winter of their enforced company with nobody else to talk to, she decided she needed to get away and be with other young people for a change. She thought she'd go mad if she had to spend another winter like the last.

She'd been with the Land Army since April, following the tractor ploughing the land ready for the crops to be planted, and removing stones and other rubbish thrown up during its progress. Although the work was hard, she enjoyed the company and the bright chatter of the other girls, and found the days passed quickly.

Breakfast, usually porridge, was served in the big mess tent erected alongside the barn, where they all slept, its interior filled with wooden trestle tables and forms at one end, and their camp beds at the other.

When breakfast was finished, they were given their instructions for the day, after which they all trooped out into the fields again. Whether it was rain or shine, they were all expected to put in a full day's work, except when the ground became too soggy for work to continue, by which time most of them were soaked to the skin.

Around midday that day, a horse and cart entered the field, a sign for them all to stop work, and get some food and a hot drink.

"I'm ready for this," Jess said to the woman working next to her, "my back's killing me."

"Mine too," the woman said, as they both stood up and stretched their aching backs.

"I hope it's something better than Spam sandwiches today. I'm getting fed up with them!"

The woman pulled a face.

"Me, too," she agreed, as they made their way back across the field, rinsing off their soil covered hands in the water butt provided.

There wasn't much talk as they all ate hungrily, even though it did turn out to be Spam once again, followed by some rather unappetising and very dry cake, but they were all so hungry that every crumb was eaten. It was washed down by some weak tea without any milk, and served in a tin mug.

"Beggars can't be choosers!" she said to the woman who was sitting next to her with a wry smile.

She'd been complaining to their supervisor about the amount of Spam they kept getting, but her complaints fell on deaf ears however, as the supervisor merely glared at her and shrugged her shoulders before walking away.

The shout came for them to resume work, but Jess decided she needed to pee first, walking into the next field and squatting down alongside the hedge. There were a number of others already there for the same purpose when she arrived.

It was as she was adjusting her dungarees and re-fastening them over her shoulders that she heard the drone of a heavy plane.

She shaded her eyes and looked up into the sky, but she could see nothing, even though the sound was getting louder, the engines throbbing loudly in the still country air.

The war was nearing its final stages, and they were in the Fenlands of Cambridgeshire, but none of them had seen, or even heard a plane for some time now.

Others around her had stopped to peer into the distance as the sound grew ever louder. Even the supervisor had stopped what she was doing, and the tractor driver was swivelled around in his seat to peer towards the horizon.

As they listened, the note of the engines began to change, and instead of a constant steady throb, the sound changed to an uneven roar, intermittently changing back to a steady throb as the engines regained their equilibrium once again.

Suddenly, a small shape appeared out of the sky over the trees some distance away, and the cry went up when it was spotted, arms pointing towards it. It seemed to be coming directly towards them.

As it drew closer, they could see that smoke was pouring from both engines on its port side as it struggled to maintain height and clear the trees, its engines beginning to splutter, and working only intermittently as it came towards them. Plumes of black smoke streamed out behind both engines, leaving a thick pall in their wake, and suddenly both engines cut out, their propellers finally coming to a complete standstill.

Giving up the struggle to stay in the air as it cleared the last of the trees, it began to nose dive towards the ground as it drew nearer. For a moment, its nose lifted slightly, and it seemed the pilot was still struggling to regain control, before it finally hit the ground heavily. There was a tearing and rending sound of metal as it bounced twice in the air before sliding along the ground and coming to rest against a slight incline, its nose still pointing skywards, just a field away from where the horrified onlookers stood watching.

There was complete silence for some moments, not even the sound of a bird, as they all stood staring, before a shout went up, galvanising them all into action.

"It's one of ours! It's a Lancaster! We need to get them out before it goes up in flames!"

They could already see fuel pouring from the plane, as they joined the rest of the throng who were running towards it. The first rescuers were already on the scene when Jess arrived, but nobody seemed to know where to begin, and what to do first.

The plane had broken into three sections, but the nose was high up in the air, too high for them to reach from the ground, and the only way in was from where it had broken away from the fuselage. That meant someone going inside the plane and making their way towards the cockpit, too dangerous when there was still a chance of it bursting into flames at any moment.

The gun turret was in the central part, which had skewed slightly to one side and away from the tail, and also the nearest part to the ground. The gunner was still encased in its battered framework, which was all but demolished. It was obvious from the state of his body that there was no chance he'd still be alive. He'd been practically shot to pieces; the remains of his head and the upper part of his body splattered all over the remaining surfaces!

One young girl nearest to the sight was violently sick on the ground, and another collapsed in a heap nearer to her.

The whole plane was completely riddled with bullet holes, the rear gunner's compartment and most of the tail missing altogether. It looked as if it had been the main target for enemy fighter planes, but luckily had already dropped all its bombs. They only hoped it had scored a hit on its own target before being attacked.

As they watched, the cockpit door began to open. A young airman in RAF uniform slithered out, helplessly sliding down the fuselage and on to the top of the wing, where waiting hands caught him as he continued his slide over its surface and down to the ground, where he collapsed in a heap on landing.

Jess ran to his side.

"Are you okay?" she asked, noticing his right arm hanging uselessly at his side, and a nasty gash on his temple, extending round towards his ear.

"I'm okay," he answered, managing a weak smile, "but my mates aren't. Get them out before she goes up. Some of them are shot up pretty bad."

He seemed to be ready to panic, but as he tried to stand, he collapsed again with the effort. Willing hands lifted him and carried him away; assuring him everything would be done to help them. They were only a few feet from the plane when there was a loud hissing sound and a jet of flame shot many feet up into the air.

The tractor driver, having positioned his vehicle just below the front part of the wing in order to access the cockpit opening, jumped down and raced from the scene. Others nearest to it followed in his wake.

"Everybody back," he shouted as he ran, "she's gonna' blow."

Just as they reached the gate, a jet of flame leapt many feet in the air and they all shielded their faces.

124

"Jack!" the airman shouted back over his shoulder. "Somebody get him out!"

But it was all too late!

Even as he spoke, one of the fuel tanks blew, and the whole plane disappeared in a blazing inferno.

Whoever Jack was, it was all far too late for him now! Any chance of rescue was impossible!

Seconds later they heard the sound of an approaching aircraft coming from the same direction as the bomber.

"Take cover," a voice shouted, as they all dropped to the ground. "They've followed him!"

The plane dropped lower as it neared them, and circled the bomber from a safe distance. It seemed as if it might be going to strafe the ground in order to take out some more innocent souls, but nothing happened, as it circled above them once again.

The tractor driver chanced a look upwards, before shouting, "It's a spitfire! It's one of ours!"

Everybody climbed to their feet and looked up, seeing the plane circle once more, as it waggled its wings a couple of times, before disappearing towards the east.

Everybody knew what that meant! He'd been one of the fighter escort on the bombing raid and he'd followed the Lancaster in order to mark where it came down. He'd now report back to base, and it wouldn't be long before the military descended on them.

They learned some time later that Jack was the pilot, a young man in his mid thirties, with many hours flying time, and a wife and three young children at home.

Dominic, the young co-pilot they'd rescued, told them later that Jack had taken a bullet in the side, and another in the arm. Injured as he was, he'd done an amazing job of getting the plane down so well.

Sadly, he'd sealed his own fate in the process!

It turned out that they'd been on a mission over Europe with their squadron of fighters and bombers, and had been spotted by enemy aircraft that had descended on them on the last leg of their journey home. The escort had bravely engaged in the battle, but several of their aircraft, how many as yet unknown, had been shot down.

Jess, and one of the other girls who had medical experience, helped him back to a bed in the barn where they made him as comfortable as possible until his unit was contacted, whilst the plane was left to burn itself out in the field.

Just over a month later, Dominic returned to the farm to thank them all for their help, and also to see if he could find Jess. She'd been allowed to stay with him until an ambulance arrived to take him back, and he'd taken rather a shine to her.

As he'd been allowed some leave to recuperate, he rather hoped she'd agree to go out with him, but by the time he arrived back, she'd already left the farm, and nobody knew where the group had been sent.

During wartime, information wasn't easily come by, as he soon learned, everything being on a 'need to know' basis, so even those he managed to contact about her whereabouts either didn't know or wouldn't say.

Jess in the meantime, had been taken to a farm in Derbyshire, this time mainly livestock and only a small part arable.

Apart from having been brought up all her life with the horses that pulled their caravans, she had very little knowledge of other farm animals. She loved the heavy horses that they kept for pulling the farm carts, and was eventually put in charge of looking after them due to her understanding of them and their needs; but she had to learn all over again with the pigs, cows and chickens they were rearing for meat.

Chickens she could never get her head around. They always seemed so scatty, always doing the opposite of what you expected, but the pigs she grew to love, even though she found the glutinous mud in the enclosures they inhabited rather distasteful. She often got very muddy herself when trying to extricate an unwilling boot from its grip.

They always seemed pleased to see her, especially when she was carrying a bucket of food, and would often rub against her for a scratch, knocking her over in the mud if she didn't manage to sidestep smartly at their approach. They would either stand quietly, or even roll over so that she could rub their bellies as well, and she was sad when they had to be taken away for slaughter.

She knew that's all they were being reared for, to 'feed the nation', as the slogan went, but she was always heartbroken when one of her favourites disappeared.

Many a night she spent sleeping with the horses. It was quieter and warmer than sleeping in the dormitory tent, and she found the whickering and snorting of the horses soothing and restful, sometimes being awoken in the morning by a soft nose snuffling against her cheek.

One of her favourites was Nero, a huge ginger coloured Clydesdale with white feathering on his enormous feet. Weighing in at over a ton, she'd been warned he was unpredictable, but they'd bonded immediately they met, and he'd been like putty in her hands. He never showed any animosity towards her, and did everything she asked of him without even thinking about it.

127

She never had any qualms about curling up against his huge foreleg and resting her head on his shoulder, sometimes spending the whole night curled up together in that way.

Seeing how much they'd bonded, and how amenable he was when with her, she quickly became his main handler, and most of their days were spent together.

She harnessed him to the cart every day and took him out into the fields with her, leaving him tied under a convenient tree whilst she was working; giving him a nosebag at lunchtime and never forgetting to return and give him water to drink a few times during the day.

One day, whilst working in the next field, she heard a great hullabaloo coming from where she'd left him. Dropping what she was doing, she raced back to where he was tethered, to find Nero prancing and rearing, in danger of trampling on the man cowering on the ground in front of him.

"Nero, no!" she screamed. "No, Nero, no!"

Immediately he heard her voice, he came down on all four feet, and turned towards her, calming down and whickering softly as she came to his side.

"What happened?" she cried, turning all around trying to find someone who'd seen anything.

The man, now standing well away from the horse, pointed towards him.

"That animal's dangerous," he shouted, "'e needs shooting!"

"He's not dangerous!" she said angrily, coming to the defence of the animal and turning on him. "Not unless you've done something to him!"

His face suffused with anger.

"They needed him in t'field and I came to fetch him. The damned brute turned on me when I tried to harness him up!"

"He wouldn't do that," she cried, fury causing her to shake all over, "not unless you did something to him first!"

"Not me," he answered angrily, "I was told he was needed so I came t'fetch 'im, that's all, and he turned on me for no reason!"

He pointed to the harness he'd been carrying, where it lay trampled in the muddy impressions created by Nero's huge hoofs.

She put her hand against Nero's neck, and rubbed her cheek against his silky one, whilst gently stroking his nose with the other hand.

All the front part of his body was liberally spattered with mud, and the animal was trembling all over. He began making small huffing sounds as she began to gentle him down, and he nuzzled against her.

Several of the others had stopped working and were standing watching as George Barford, the farm manager, strode through the gate.

"What's happening here?" he asked. "Why have you all stopped work? It's not lunchtime yet!"

Carl started ranting at him now.

"I was sent to fetch the 'orse!" he spluttered. "It were wanted in t'next field, and when I tried to 'arness it, it turned on me! Damn near killed me! Would 'ave done if it'd 'ad a longer rope!"

"What happened?" George turned to ask Jess.

"I was in the next field – I didn't see anything. I came running when I heard the noise," was all she could say.

Just then, their supervisor, Jennifer Sutton, who'd been following George, strode in through the gate, and looked at the mud covered man standing in front of the horse.

"Well, Carl," she said, "are you going to explain, or do I have to? I saw everything!"

Carl had the good grace to blush, although none of them were able to see it under its liberal coating of mud.

"I . . . I . . ." he blustered, not finding any words of explanation.

His previous aggressive mood was wilting, and realising his actions had been witnessed, became replaced by one of complete embarrassment.

Picking up a stout tree branch from where it lay to one side of the horse, she brandished it towards him.

"I'd say this had a lot to do with the horse's behaviour – wouldn't you?"

At the sight of it, Nero became restless again, and Jess had to calm him down once more.

"Wouldn't do as 'e was told," he muttered. "Kept turning 'is 'ead away and wouldn't let me put it on."

George's face was scarlet as he looked at the man.

"Get off my farm!" he said in a low and threatening voice. "If I ever see you round here again, I'll personally shoot you myself! I won't have any animal treated that way!"

Carl looked as if he was about to argue, but one glance at the angry and determined face of the man standing in front of him was enough to make him change his mind.

As he slunk away, George turned to Jess.

"Check the horse over and see that he's not injured will you, then take him to where they need him. You'd better stay with him for the rest of the day and make sure he behaves properly. I know he can be awkward, but there's no need for that kind of treatment from anyone."

After everyone had gone back to work, Jess gentled her way round Nero, checking for any serious damage, running her hands gently down his legs to his fetlocks, and sliding soothing hands over his whole body as she checked around him. Shivers of pleasure ran through his body as he occasionally whickered at her, and she finally found the offending wounds just behind his right shoulder.

The branch had caused several abrasions to his right flank, the main damage being the one behind the shoulder, where the jagged end of the branch had cut into the skin, causing a deep wound which ran for about six inches downwards, little droplets of blood oozing from it.

"You poor fella'," she soothed. "No wonder you were so aggressive – and who could blame you? I won't ever let anybody treat you like that again!"

Once he'd calmed down, and she'd wiped the cut clean with some water from the butt, she fitted his head harness and led him into the next field, where the workers had been appreciating the time it had given them for a rest. He was placid and gentle with Jess leading him, and did the job he was needed for without any further problems.

That night, returning to the stables, she bathed the wound with some warm soapy water, and covered it in antiseptic cream, before going back to eat her evening meal.

Some of the girls were going to a dance in the local village hall, but she wasn't really interested in dancing, and returned to the stables, where she managed to get astride Nero and take him for a steady stroll around the fields.

More used to a harness, he was surprised by her jumping up on his back, even without a saddle, but took no offence, and trotted amiably around with her sitting astride.

Once they returned, she gave him a drink and prepared to bed down alongside him, using a horse blanket to cover herself.

It was several hours later, and the whole farm was completely silent, that Nero suddenly reared his head up from underneath her and whinnied loudly. Taken by surprise, she rolled away from his side in case he inadvertently caught her with one of his giant hoofs. The animal lay with his head up and ears pricked for some seconds before whinnying loudly again and lumbering to his feet.

"What's up boy?" she asked, going to his side and putting a hand on his shoulder.

His answer was to swing his head around in her direction, catching it against her shoulder and snorting loudly, his eyes flaring wide in alarm.

She turned her head in the same direction, and then she smelt it! A distinct whiff of wood smoke!

"Ok boy!" she said. "I smell it too!"

Leaving his stall, she hurried outside where the smell was becoming stronger, and it was there that she saw the flames licking up against the wooden stable side, which was already well alight.

Dashing back inside, she took hold of Nero's shaggy mane and led him outside, where she tied him to a tree well away from the stables.

She didn't have time to gentle and reassure him, but he seemed to understand and stood quietly, snorting every so often as the smell of the smoke reached his nostrils.

The others too had smelt the smoke and were beginning to panic, and it took her several minutes before she was able to get a halter on them and lead them outside, where she let them loose into a nearby field before running to the workers tent. Everybody was by now sound asleep, and she raised the alarm.

Luckily, the house was too far away from the fire to be under any threat, but the tent was within easy reach of the flames if the wind carried them in that direction, and she ran inside, screaming at the top of her voice.

"Fire! Everybody out! The barn's on fire! Everybody out – quickly!"

Bleary eyes opened in surprise, and soon everyone was making for the opening to the outside, most still in their pyjamas, but others having picked up dressing gowns and shrugging into them even as they pushed their way through the flap.

Panic reigned as their supervisor appeared, shouting out orders and pointing out taps and buckets as they formed a line under her supervision and tried to put out the fire – but it was all too late! Fanned by a light breeze, the dry timber had taken light easily, and the roof was now well alight as a cat suddenly shot out from between two burning planks. Its fur was already beginning to smoulder, and only the quick thinking of a young woman nearest to it saved its life as she threw a full bucket of water over it.

The cat stopped in mid flight, seeming dazed by the dousing of water, and after shaking itself wildly, it gave her an angry glare and shot off into some nearby bushes.

"Well, there's gratitude for you!" she commented to no one in particular, smiling before continuing her efforts to douse the fire.

Soon it became clear that they were fighting a losing battle. Their efforts at throwing buckets of water weren't able to reach far enough up onto the roof, and it wasn't long before the crackling timbers began to fall into the interior, as they stood back and watched helplessly. There was nothing further they could do except watch the structure collapsing in on itself, and it was well towards dawn before the last smouldering embers burnt themselves out, leaving wisps of smoke drifting into the air, covering the whole farm with the smell of wood smoke.

Luckily, the breeze had been in the opposition direction to their sleeping quarters, and apart from discolouration of the canvas by singeing, seemed to have received no other damage.

When it was all over, the workers made their way back to bed, being told they could have an extra couple of hours sleep that morning to make up for that they'd missed during the night.

"Great!" one of the girls said in an aside to her nearest companion. "We were out at the local hop last night and we didn't get to bed until after midnight. We only had a couple of hours sleep before we were woken by the fire – and all they give us is a measly couple of hours extra! I feel is if I could do with a couple of weeks extra!"

Carl stood on the edge of some trees nearby and watched the fire take hold, grinning and chuckling to himself as he watched their puny efforts at putting it out as he tried to get closer.

He'd been working on the farm for several years, and he wasn't going to be brushed off so easily from his employment by someone like George Barford, a relative newcomer to the farm, as he considered him.

Carl had been called up to war at the age of 24, along with the rest of his friends and colleagues at the factory where they all worked, being invalided out two years later after receiving a bullet wound to the leg.

He'd spent several months in hospital, the bone being shattered into several pieces, and when it healed he was considered unfit for duty as it was obvious he'd never walk properly again, having been left with a permanent limp.

The factory where he'd worked had been severely damaged during a bombing raid, and was no longer in production, so after a period of convalescence at home, his father had finally found him a job on a local farm.

It wasn't far from his home and he could cycle there and back easily each day, and he found it more to his liking than factory work.

It was easy to shirk off when there was a job he didn't want to do, and when he didn't feel like working, he could always make himself scarce for an hour or so. There were plenty of places he liked to use, knowing there wasn't any likelihood of being caught, and it was always easy to make up an excuse as to where he'd been and what he'd been doing.

Having been invalided out of the army, he had been considered a bit of a hero – permanently injured in the line of duty – as they all thought of him; but that was far from the truth.

Carl had, in fact, been in the act of deserting from his platoon.

He'd come across a small German patrol whilst trying to make his way to freedom.

He thought they hadn't seen him, and quickly pulled back into the cover of the trees he'd just left – but he was wrong!

They were a small scouting party who'd been sent on ahead, and who were now waiting for the rest of the platoon to catch up with them. Spotting him, they thought they'd have some fun by 'bagging another Tommie' as they laughed and jeered their way after him.

Having been on the run for some hours now, he was tired and they, having rested whilst waiting for their platoon, were much fresher than him. They were gaining on him, firing their weapons indiscriminately into the trees as he zigzagged from side to side, hoping to avoid a stray bullet.

He knew his best chance was to find a hiding place until they'd passed him, but he also realised they'd have to return in the same direction to reach the road again, and their waiting vehicle. He'd need to stay put until after their return before he could consider it safe once again.

A small depression in the ground caught his eye. It was filled with thick undergrowth and brambles, and he hoped that by rolling into it, he might hide himself whilst not getting too many scratches.

He soon found why the growth was so lush when he rolled into six inches of water at the bottom, and lay shivering in it until their return.

As they passed him by, he held his breath, hoping they wouldn't still be looking for him, but just at that moment, an unwary rabbit ran across their path, and laughing loudly, they took aim and fired at it. The bullet missed the rabbit, but unfortunately for him, ricocheted off a tree and into the clump of brambles where he was hiding, hitting him in the leg.

He bit his lip, trying not to cry out with the pain, for that would have meant his instant death, and the blood from his lip ran down his chin, filling his mouth with the salty, acrid taste.

He lay in the depression for some time before he heard their platoon catch up with them. Most of the other soldiers took the opportunity to enter the woods and relieve themselves; and all the while, he expected his hiding place to be discovered. He finally heard the vehicles starting up once again, and breathed a sigh of relief as the sound of the tanks and the shouting voices rumbled away into the distance.

It was some time later that that he heard the sound of English voices coming towards him through the trees as he peered out through the brambles.

"Over here!" he shouted wildly, as he saw British uniforms streaming out of the trees, and he screamed loudly as they dragged him out.

It wasn't his own platoon but another that had been in the area, and it was after that that he had swiftly been taken to a medical station. Following treatment, he had been repatriated to Britain for his long stay in hospital.

His story was that he'd got separated from his own platoon and become hopelessly lost – the story he was sticking to – but it was far from the truth!

Now, as the fire died down, the building only a heap of burnt out timbers littering the ground, he chuckled once again.

"That'll teach you!" he muttered to himself, hoping the horse that had caused the trouble had gone up in smoke.

He made his way back across the fields from his hiding place in an old dilapidated barn where he'd been biding his time. We wanted to see the damage he'd caused, in the hope of seeing the burnt carcass of the horse being brought out, but he wasn't aware in the darkness that the horses had been brought out in time and let loose in the same field where he now was.

Nero, lifting his head, took a sniff of the air and sensed the presence of Carl, the man who had inflicted so much pain on him, as he saw his outline creeping along the hedgerow towards him. Carl, however, hadn't seen the stationary horse standing in the darkness under the overhanging branches of an ancient sycamore, and continued coming towards the animal.

Nero stood stock still, eyes rolling and expecting something bad was about to happen to him once again.

Carl still crept along the hedge line until he was almost immediately behind the horse, before suddenly becoming aware of his silent presence; but by that time it was far too late. Nero, in his panic stricken state, let out an angry bellow and reared up on his front legs, bringing them down hard on the ground, and kicking out backwards with both rear legs, putting all his mighty strength behind it.

One hoof caught Carl full in the chest, crushing his rib cage to a pulp, the other catching him on the side of the head and crushing his skull.

He was catapulted through the hedge behind him, landing in a murky stagnant pond on the other side, where his body almost immediately sank from view.

Jess heard Nero's bellow, and left the tent where she was to spend the rest of the night, anxious to check whether he was all right, but when he contentedly trotted

138

up to her out of the darkness and nuzzled against her, she stroked his nose for a while and returned to her bed.

Whatever had disturbed him, he seemed to have settled down again and no longer felt under threat.

Nobody missed Carl, as he'd already been told to leave the farm many hours ago, and when his father came searching for him several days later, they could all say with absolute truthfulness that they had no idea where he was.

CHAPTER 14

Amy Taylor sat on her bed, staring out of the window of her little flat overlooking Sefton Park. There was a well-tended garden below, full of summer flowers, but she saw none of it.

Her face was blotchy with crying, and her sodden handkerchief lay in her hands, leaving a wet patch on the skirt beneath it.

She and Peter had become engaged during the war years, and had seen very little of each other since. She worked as a secretary in the Air Ministry, and he as an Army Captain stationed somewhere in the middle east. She never knew where he was at any one time, and secrecy was of the utmost importance with the job he was doing, so he wasn't able to tell her. They intended to marry as soon as the war was over, and she often went over her new name, Mrs. Peter Lacey – Amy Lacey – as she would become, and felt it had a nice ring to it. It gave her a warm glow inside when she repeated it aloud.

He'd already told her about the farm his father, Ben Lacey, owned in Lancashire, saying he wanted to return and work on the farm after their marriage. She wasn't opposed to the idea, in fact, she quite liked the idea of having a country cottage somewhere on the farm where they could build a cosy little home and rear their three, or possibly four, children.

His father had already told him the farm would become his after his death, so she had the prospect of living in the farmhouse sometime in the future.

Her brother, Harry, a sergeant, was serving in the same platoon as Peter, and it was his letter she had received this morning. She stared down at it for some time before picking it up once again, and re-reading the dreaded lines for the umpteenth time, although she'd read it so many times, she already knew what it said by heart:

'My dear Amy,
I'm so sorry to have to tell you that Peter has sadly been taken from us. He died from gunfire during a battle, but that is all I'm able to tell you for the moment . . . '

It was only a short letter, written some weeks ago, having only just reached her. There were a few more platitudes of sympathy, which she had previously read, but now she couldn't seem to read any further, as her throat constricted once again. Those few words would haunt her forever!

All those weeks he'd been dead, and she hadn't known a thing about it – how she wished she'd known sooner – but there would have been nothing to be gained by that either. He'd still be gone, whichever way you looked at it.

They weren't officially a couple, so none of his belongings would be returned to her, and she'd have nothing left to remember him by – except her lovely sapphire engagement ring which she fondled lovingly. She'd wear it always!

She didn't know if he had any brothers or sisters, and she'd never met his parents as yet, so there was nobody to ask for a memento to remember him by, and he himself had lived in a rented flat.

There seemed nothing left except to continue living as she was for the rest of her life; a sad and lonely spinster.

Rousing herself finally, she went to the small kitchenette and made a cup of tea, where her pet cat, Studibaker, started rubbing against her legs and calling for food.

She lifted up his dish and filled it with food while the kettle boiled, deciding to go for a walk to try and clear her head. She found that whenever she had troubles, a walk often helped her think more clearly.

Leaving the house, she walked blindly in no particular direction, letting her feet take her where they wanted, not really noticing her surroundings, until she found herself on the main road.

Glancing to her right, she saw a tram coming towards her and without thinking what she was doing; she walked straight out in front of it.

The tram driver shouted out a warning, but being unable to stop the progress of the vehicle in time, he watched horrified as he saw her disappear under the front of it.

When they got her out, a doctor who was driving in the opposite direction stopped immediately and went to attend to her, but even from a swift glance at her injuries, he knew life was already extinct!

CHAPTER 15

It was now two years since the war had ended, and Frank had been made a supervisor at the Corporation yard, Callum having been made his deputy, with a wage increase for both of them. Calls for replacement housing were never ending, as well as the repairs that were in constant demand, and the workforce had to be increased to more than twice its normal level.

Nobody had ever queried Frank's ownership of his brother's house, and eventually he'd changed all the utility bills and other documentation into his name. Maura had worked wonders on the interior with the increased amount of money he and Callum were now bringing in.

Coming home from work one night, Maura handed him a letter.

"Looks official," she said, turning it over and indicating an address stamped on the reverse, "it's from a firm of solicitors."

His heart sank. Had he been wrong about the ownership of the house? Did it still belong to him – or had somebody else come forward with a more compelling right to its ownership? Although he'd never found a Will throughout his searches of the house, had somebody else perhaps come forward with one?

It was with trepidation that he rang them from work the next day. They weren't allowed to make private 'phone calls, but as he was on his own in the office, he decided to chance it.

"Smith and Smallwood – how may I help you?" a female voice answered.

His hand trembling, he went on to explain about the letter he'd received, and was asked to wait a moment while she looked through the records.

"Yes, I have it here. Mr. Smallwood has a matter he'd like to discuss with you. When would it be convenient for you to call and see him?"

"I could possibly make it on Thursday afternoon," he answered, feeling even more worried than ever. He was allowed one half day off a week, so if he worked all day Saturday, they'd probably allow him to take his half day on Thursday.

He heard her turning pages before she came back on the line and said, "Mr Smallwood is free at three thirty if that would suit you?"

"Yes, that shouldn't be a problem."

If he left work at one o'clock that would give him time to get changed and catch a tram to their offices in the city centre with plenty of time to spare. He decided not to try and use the car as the city centre was still in a very bad way. Clearance of the debris was still taking place, with many roads impassable, and buildings still liable to collapse. Only last week a woman had lost her life when, without warning, the whole front of a building had collapsed on top of her as she was walking past.

There was no problem when he asked the manager for time off, but he was a worried man when he descended from the tram in Victoria Street, in the heart of Liverpool's most prestigious city centre office buildings.

144

Most of these had been erected by wealthy merchants and bankers during Liverpool's meteoric climb to world-wide importance as a shipping and trading port; often on the backs of the slave trade, through which many slave ships had passed during its long history.

He'd allowed himself half an hour to find the office he wanted; most buildings bearing brass nameplates at their entranceways, some up wide flights of steps before they could be read, announcing the businesses housed within, and which floor they were situated on. He managed it well before that, and had a twenty minute wait before he was called into Mr. Smallwood's office.

The man wasn't very tall, possibly around fifty and slightly rotund, with short dark hair and a clipped moustache to match, however, he was friendly in his manner and Frank hoped it wasn't the calm before the storm.

"Our enquiries have led us to believe that you are related to Benjamin Lacey. Is that correct?" said the solicitor, referring to papers laid out in front of him when they were both seated.

"Yes, George was my bro . . .," suddenly stopping himself in mid-sentence. "Did you say, **Benjamin** Lacey?"

Mr. Smallwood nodded.

"I'm sorry, I thought this would be about my brother George – he was killed during the war."

Then pulling himself together once more he said, "Yes, Benjamin Lacey was my uncle, but he was also killed in a bombing raid during the war."

"Yes, I am aware of that," Mr. Smallwood replied, "which is why I have asked you to come and see me.

It would appear that Mr. Lacey only had two sons, one of whom was killed in the same bombing raid as his father and mother; and the other, a Captain Peter Lacey, was serving with the armed forces overseas. Captain Lacey was killed very near the end of the war, and our enquiries have led us to believe that you are now Benjamin Lacey's only surviving heir."

Here the solicitor paused, allowing Frank to take in and digest what he'd just said, before he continued once more.

He wasn't a wealthy man, but he did own a farm and a good amount of acreage to go with it, which was used by the army during the war, under an agreement previously signed by Captain Peter Lacey. However, the army now has no further use for it since the war has ended and has relinquished that agreement. It would seem that it now belongs to you solely."

Frank couldn't for the moment believe what he was hearing, and his mind was reeling with the possibilities as he left the building. Uncle Ben's farm was now his – what was left of it! He'd need to rebuild the house if it was to be of any use to anyone, and he almost missed his stop on the way home trying to think of a way to get together enough money to be able to do so.

Maura and Callum were delighted when they heard the news, and after a great deal of thought, it was Callum who eventually came up with the answer.

"Why not sell this place and use the money to rebuild the farmhouse? We could rent somewhere until it's completed and travel up every weekend to check on its progress. I could chip in with the rent, and once the house is finished we could run the farm between the three of us." Frank and Maura looked at each other. They were both overawed with the idea, thinking it definitely had promise, until Frank suddenly thought of another problem.

"We don't know yet if George's house legally belongs to me, and if there are deeds to the property, they won't be in my name."

Callum thought again for a moment.

"You need to make another appointment with Mr. Smallwood and see if he can sort it out for you, but I'm pretty sure if it legally belonged to somebody else, they'd have been knocking on your door long before now."

Frank sighed contemplatively.

"Lad's right," Maura chipped in. "No use counting your chickens before they're hatched! You need to sort the legal position of the ownership before making plans."

Frank was worried about bringing the problem of his ownership out into the open. They could open a can of worms if it turned out he wasn't legally entitled to it. They'd probably have to leave if another owner was found, leaving them with nowhere to live once again.

What if it was only a rented house and the owner hadn't realised they'd been living in it since George's death? Everything had been in such turmoil during the war, the owner might possibly have overlooked the fact that they'd moved in. He may even now be making plans to find another tenant for it, or even to sell it.

When he voiced these doubts, it was Maura who chipped in this time.

"You've already decided to sell this place and rent somewhere else while you have the farm rebuilt, so what would it matter if we did have to move out into rented accommodation? If we had nowhere else to live, you'd be entitled to apply for a Corpy house, and with you both working for them, I can't see them turning you down.

They're modernising that estate where the Corpy yard is. It's only quarter of a mile from here and there'd only be a short walk to work no matter where they housed us on the estate.

There are some nice three bedroom semi-detached houses, with gardens front and back. I wouldn't mind living in one of them."

"But what about the farm?" he asked, seeing the logic behind her thinking.

"We'd have to sell it," she said flatly. "Wouldn't fetch a lot with the state the house is in, but it would be enough to see us comfortably off for a good while. There should be plenty of takers for the amount of land it has with it."

Frank realised she was talking a lot of sense. She obviously had it planned out in her mind, and he had to admit, they were certainly nice houses she was talking about – he'd worked on them often enough during their modernisation. The streets were wide and tree-lined, with good-sized gardens front and back, and he wouldn't have minded living in one, but he still longed for the wide open countryside once again, and to be able to re-build the big old stone farmhouse. It felt like something he really wanted to get his teeth into.

He eventually plucked up the courage to go and see Mr. Smallwood again, who said he would start making enquiries into the ownership of the house immediately, and came back some weeks later with the news that Frank had been hoping for. The house did in fact legally belong to him, as they'd been unable to trace any other person who might be entitled to a share in its ownership. It seemed it had been left to his wife, Flora, by her parents when they died. She herself was an only child, and as she was already dead, had now legally belonged to George.

The papers were drawn up, and Frank duly became the new legal owner of the property.

After making enquiries at work, he was told that already being a home owner; he wasn't entitled to a Corporation house. A colleague, however, did give him some help in finding private landlords who rented out their properties, pointing out that their rents would be somewhat higher than those the Corporation charged.

In his eyes, that didn't matter. He was now the proud owner of two properties, and when his own house, as he liked to think of it, was sold, he'd have enough capital to start work on the farm.

He'd come a long way from losing his job and his home, and being reduced to living in a wooden shed on a farm, to now being the owner of not one, but two properties, of his own.

When he voiced these thoughts to Maura, she brought him back to earth with the sobering thought that although he was now the owner of two properties, in the process, he'd lost both his brother and his uncle.

A sobering thought indeed!

CHAPTER 16

Jess stayed on the farm in Derbyshire until the end of the war, and their group was finally disbanded. However, as the work of the Land Army still continued, they were given the choice of staying on if they wished. Most of them decided to return to their homes, as their husbands and sons would soon be demobilised, but a lot of those who'd lost their loved ones had decided to stay on. Life had become a lonely prospect for them!

They had decided not to rebuild the stables, as the owner had invested in a tractor, which was able to do the work of all three horses, and much, much more, but in far less time. Instead they built a wooden loose box alongside the side wall of the farmhouse for Nero, where it was easier to keep an eye on him, and sold the other two horses. If the tractor broke down, as it frequently did, they still had him on hand to pull the carts.

Jess, having nowhere to return to herself, had decided to stay on. She had no wish to return to her family and face her fathers' wrath, and became Nero's sole carer.

She was sad to see the other two horses go. As they were both quite elderly, she felt sure they'd go for horse meat, but she was determined that wouldn't happen to Nero, even if she had to steal him herself and ride off into the night with him.

There was a small area at the side of Nero's stall where his tack and harness was kept, and there was just enough room for her to set up a camp bed and an old apple box at the end of it for her meagre belongings.

Apart from her clothes, which were washed weekly on a communal wash day in which all the girls participated, she needed and owned very little else, and what she did own fitted easily on the top of the box, or hanging from a few hooks in the wall.

One day, returning from a day's apple and pear picking, she found the farm owner, Harold Jayston, standing looking into Nero's stall, with another man she didn't recognise.

As she walked towards them, they heard the sound of her feet on the cobbled surface, and both turned towards her.

"Ah!" Harold said, "Now here's the lady you need to talk to!"

Puzzled, she took a few steps nearer and stopped, a worried frown creasing her face.

"Jess," he continued, "this is Paul Archer. Paul has set up stables in Lancashire where they intend to breed these heavy horses."

Now she definitely had cause to worry. Was he intending to sell Nero to this man? She couldn't conceive what her life would be like without him, or what she'd be able to do with herself in that eventuality.

Paul smiled and held out his hand to shake hers. She had to admit he was rather good looking – in a rugged and weather beaten sort of way.

"I'm pleased to meet you," he said, "I've been hearing a lot about your prowess with horses. I hear you're a natural with them."

Just at that moment, even without hearing her voice, but sensing her presence, Nero pushed his huge head through the open door and whinnied loudly, brushing Paul to one side as he did so.

"I'm so sorry," she cried, catching Paul's arm as he staggered sideways and helping him regain his balance.

But instead of being annoyed, he laughed loudly.

"Well, at least he's pleased to see someone! All he's done is hang his head while we've been standing here."

She reached out her hand to Nero, and he snuffled against it, reaching forward to rest his head against her shoulder.

"Do you think you could manage to get him out and show him to Paul properly?" Harold asked.

Unhappily, she nodded, and went inside to fetch a halter, quickly and expertly fitting it onto his head and leading him outside. It looked very much as if he was to be sold after all, otherwise why would the man be here, and why did he want the horse paraded in front of him?

Nero was a little frisky at first, sensing something wasn't quite right, but under her soothing words, he quickly settled down.

The two men were talking quietly, but she couldn't hear what they were saying, as the sound of the horses' hoofs on the cobbled surface drowned out their words.

"Thank you Jess," Harold called out after a few minutes, "could you bring him over here now."

Obediently, she did as he asked, and Paul walked all round the horse, examining him from a distance, before stepping forward and attempting to lift one of his shaggy forelegs to examine his feet.

Nero turned a rolling eye towards him, but refused to lift his foot, and no power on earth was going to make that happen if he didn't want it to. Paul exerted all his strength in the effort, but still the foot didn't move an inch. If anything, Nero seemed to be putting all his weight on the foot he was trying to lift.

Jess hid a smile.

"Would you like me to try?" she asked innocently.

A red faced Paul stood back and held out a chivalrous hand towards the leg.

"Be my guest!" he said.

Jess obligingly walked round to the foot, and standing in front of his shoulder, she bent down and took hold of it.

"Up!" she said in a commanding voice, at the same time taking hold of his fetlock.

The foot came up immediately and she braced it against her knee as a surprised Paul came round to examine it; the now amenable Nero repeating the process for all four feet.

As she held the horses head, Paul examined the rest of his body, eventually lifting his tail to manipulate his testicles. Jess was worried that he might kick out when he started doing that, as his eyes were rolling, and he was trying to turn his head again, but soothing words from her ensured that the examination went off without a hitch.

"You have a lovely touch with the animal," he said, coming to the front of the horse and examining his mouth, nose and eyes. "You can put him back now."

She took Nero back into his stable and gave him a few carrots and an apple she had in her pocket as a reward, but when she came out again, the two men were nowhere in sight.

When she returned from work the next day, she found a note pinned to the stable, asking her to call at the farm and see Harold after their evening meal, and it was with a heavy heart that she made her way to the mess tent.

There were only six girls left working the land now, the rest having returned home, and although she was friendly

153

with all of them, she hadn't really made a special friend of anyone. From her morose attitude they all realised that something was wrong.

Afterwards, she made her way back and knocked on the door of the farm, which was opened almost immediately by Harold.

"Come in, Jess," he said, stepping back and waving her inside, motioning to a chair at the kitchen table, and pulling out the one opposite for himself.

Without further ado, he came straight to the point.

"As you've probably guessed, Paul Archer is interested in buying Nero."

Her heart fell, and she gulped inadvertently.

"Having bought the new tractor, I've seen the advantages it brings over those of horses, and I've decided to buy another. The government are providing grants to get the country back on its feet again, and I've decided to take advantage of it, so I really don't need to keep a horse any longer."

Seeing she was near to tears, he continued quickly, putting a hand on her arms crossed in front of her on the table.

"Nero won't be going alone – if you'd like to – you'll be going with him!"

"What!" her eyes almost popped out of her head.

"Horses are still needed in places where it isn't possible to use tractors, especially in forestry work, where they can't be used amongst the trees. These heavy horses can be harnessed to whole trees and they can drag them through the undergrowth with ease.

Paul is setting up a breeding programme to find some good strong stock for such work, and Nero is just the type of horse he's looking for as a stud."

154

She was delighted with this outcome. Nero's life would become very different from now on, and come to that, so would hers.

"Paul is also going to buy one of the carts we no longer have any use for. Would you be happy to take Nero all the way to Lancashire pulling the cart?"

He looked surprised when she laughed, and explained her laughter by telling him about her upbringing in the gypsy community, which brought him to laughter as well.

"Well that's one problem solved!" he stated as their laughter subsided. "I was worried about you being able to manage all on your own, but obviously you should be well capable of the task."

The following weekend saw her harnessing Nero ready for their trek towards Lancashire, Harold having furnished her with a map, on which Paul had already marked the position of his stables. It was just on the fringes of a village, and as there was only one road through, which led straight past the stables, there was very little chance of her missing it.

It took quite a few days to get there, the weather staying unseasonably kind to them. They took frequent breaks along the way, and found the farm easily by the sign arching high above the gateway proclaiming the entrance to **'Archers Heavy Horse Stud'**.

Turning in, she was impressed when they drew up before the stables.

No longer a wooden lean-to against the farmhouse wall, but a purpose-built block of three loose boxes to house the breeding stallions; one of them already bearing the name **'Nero'** painted above the door.

The flat fenced paddocks stretched as far as the eye could see, and it was while she was gazing across the acres of lush green meadow that Paul came to find her.

"Good to see, isn't it? My father was lucky to find this place."

"Your father?" she queried, looking at him in surprise. "I thought you owned it?"

"Oh, I do – with some financial help from my father. He owns a haulage business in Liverpool, and they do a lot of heavy haulage and furniture removals. They'll eventually move into motorised vehicles when there's enough petrol available, and the roads have been repaired after the bomb damage, but until then, they'll go on using heavy horses, which is why he saw the potential in my idea of breeding them. There's still a lot of work out there for them in the community, and we've already had loads of interest from all over the country."

As he spoke, she'd already stepped down from the cart and stretched her stiff limbs. Knowing she was nearing her destination, she'd completed the last few miles without a break, wanting to reach it before nightfall, and was now feeling extremely tired.

"Nero's box is all ready, so if you get him unharnessed, we can settle him down and I can show you your own quarters," he said, as he walked round examining the horse and also the cart, for any signs of damage.

Nero nuzzled into her as she undid the buckles and unharnessed him, before giving him a bucket of water. She went into the loose box ahead of him to show him there was nothing to fear in this strange place, but she needn't have worried as he trotted happily after her, appreciative of the smell of fresh hay in the rack. When she left him a few minutes later, he was happily tucking in without a backward glance, and it seemed that he'd accepted his new home immediately.

Walking across the yard and round to the other side of the house, they found another block of four stables with a tack room at the end, which Paul explained was to house the mares when they were brought to the stallions.

Beyond that was a large open storage barn already housing a small tractor, some bales of hay, and sacks of horse feed held above the floor on wooden pallets.

"Your quarters are above the stables," he said, seeing her taking everything in before leading her round the corner to the back of the building, where a stone staircase ran up towards a door at the top.

He went up first and she followed, gaping in awe when she stepped inside and looked around. She'd never had living quarters like this before in the whole of her life.

It was one large room with a kitchen area to the left; a window above the sink looking out across the paddocks, and a wooden table and four chairs set around it.

In the centre of the room, flooded with light from two windows overlooking the stable yard, was a sofa, rather past its best as Paul admitted, and two armchairs – not matching, but perfectly serviceable.

To the other end of the room stood two doors, which Paul opened to show her two bedrooms, each identical, and each housing two single beds, two small wardrobes, and two bedside cupboards, with a sink in one corner.

"I've had a lavatory installed," he said, rather apologetically, "but there wasn't room for one up here. You'll find it at the back of the tack room, which also has a door on this side of the building, so you won't have to walk right round the stables to get to it."

It made no difference to her, she'd never used a proper lavatory in her life, so didn't even know how they worked, except that people she knew who'd used one said they were wonderful, and they didn't smell at all. Having buried all their excrement in pits while with the gypsies, there had never been any smell, but they'd had an earth toilet at the farm, which did on occasion smell a bit ripe.

"Will there be more girls then?" she asked, noting there were four beds.

"Yes, or should I say, four girls at any one time," he answered. "There'll only be you and one other for the time being, but if things get busier, I may hire another two. She'll be starting next week, so I guess you have the place to yourself for the time being, so you can pick which room and which bed you want as well."

He showed her where everything else was kept, and had even filled the cupboards with stock items such as tea, sugar, salt and pepper, and a few tins of baked beans and soup, showing her a small loaf of bread and some margarine in the metal bread bin.

"There's a small shop in the village if you need anything else. They don't have a great deal to offer, only the basics, but you can take the cart into town and do a bigger shop in the next few days. There won't be a great deal for you to do here for the next few weeks before we get up and running properly as we're still finishing off the stable block."

When he'd gone, she chose her bed and lay down on it, luxuriating in the softness of its mattress. It was only utility furniture, most of it bought from a second hand shop, although the mattresses, bed linen, and blankets he'd bought from new. The mattresses were only flock, but

158

never having slept on a proper bed before, it was luxury indeed, and she soon found herself fast asleep.

After what seemed only minutes, but was in fact two hours later, she was awoken by a knock on the door, and she heard Paul's voice calling.

"Jess, are you in there?"

"Yes, just a minute," she called back, realising it was already dusk.

Stretching and climbing off the bed, for the moment wondering where she was, she answered the door.

"There's only the two of us here tonight, and I wondered if you'd like to eat with me. I have a pan of stew simmering on the stove."

She hadn't realised before, but she did now, that she was extremely hungry, and accepted his offer with gratitude.

"Yes, I'll be down in a minute. I just want to check on Nero first – just to make sure he's settled in."

"Ok, I'll have it on the table in half of an hour," and he made his way down the steps, while she returned to the bedroom to have a wash. They'd had running water on the farm she'd just left, so she knew how to use a tap, but having it in the bedroom was a great novelty – and having a bar of Pears soap to clean your hands was luxury indeed. Even more so was a soft towel to dry her hands afterwards; usually the whole crew had used the same old bit of rag or sacking for all of them. She found herself wondering where they'd be able to wash all these things when they became dirty – the sink was far too small.

When she reached Nero's stall, he was lying down, but lifted his head and gazed at her with a baleful eye for a moment, before resting it down again onto the straw. If he was contented with his new surroundings, then so was she.

159

CHAPTER 17

Maura was busy baking one Saturday afternoon when she heard a knock at the front door. Rinsing flour off her hands and wiping them on her apron, she hurried to answer it, just as the caller knocked once again.

"Sorry," she said as she opened the door. "I was baking and my hands were covered in flour."

"On the contrary, dear lady, it is I who should be sorry for disturbing you from your labours," said the man standing on the doorstep, as he took off his black trilby hat and doffed it towards her.

He was tall, and dressed all in black, from his woollen overcoat to his black trousers and shoes, and looked every inch the elegant gentleman that he was.

"Can I trouble you to fetch Mr. Lacey for me?" he now asked.

A little flummoxed by such an affluent looking gentleman standing on her doorstep, she left the door open while she went to look for Frank, finding him in the back room reading his newspaper.

"There's a gentleman at the door asking to speak to you," she said, somewhat annoyed that he hadn't answered the door himself when he knew she was baking.

"What's his name?" he asked, not expecting any callers on a Saturday afternoon, and she realised that in her awed state, she'd forgotten to ask his name.

"I forgot to ask," she said, lowering her voice as she added, "but he's a real toff – ever so well dressed!"

Folding his paper and putting it down on the arm of his chair, he followed her out and went to the front door while she returned to her baking, leaving the door open so that she could hear what was said, and almost forgetting about the scones she'd left in the oven. Luckily, the smell alerted her to them, and they were only slightly too brown on the tops.

"Good afternoon," said the gentleman, doffing his hat once more as Frank appeared at the door. "My name is Grant, Frederick Grant," as he handed him a plain white business card with black lettering stating simply: **Frederick Grant**, and below it: **Cotton Broker**.

Without waiting for Frank to ask any more questions, he continued.

"I am led to believe that your house is for sale, is that correct?"

Frank nodded. The signboard hadn't even been put up outside yet!

Seeing his astonishment, the man smiled.

"My brother is in charge of the Corporation department where you work, and it was he who passed me the word that you were selling your house. May I come in and look around if it's convenient?"

Frank stood back and allowed him to enter.

"I'm afraid it won't be very tidy," he said. "We weren't expecting your visit."

"No matter! I don't need it in a pristine state of tidiness, the suitability is all that I need to ascertain!"

Frank took him round, noting Maura's state of disarray in the kitchen. She'd heard what was said at the door, but it was too late for her to do anything about it.

Frederick Grant made no comments as he looked perfunctorily into each room, and she was glad she'd made the beds and tidied the bedrooms before starting on the baking.

When they returned to the hallway once more, he turned to Frank and held out his hand.

"Your house is eminently suitable. Congratulations – you've sold it even before it's been put on the market. You can now tell the estate agents you've changed your mind and decided not to sell it, and all you'll have to pay is their out of pocket expenses, with no commission due on the sale!"

Frank and Maura looked at each other, neither knowing what to say, before Maura gathered her wits about her and asked if he'd like a cup of tea while they discussed it.

"I don't mind if I do – and some of your excellent home baking wouldn't go amiss if the smell is anything to go by."

She smiled at the compliment and busied herself getting things ready while the two men went into the parlour, the room always kept neat and tidy and usually reserved for visitors.

Maura made the tea and picked out the scones that hadn't browned too much, using some of her precious margarine ration and her own home-made blackberry jam to cover the meagre spread of margarine.

When they were all seated and had drunk the tea and eaten the scones, Frederick proceeded to give an explanation.

"The house isn't for myself," he said. "My daughter and her fiancée have both been serving in the RAF during the war; he as a pilot of Lancaster bombers, and she as an operator in the control tower. They have both been recently demobbed, and have decided to get married straight away. I feel the least I can do is to buy them a house in which to start their married life as a small token of my gratitude for their efforts during the war. They were both in a great deal of danger at all times, and I feel I need to do something for them."

Frank and Maura were both in awe of his reasons and admired the man for it.

"Unless you have any more questions, I'll be on my way now. I will appoint a surveyor to check the house over next week, but barring any complications, the sale will go ahead as planned. I will be paying cash for it so things should go through very quickly."

He shook hands with them both at the door as he was leaving, and congratulated Maura on her delicious baking, saying he only wished his wife could cook as well.

Sure enough, the surveyor appeared the following Wednesday morning, and by Friday they'd had a letter from Mr. Grant's solicitors informing them that the sale was going ahead.

Six weeks later found them living in a small flat above a hairdresser's shop just around the corner from the Corporation yard where they worked.

The message about its availability was passed to him through the channels by his boss, Arthur Grant, the brother of Frederick, the man who had bought their house. It seemed that his daughter owned the salon, and also the flat above.

It wasn't very big, consisting of one large room acting as kitchen, dining, and sitting room combined, with two small bedrooms, and a lavatory at the bottom of the stairs in a small yard at the back, which they shared with the hairdressing staff, but they counted themselves lucky to have it. There were so many families looking for accommodation after being bombed out that any kind of property was snapped up immediately it became available, even before they'd seen it.

As it was early summer, the builder he had hired to re-build Beech Tree Farm had told him they hoped to have it completed within three months. There was much he could salvage from the previous building and plenty of second-hand building materials to be had from bombed out premises which weren't, or couldn't, be rebuilt.

However, the smallness of the flat was something they could learn to live with for the time being; Frank and Callum still working long hours on the repair and rebuilding programme for the Council, and Maura busying herself browsing the shops for furniture, carpets and curtain materials, which filled up many of her days.

The flat, being so small, took little time to clean, but having windows both front and back, was nearly always filled with light, giving it a pleasant atmosphere.

Most of their weekends were spent going out to the farm to check on its progress, and to lend a hand where they could. Petrol was becoming easier to obtain, and as Frank and Callum were able to walk to work, it was all conserved for their weekend outings, noting more and more progress as the weeks went by.

It was nearing the end of July that the builder announced it should be ready for occupation in two weeks time, and they had to give in their notice at work. They were told that other Councils were always looking for qualified tradesmen, so Frank at least, should have no trouble finding a job.

The Lancashire coast hadn't been hit as hard by the bombing as Liverpool had, and it did seem that people now wanted to move out of Liverpool and live further out in the suburbs. There was a constant need for more housing to be built, especially where people had been housed in prefabricated buildings, and had enjoyed a less hectic life than living within the confines of the city. These were to be demolished and rebuilt as more substantial dwellings, where tenants were readily available.

Callum and Gina said their final goodbyes on the night before leaving, sitting on a seat overlooking the neat flower beds in the local park.

"We still have the car, so I should be able to get back and see you at weekends, but it won't be for a while, as there'll be a lot to do when we move in," he said sincerely.

"I know," she replied. "I'll still be here when you can. Dad's having a telephone installed, so I'll write and give you the number and you can let me know when you're coming."

They both knew that they probably wouldn't see each other again. They'd enjoyed each others' company, but just lately it had become more a friendship than a romance, and Gina had already been seeing another boy while Callum was working so many long hours.

She enjoyed his company, and he'd taken her out a lot more than Callum ever had. Working in an office, and putting in far less hours than Callum, he always had his weekends free.

165

Whether she'd ever write with the number, or he'd ever arrange to come back and see her, was something that neither of them was too sure about. Callum knew that for the foreseeable future, there'd be a lot of work to be done on and around the farm to get it back on its feet again, and he still had a hankering after Jess – something that had never left him, and he doubted it ever would. He knew the gypsies visited Lancashire from time to time, and hoped there might be a chance they'd come across each other again, not knowing that she wasn't with them anymore.

They allowed themselves a month to settle in, before Frank and Callum started looking for work, and both were given a job immediately by the local Council. Neither could believe their luck when it turned out to be working on the prefabs opposite the farm – where Maura had once lived. They were to be torn down, and three bedroom semi-detached houses were to be built in their place, similar to those Maura had admired in West Derby.

"How many houses will there be?" she asked one evening while they were sitting by the stove one particularly chilly autumn evening.

"I believe about three hundred," he answered absentmindedly, engrossed in his evening paper.

"I've been thinking," she continued. "With so many houses being built, we'd have plenty of custom if we were to build a farm shop again near the gate. It'd be a ready market for our home grown produce, and we could buy in other goods to sell alongside them. I always found lots of people around making their own jams and chutneys."

166

Still holding his paper, he dropped it down to his lap and looked across at her.

"And where would we get the time for that?" he said, annoyed at being disturbed, and immediately ready to reject her idea.

"You've already thought about hiring in labour to get the land ready for spring planting next year, and we've still got money left in the bank from the sale of the other house, so we could start off with a small wooden structure and work our way up from there. A large shed shouldn't cost too much, and I'd enjoy running it and meeting my new neighbours for a chat. Who knows, we might even be able to stretch to one of those new tractors to make life easier."

He began to mull it over. They had almost a whole year before there'd be enough produce to sell. They could easily rebuild the wooden shed he'd lived in with Callum and Alison. It could house itinerant workers, as it had once before, and they could help with getting the land ready for the spring planting.

On further consideration, it didn't seem such a crazy proposition as it had first appeared!

CHAPTER 18

Jess had been employed at the stud for about a week, work still being carried out on some of the loose boxes by Paul and his crew, when Susan Howarth arrived.

She'd been a bit bored and lonely for most of the week. Nero was as yet the only horse there, and apart from his feeding, cleaning out and exercising, there was little else for her to do.

Susan was a little morose and uncommunicative when she first arrived, but after Jess had offered to help her move in and take her belongings up to the flat; she thawed out a little and gladly accepted a share of Jess's beans on toast.

When they'd finished, Jess made them a mug of tea each and they sat down in the armchairs facing each other while they drank it, using the window ledge to rest their mugs on.

It was raining heavily outside, and rain coursed down the window, giving the fading daylight an eerie feel.

"Makes you feel as if a ghostly spirit of some long dead soul will appear at the window any minute, doesn't it?" Jess said, pulling a grisly face. "Shades of Heathcliffe and Cathy! We really must get some nice bright curtains when we get time to go and shop for material."

For the first time, Susan gave a slight smile as she nodded.

Seeing her beginning to thaw out, Jess continued, picking her tea up and taking another mouthful.

"Can you sew?" she asked.

Susan nodded again.

"Yes, my mother was a seamstress, so I learned from an early age."

"D'you think she'd do them for us if we asked her nicely?" Jess asked. Her sewing prowess wasn't up to much, so she rather hoped the answer would be yes.

Susan seemed to shrink back into herself when she heard the suggestion, and shook her head sadly.

"No, she definitely wouldn't," she replied adamantly.

Jess knew she'd touched on a raw nerve, and tried to recoup the situation.

"Oh, well, I guess you're going to have to teach me then," she said, laughing. "I've never been much good with a needle and thread – and as for a pair of scissors – it isn't wise to let me loose with a pair of **them**! Anything could happen!"

This once again seemed to lighten the atmosphere a little and Susan smiled at her joke.

"A nice bright yellow would look nice in here," Jess continued, looking around, "and some pale green on the walls."

Susan roused herself and looked around, before picking up her mug and finishing her own tea.

"You might be right – it'll brighten the place up a bit, and hide this depressing rain."

As Jess had made their meal, Susan repaid the favour by doing the washing up, whilst Jess went out to check on Nero before going to bed.

When she arrived back, Susan had found a tin of cocoa in the cupboard and made them both a cup.

169

"I hope you don't mind," Susan said, holding up the cup, "I thought you might like some before bed. As soon as I get time, I'll find a shop and buy some food myself."

Jess was appreciative, and having hung up her wet raincoat behind the door, she brought out a packet of chocolate biscuits from the back of the cupboard before she settled down in an armchair. Before either of them had noticed, the packet was empty.

"Oops!" Jess said. "We've rather made pigs of ourselves, haven't we? But it was only three quarters full anyway."

This elicited laughter from Susan for the first time since she'd arrived, and seemed to open the first steps to a friendship between them.

"I don't know what you must think of me," Susan said, as she curled her legs under her and sank back into the chair.

Old and saggy the chair may be, but it was certainly comfortable to curl up in, as Jess did likewise with her own chair.

"I'd like to explain," she continued, more morose again. "I met Robert during the war years, when he had a spot of leave from the army. We kept in touch all through the war, and to cut a long story short, I got pregnant just after he was demobbed.

Mum and dad were furious, and being staunch churchgoers, they told me I was bringing shame on them and the rest of the family. They insisted we get married immediately, but a week before the wedding, Robert announced that he didn't want to marry me any longer, and to tell the truth, I was relieved to hear it.

I realised that I no longer loved him the way I thought I did, and when I faced mum and dad to tell them, they were so furious, they told me to pack my belongings and leave immediately.

I stayed with a friend for a few days, but then she told me about working on a farm during the summer months when labour was always in short supply, and usually accommodation was included. She introduced me to the farmer, and I've worked there all summer, but they've no need of me now that winter's arriving.

Then I heard about Paul and the stud farm. I've always loved horses, and I used to volunteer at the Co-Op stables in Liverpool when I was younger, where I worked most weekends. They used to use horses for their bread deliveries.

Hearing that I was used to horses, he told me he needed staff and was willing to give me a trial."

"But what about the baby?" Jess interjected.

Susan dropped her head, and when she lifted it again, her eyes shone with tears.

"I miscarried in my fourth month – so there is no baby anymore."

"I'm so sorry," Jess said, feeling that she'd gone too far and shouldn't have asked. It should have been obvious that something had happened to the baby when she'd arrived alone.

"Never mind - I'm over it now," Susan said, briskly picking up the cups and taking them to the sink to wash. "I didn't know how I was going to look after it anyway, and probably things have worked out for the best in the long run."

Susan chose to sleep in the second bedroom that night, saying that when somebody else came along, she'd move in with Jess, seeing as they were beginning to get along so well; but Jess suspected that wasn't the real reason when she heard her sobbing quietly.

Next morning, Susan was already up and about when Jess showed her face. She was never very good in a morning, and it took her a good hour to wake herself up properly; but Susan was obviously a morning person, as a pot of tea and some toast was already waiting for her when she emerged from her room.

"That's a welcome sight," she said, as Susan poured the tea and tucked into her own toast.

"I'm sorry I heaped all my troubles on you last night," she said, as they were finishing off. "I promise not to do it again. I think I've got it out of my system now."

Jess smiled.

"And will you make it up with your parents now?"

A frown creased Susan's face.

"No – never!" she answered emphatically. "What parent turns their back on a child in their hour of need? I'd never do that to any child of mine! They'd always know they could turn to me in any emergency. I'd always be there to help – no matter what."

She was so vehement in her reply that Jess decided not to push it any further.

"Come on," she said brightly. "Let's clear up here and go and find Paul – see if he has any jobs for us today, then you can come and help me feed and muck out Nero's stable. I want to see what he makes of you. I hope he takes to you too!"

Paul, busy as ever, greeted them on his way out, shrugging into his jacket as he came through the door.

"Sorry to dash," he said, "but I'll see you later. Jess will show you around," and he was gone.

She handed Susan a carrot for Nero, and they made their way to the stable, where his huge head poked from the opening as he heard their approach, huffing and whickering when he caught her scent.

"Wow! He's a big boy, isn't he?" Susan said, going straight up to the horse with her hand held out offering the carrot.

Nero rolled his eyes at first as he realised it was a stranger, but then suddenly changed his whole attitude and took the proffered carrot from her hand.

As he chewed, she stroked his head, from his forehead right down to his nose, gently murmuring to him as she did so, and Jess, with a slight pang of jealousy, was glad to see he'd accepted her. She had to get used to the idea that Nero would have to be handled by other people in the future – he wasn't solely her horse any more.

It soon became clear to them both that things weren't going to be plain sailing for Paul in his new venture.

No new girls joined them, and for the rest of the winter, she and Susan had the flat to themselves.

The rest of the stables were completed, and the building workers left, the only mare having been installed in them was Krista, Paul's own horse. He'd had her since his late teens, and although she'd had several foals when younger, she was far too old now to have any more.

Over Christmas, Paul returned to spend a week with his own parents and family. Jess and Susan, not having any family to return to, spent Christmas together in the flat, assuring him they'd take care of Krista while he was away.

The flat was now much more homely, having bought some pretty curtain material with which to adorn the windows in each room.

Jess's efforts at sewing being slow, and not very productive, they came to the arrangement that Susan would complete the curtains, while she painted the walls. That seemed a much better arrangement, and suited their respective talents better.

When Paul returned in the New Year, it was to announce that he'd made a couple of new contacts whilst at home, and a man would be arriving in a couple of weeks to have a look at Nero as a prospective sire for the two mares he wanted to put in foal that year.

Jess was a little worried by this. Although she knew Nero had been used at stud before, it was some time ago, well before she'd arrived at the farm, and she was a little nervous about how he'd behave. He was in his mid teens now – would he still be interested, or would he be over zealous, in which case, he might be hard to handle with his great size and weight.

The man arrived and looked at Nero, seeming surprised that Paul only had one stallion to show him, however, he seemed pleased at what he saw. They haggled over the stud price, and eventually settled on one quite a lot lower than Paul had hoped for, but he knew that if this was successful, other contacts might follow.

When it came time for the mare to be brought in, Nero seemed to get a whiff of her presence immediately, lifting his head over the stable door and scenting the mare as the trailer came in through the gate.

However, when it came time for him to serve her, he was the perfect gentleman and performed with all the aplomb of a seasoned performer, despite not having served a mare for quite a number of years.

Paul had already had Nero's fertility tested, and both he and the vet were happy with the outcome. Whether it had taken or not; only time would tell.

They were all pleased to hear some weeks later that the mare was definitely in foal, and this news was followed a few days later by the booking for another stud.

Paul, however, wasn't too pleased by the way his new venture was progressing.

If he didn't have at least two stallions to show prospective breeders, they would look around for where there was a better choice, but he also knew that it would be risky to buy another stallion when money was so tight. He'd expected far more interest than had been shown at present!

CHAPTER 19

Silas and Kyla had liked the small camp site they'd found in the quarry in Wales, and had stayed there for almost two years now. It was sheltered from the worst of the weather, and as the ground around them was very porous, it never became muddy underfoot, even during the wettest of weather. The children were able to roam around and play to their hearts content without hindrance from anyone.

Silas was able to forage for food in the nearby woods, always coming back with something, as there were plenty of edible fungi throughout the different seasons, rabbits and pheasants also being in plentiful supply. He even managed to catch a couple of grouse on the moorland above the quarry, but they weren't in plentiful supply.

He'd also caught a small deer at one time in the woods, which fed them for over a week, and although Kyla had cooked and wrapped the meat in plenty of large leaves and left it in a deep cleft in the rock face which was cool and damp, they'd eventually had to throw the remains away.

One day, Kylas's roaming instincts getting the better of her, she mentioned it to Silas when he returned from his latest foray into the woods, having brought with him a couple of plump wood pigeons.

"You know, I love this place," she said, as she plucked and cleaned the birds, "but I really feel the need to move on again."

"Me too," he said, "I've been feeling the same as well just lately. Where do you want to go?"

"I did think about going down south to catch up with my own family," she replied.

"No, that's the first place my father would think of looking. He's probably already been making enquiries amongst other families coming from that direction, and he'd soon find us, especially as that's where you told him you were heading. How about we go further north? There's a rather nice wooded place we used to go to once. It's near the beach, and there are miles of sand hills. The children might enjoy that for a change."

She agreed immediately. She felt she might enjoy that herself for a change, and with summer just beginning, they could stay for a good few months before returning here to overwinter in the relative shelter of the quarry.

Just over a month later, they found the open clearing in the woods near Southport, obviously having been used as a campsite previously. The sandy ground was well trodden, and even though the fires had been extinguished well before the others had left, there were still the ashes to be seen littering the site.

The children, excited by the proximity of the beach, wanted to go down to it immediately, and Kyla agreed, Silas following behind to make sure they came to no harm. It gave her time to make preparations for their stay and to start cooking a meal.

It wasn't far off sundown, so Silas brought them back before it was too dark to find their way back, smelling wood smoke, and a delicious aroma of cooking food wafting towards him as they made their way through the trees.

They'd always been used to doing farm work, or other non-skilled jobs wherever they camped, to pay for clothing and food they couldn't forage for themselves, and it wasn't long before news of work not far from their camp filtered through to them.

Silas took himself off early one morning to find where it was, and the man who seemed to be in charge of the labour force informed him they were lifting potatoes and cabbage.

Having done this type of work many times before, Silas was set on straight away, being surprised at the cart pulled by a tractor and not a horse. He didn't much care for the amount of noise it created, but that was far outweighed by how much quicker and easier it was to get the job done with its use.

Two weeks later he returned to their camp site early. It had rained most of the day, and the ground had become too muddy to work, so they'd been laid off for the rest of the day.

There was no sign of Kyla or the children, and after an hour's anxious wait, he decided to go and see if he could find them.

Although it had stopped raining, the day was too cold to be on the beach, and he made his way through the woods, calling out to her, wondering if she might be foraging for something tasty for their meal. At first there was no sign of her, but suddenly, a hand shot out and grabbed him by the shoulder.

"Over here!" hissed Kylas's voice. "Don't make a sound!"

Used to this sort of behaviour, as gypsies weren't always welcome during their travels, he followed her into the shelter of some bushes, where he found the children sitting on an earth bank and waiting quietly.

Putting her finger to her lips, and motioning the children to stay where they were, she led him through the trees, where he became aware of an increasing amount of noise and human voices.

Stopping him, she pulled him behind a thorny bush and pointed through a gap in the trees, where four gypsy caravans were parked.

She said nothing, but motioned him back through the trees to where the children waited.

"It's your people!" she said, stating the obvious, as he'd already recognised the caravans.

"Your father isn't with them yet, but he's bound to be along soon with the rest of them. We need to get out of here quickly before he arrives. Otherwise there'll be a real ruckus."

Packing up as quietly as they could, and hitching up the horse, they made their way towards the edge of the woods. They pulled in amongst the trees a couple of hundred yards from the entrance, and told the children to stay inside the caravan until they returned, making as little noise as possible.

"They'll have to come past the end of this road to get to where the others are camped, so we'll wait here until they all arrive, and then we can make good our escape," she said, speaking quietly against his ear.

They crept through the trees and waited until the rest of the group arrived, his fathers' being one of the last.

"How many of them are there?" she asked at last.

"That's it!" he stated. "There won't be any more."

179

"Yes, but if there are any new ones, they're bound to tell the others they've seen us. We can't just be travelling through. This road stops about quarter of a mile further on, and it's nothing but woods and beach after that."

Bearing this in mind, they waited another hour, before deciding it was safe to carry on, reaching the main road without seeing another caravan.

"That was a close shave," he said, as they stopped at the road. "Now which way? Left, right or straight on?"

"Perhaps if would be safer to go straight on and stay off the road for a while, just in case there may be some stragglers," she answered, as he urged the horse into a trot to cross the road.

Not many ordinary families owned motorcars yet, but they were becoming more and more popular amongst those with a bit more money in their pockets, and the use of lorries for carrying goods was increasing all the time. Used to horse drawn transport, they thought these motorised vehicles drove far too fast on the roads, and he whipped the horse into a trot to cross it as quickly as possible.

They travelled on for as far as they could before dusk began to approach, finally coming to an area of open ground overlooking a duck pond, the only thing they'd passed on the road being a hay wagon, piled high with the fruits of the days labours, and accompanied by its driver and two workers sitting on the back. They'd exchanged a few words before continuing on their separate ways, but not delaying too long as both parties were anxious to reach their destinations before nightfall.

There was enough cover to hide the caravan from the road, and they all enjoyed roast duck for their supper that evening; the unwary creatures, not being used to human company, straying too near the edge of the pond for their own good.

Continuing on their journey the next day, within minutes they came to another main road, again crossing their path at right angles, but this time there was no road straight ahead of them.

All signposts had been taken down during the war in case of invasion, and as yet, not all of them had been replaced, this being one of them. They weren't too sure which way to go.

"Judging by the position of the sun," Silas ventured, "I'd say north is to our left, meaning we'd be heading towards Southport. That leaves Liverpool to our right. Which way do you want to go?"

After a few minutes discussion, they decided farm work would be easier to come by around Southport, so decided on that direction, finding a farm entrance within ten minutes of setting off.

A man was working on a fence alongside the entrance, and they asked if there was any daily work available.

Stopping to mop his brow with a grubby handkerchief, he pushed his cap back on his head and eyed both they and the caravan.

"Plenty, if you've a mind to work, but boss only hires on a daily basis, and you'll be off with a flea in your ear if there's any thieving! Won't have you back neither if you don't pull your weight."

"We don't mind a bit of hard work," Kyla replied indignantly. "We'll both do a fair day's work for a fair day's pay, and we've a couple of strong boys that'll help."

Not having seen the children inside the caravan, the man wasn't sure whether the boss would set them on as well, but told them to go on up the track to the farm anyway. That wasn't his decision to make!

The farmyard was deserted except for a cluster of hens waddling around and pecking at anything in sight; and their knocking on the door elicited no reply, so they decided to try looking around the fields.

Just opposite a man appeared in an open gateway, sluicing his dusty hands off under a tap. He turned as they approached, a frown creasing his face as he dried them off on a piece of sacking and turned in their direction.

"What can we do for you?" he asked peremptorily, noticing the caravan behind them, not at all pleased with having gypsies on the site. They spelt trouble from previous encounters he'd had with them before.

"We're looking for the boss man," Silas said, stepping forward. "We're looking for work."

Silas had seen the way he looked at him, and was trying to put on his best front.

"I'm up for hiring and firing here," the man stated. "We've had trouble with your sort before. I wouldn't hire no gypsies – except we're short of workers this week. I'll give you a chance, but any sign of slacking or trouble and you're out."

"We can do a fair days work!" Silas replied, determined not to be cowed by this man. "And we've two strong lads to help out as well!"

Four workers in one go! The man was delighted, but wasn't going to show it.

"How old are they?" he asked. "Don't want young kids running around and making a nuisance of themselves."

"Old enough, and well used to farm work," Kyla chipped in determinedly.

This wasn't strictly true as they'd only done a small amount of farm work during the last couple of years, but they'd soon buckle down to it after a few sharp words from her. Their staying on the farm for the rest of the season depended on it and that would be made very clear to them both!

He pointed out an area of hard baked ground near a cattle trough where they could leave their caravan, and left them to get settled, telling them where to find him when they were ready to start work.

"I suppose that means today," Kyla said when he'd gone. "He intends to make sure we do some work as soon as possible, doesn't he?"

When they found him, he and three other workers, two of them Polish immigrants, and one a middle aged man from the local village, were picking runner beans.

"There's bad weather on the way," the man who styled himself as foreman, told them, "so we need to get the last of the crop in before it arrives. We'll lose the lot if there's high winds with it."

The boys had never picked beans before so Kyla took them well away from the others and showed them how to do it, saying they were going to start from the other end so as not to get in anybody else's way.

Silas quietly applauded her. Under her tuition, nobody need ever know their lack of knowledge.

At the end of the day, they were informed that an early start would be made the next day on the last of the pea crop, as both crops were to be sold at market on Saturday. They were to start at dawn!

The day stayed fine, and they managed to finish the picking by late afternoon, but as they returned to their caravan, Kyla spotted someone looking in the back of it.

"There's someone poking around the caravan," she said quietly, taking Silas's arm and stopping him in his tracks. They both stopped to look, and the lad disappeared round the other side, as Silas told them to stay where they were while he found out what the lad was up to.

He was still round the other side when Silas reached it, calling out loudly, "Hey you, what do you want with our caravan?"

The lad appeared from the other side, a smile spread across his face, as he stepped over the empty shafts and introduced himself.

"My name is Callum, and my father owns this farm. We lived with a band of gypsies for a while just after the war. I don't suppose you know them – Giovanni was their leader."

"Yes, I know them, but I don't remember seeing you with them," Silas replied a little warily.

Callum went on to explain how the farm had once belonged to his uncle, and how they'd worked there after losing their home in Liverpool. He finished by telling him how they'd come to join up with the gypsies and travelling with them for a couple of years, before returning to the farm and finding that too had been bombed out, and his uncle's family had perished. As his father was now his only living heir, he had inherited the farm.

Silas realised after a while that he had nothing to worry about with this lad. His family seemed to have no connection to the gypsy community now, and he began to relax in his company.

When Callum had finished, Kyla went inside and brought out some mugs of elderberry juice she'd made the previous year, before Silas went on to tell the story of how he was betrothed to a gypsy girl when she was only two years old and he just twelve. Their fathers were cousins, and he was to wed her when she reached the age of eighteen, but he'd met and fallen in love with Kyla when she joined their community after her husband died.

He then went on to explain the plot he and Kyla had cooked up to escape together before the wedding, already having spoken to the young girl he was betrothed to, who didn't want to marry him any more than he wanted to marry her.

There was a long silence when he'd finished. Callum's demeanour had changed, as he looked across at Kyla and then back at Silas. They were both wondering why he looked so strange.

"Was her name Jess?" Callum finally asked quietly.

"Yes, it was," Silas said. "Did you know her?"

He nodded without saying anything for a while.

"Jess and I loved each other. I still love her, but she couldn't bring herself to leave her parents or the gypsy way of life – she'd never known any other," he finally said, in a quiet and sad voice.

Silas and Kyla glanced at each other again. They'd both heard of Jess's lost love, but never dreamed that they'd ever meet him under such circumstances. What a coincidence this had turned out to be!

It was fully dark when Callum finally returned home, and Maura placed a plate of food in front of him that she'd warmed up.

He was full of the news he had to tell them, and they were both interested in the tale he told, but neither of them having met either Kyla or Silas, it wasn't as exciting to them.

Callum went to bed that night thinking of renewing his efforts to find Jess once again.

She hadn't married Silas, so he wondered if there was still a chance of them getting together again – that's if he could find her!

CHAPTER 20

It wasn't very long before Paul realised that he was never going to make his fortune from breeding Shire horses, and his mind began to wander to some sort of diversification. Money was starting to become tight. The stables were expensive to run, as were the feed and farrier bills for the two horses. Nero was still as yet the only stallion he'd been able to buy, and wages for the two girls were an ongoing expense. As for the loan he had to repay to his father; that too was becoming a persistent worry.

Having spoken to Jess and Susan about this, it was Jess who finally came up with an idea, which she and Susan had talked over before speaking to Paul about it.

Both of them seemed to have found something they'd been looking for for a long time; a place of their own to call home, and a friendship which they didn't want to lose so soon after finding it.

"There are a lot of young people around who'd love to own a horse of their own, but who don't have anywhere to keep it, and you have three loose boxes sitting empty, with plenty of grazing land going to waste," Jess said to Paul, acting as their spokesperson.

"How about we put them up for rental at a weekly fee? They could keep their horses here, and clean and feed them in the evenings after work or school. All we'd have to do would be to keep our eye on them during the day.

We already have to do that with your horse and Nero, and it would give us something more to do ourselves."

He mulled this over during the evening, and things certainly seemed to stack up. It would cost him no more to run something like that, and it would bring in some much needed extra income.

He wouldn't need any more labour. The customers would be paying all the overheads for him, and doing all the feeding and cleaning themselves. It certainly seemed a very promising idea!

An advertisement in the local paper brought in six applicants within a week, and he rapidly realised the potential in their idea; all three stables being occupied within the following week, and the money slowly began to flow back into the business.

Within the month, with more enquiries still coming in, he decided that this was the way to go in the future, and borrowed some more money from his father to build another four stables behind those already in use. His father was a little sceptical at first, having already lent him a considerable amount, but seeing the books and realising the amount of extra money they could bring in, especially when he saw the letters asking for stabling, he agreed to the loan.

Within six months they too were up and running, and he'd built another two stables alongside his own house where he kept Krista, with another for the few mares who still came for stud. This kept them away from the business side of things, and still allowed free access for the large horse boxes that were needed for these mares. The money was at last beginning to roll in!

However, people coming and going at all times was often a hindrance to Paul, as they were using the main farm entrance, so he decided to install another entrance on the opposite side of the stables. There was already a small gate and a track leading from the road on that side, so all he needed to do was widen the gateway and lay a concrete roadway, which the local building firm installed within a week. All that was needed now was to put up a few signs to make sure owners and feed delivery vehicles used the new entrance.

While this was in progress, he'd also decided to change the main entrance sign to: **'Archers Livery'**, with another on the side pointing towards the entrance further down the lane.

As the first sign had cost a lot of money, he decided to design and paint his own, for which he enlisted the help of Jess, and they'd soon come up with something, perhaps not as showy as the previous one, but just as eye catching.

When it was finished, and the paint was drying, they both stood back and looked at it.

"Even though I say it myself," Paul said, "we've done a good job on that!"

Jess had to agree, as did Susan when she too saw it being fixed in place. This one wasn't over the entranceway as the other had been; often causing consternation that the larger horse boxes would knock against it, but stood on a large signboard alongside. It was lower down, and easier to spot when coming towards it.

In light of how good that looked, they erected a second one alongside the customer's entrance.

Whilst working with Paul, Jess felt a real affinity with him, and they got on well together, often seeking out each others' company during working hours, and she was surprised one afternoon when he asked to take her out to dinner the following evening to thank her for her help.

Without a moment's hesitation she agreed. What harm could going out for a meal with him be – but during the following day, she began to have her doubts.

Although she liked Paul and they worked well together, she held no romantic aspirations towards him; but was he perhaps seeing her in a different light? If he was, would a rebuff sour their relationship?

She still regretted her decision not to leave with Callum when he'd asked her, and, knowing he'd been coming back to work on his uncle's farm in Lancashire, she still hoped that one day she'd be able to find him.

Knowing Paul had already booked the table, it would have seemed churlish to back out, so she decided to keep things on a light note right from the start; but she needn't have worried, as he didn't seem to have anything like that in mind. He talked endlessly about his plans for the future, with prospects for building more livery stables when money allowed.

She enjoyed the home cooked food, and listened to his plans, finding herself being drawn in, and interjecting with some ideas of her own occasionally. She found his plans interesting, and enjoyed the evening.

As the pub was only half a mile from the stables, and it was a fine evening, they'd walked down, and were glad of the walk back to help digest the large meal they'd both consumed, still talking animatedly.

It was a little after ten o'clock when she opened the door to the flat, expecting Susan to be sitting in her pyjamas with a mug of cocoa as she usually was at this time of night – but she wasn't there.

Popping her head round her bedroom door, thinking she'd gone to bed early, she was surprised to find she wasn't there either.

Neither having friends in the area, they often went for walks in the evening together if the weather was fine, and always checked the stables and the horses out in the fields before settling down for their ritual cocoa before bed.

She went back outside to see if Susan was still checking the stables, but there was no sign of her there, and she patted Nero as she passed his stall, his huffing from inside showing he'd sensed her presence. Usually the top of the stable doors were closed at night, but as it was so warm, she wasn't surprised to find his still open.

Checking the nearest field, where she knew there were only two quiet and elderly mares left out at night, everything there seemed to be in order, so she returned to the flat.

There was still no sign of Susan when she opened the door! It was just as she'd left it, and it was now well past eleven o'clock.

Going into Susan's bedroom, she checked the wardrobe and the small bedside cupboard they used for clothing, but her clothes were still all there.

They were both up at six every morning, so usually in bed shortly after ten o'clock every evening. Where could Susan be at such a late hour?

It was shortly after midnight that she heard the rattle of a key in the front door to the flat, followed shortly by the sound of Susan's bedroom door opening and closing.

She considered getting up and asking her where she'd been until then, but dismissed the thought immediately it entered her head. Susan was a grown woman and older than her! She could do what she liked, and whenever she liked! It wasn't up to her to pry. Susan would tell her soon enough if she intended to.

The next morning, Susan was up at her usual time, and they ate their breakfast together as normal. She did seem a little subdued, but Jess put this down to lack of sleep. She didn't say anything about her late arrival home, and Jess didn't admit she'd heard her come in.

They worked together as normal during the day, talking to those people feeding and watering their horses before going to work or school, and then sweeping and hosing the yard down after they'd all left.

Just after ten o'clock, Paul sought Jess out and told her he'd heard of a farm that could provide excellent hay and carrots by the sack for feeding the horses.

"If we bought in bulk, we could keep it in the barn and charge the livery customers to provide them with feed as well. If we could buy in cheaply enough, we could even make a profit from selling it to them. They wouldn't have to source their own food and bring it here with them."

"Good idea," she answered, seeing the logic of his idea immediately. "But what about winter feed? A lot of people like to feed extras during the winter months."

"I had thought about that," he replied. "I'll have to make enquiries about that later on, but for the time being, let's see how I fare trying to do a deal at the farm. We have the rest of the summer to think about winter feed – and also straw for winter bedding."

As it wasn't too far, he decided to ride over on Krista, saying she could probably do with the exercise, as he didn't ride her often and she tended to spend most of her days out in a field.

He hadn't returned by lunchtime, so Jess and Susan returned to the flat and made a sandwich, deciding to have a long, leisurely lunch for a change. Everywhere was spick and span, so they wouldn't be missed down at the stables.

After they'd eaten, Susan, making them both a second pot of tea, sat down once again in her chair opposite Jess. It was obvious that she wanted to say something, so Jess sat patiently for a while, before looking at her questioningly.

"Is there something on your mind?" she asked.

It was what Susan seemed to have been waiting for, and putting her cup on the window ledge, she looked over at Jess calculatingly before she spoke.

"I suppose you're wondering where I was last night," she stated.

Jess grinned.

"I was rather, but I'm not your keeper, and you don't have to tell me anything if you don't want to."

"Oh but I do! You're probably the only person in the world that I could trust with my secret – I've never told a soul before now – but there's something you need to know; but it may mean my leaving here."

Dismayed, and at the same time intrigued, Jess sat and looked at her, waiting for her to continue, but Susan looked down at her lap, as if still in two minds as to how to continue.

"You have to promise you won't say a word to anyone else if I do tell you – not even Paul. I know you and he have been getting very friendly just lately."

"Hey! Steady on!" Jess cried. "There's nothing going on between Paul and me! I still love Callum, and I still want to try and find him if I can. Paul and I are only working together on increasing the business, bouncing ideas off each other as we think of them. You're very welcome to chip in with ideas of your own at any time!"

193

Hearing this seemed to give Susan an impetus as she began to speak.

"First of all, I have to tell you that I lied to you about my past – but not all of it!"

Jess sat back and curled her legs under her, prepared to listen to what she had to stay, as Susan continued.

"The part about meeting Robert during the war, and becoming pregnant after he was demobbed is perfectly true, as was mum and dad's anger when they found out.

Under pressure from both sets of parents, we **did** eventually marry, and we didn't go our separate ways as I told you, but it was the worst mistake of my life! Things went well for the first month before the newness of our relationship wore off and we began to argue.

We were living in a small and horrible flat, with damp walls and a tiny kitchen which was always full of condensation whenever I cooked anything. I hated it, but Robert was doing his best to find full time work and to keep paying the rent. He wasn't skilled in anything, and after the war, there were lots of men looking for unskilled jobs, and more than a few days work was hard to come by. I was also doing cleaning jobs to help out, and worried a lot about what would happen when the baby arrived. We could hardly scrape together a living for ourselves, let alone afford another mouth to feed.

One day I fell down the stairs when I was cleaning in a big house, and I lost the baby a couple of days later. Robert was furious, and that was the first time he hit me, blaming me for the loss of our baby. I hadn't realised until then that he actually wanted our child.

Things went from bad to worse, and we argued constantly, with the neighbours often knocking on the walls and telling us to keep the noise down, but he kept

194

hitting me more and more frequently. I retaliated on several occasions, but it only made him angrier and made the beatings worse: but he was always careful to hit me where it wouldn't show. On several occasions he hit me so hard in the kidneys that there was blood in my pee for days afterwards.

One day, the fear of another beating became too much.

We'd been arguing all Sunday afternoon, I've no idea what about now, and when he followed me into the kitchen and raised his fist towards me yet again, I reached out for something to defend myself with. Unfortunately, the nearest thing to hand was a kitchen knife, and in the heat of the moment, I lashed out with it.

He was so angry, he hadn't realised what I was holding, and I don't think I had at the time, but he kept on coming towards me, with the result that he ran straight onto the knife."

Here she paused for breath, and Jess, anxious to hear what had happened next, exclaimed in horror.

"You didn't kill him, did you?"

"Luckily not," Jess continued, "or I wouldn't be here today."

"What happened then?" Jess pressed, anxious to hear the rest of her story.

"Being pretty fed up with the noise of our arguing, one of the neighbours had seen a policeman passing on his beat, and had called him in. They broke in the door and found Robert in a pool of blood on the floor, and me still holding the knife. To the police it was a cut and dried case.

The neighbours gave statements to the police about all the arguments they'd heard, as well as all the thumping and banging coming from the flat over the time we'd been living there, and instead of being tried for attempted murder, I was tried for grievous bodily harm. The Court accepted my plea of mitigating circumstances after seeing the bruises and abrasions on my body photographed by a doctor and shown to the jury. I was given a prison sentence of ten months, but I was released after six for good behaviour."

"And what happened to Robert?" Jess now asked.

"He had a punctured lung. They said the knife only missed his heart by a fraction, otherwise I could have been tried for murder, and I could have hung."

Jess could see the tears shining in her eyes, her voice now beginning to break. Giving her time to compose herself, she got up to pour them both another cup of tea.

When she sat down again, Susan was holding a handkerchief in her hand after having blown her nose and wiped her face, but Jess said nothing about it, waiting for her to tell her the rest.

"Is there any more to tell?" she prompted.

"The rest you know – more or less. My parents wouldn't have anything more to do with me, and Robert had moved back in with his own parents, who lived in Manchester, when I was released. As I've told you previously, I stayed with a friend for a while before moving on to farm work, and then arriving here."

Jess thought for a while before remembering Susan's cryptic remark at the beginning when she'd said she may have to move on again.

"Has something happened since to make you think you'll have to give up your job here?"

Susan nodded.

"Last evening, just after you and Paul left for your meal out, a motor car arrived at the house.

A man and a young girl got out of it, and I recognised him immediately – it was Robert's brother, Matthew!

I was still in my scruff sweeping down the yard, and wearing overalls and wellingtons, with a headscarf holding back my hair. Without making it obvious I was trying to avoid him, I had no choice but to continue.

He called out to me when he couldn't get a reply at the house, but luckily he was looking towards the setting sun, and I was in the shadow of the trees.

He said that he was after livery for the horse his daughter wanted for her birthday, and asked if we had any vacancies. Knowing the sign for vacancies was still showing at the entrance, I had to say that Paul was in charge of that sort of thing, and he wasn't back until late.

He said he was on business in the area and would call back later if he could, otherwise it would have to wait another week or so.

Later on that evening, just before you arrived back, I was checking the horses when I saw his car pull back in again, but this time, after knocking at the door, he started looking round the stables.

He hadn't seen me, so I decided to get away for a bit until all chance of him coming back that night was gone.

It was pretty dark by now, so I used the shadow of the hedge to make my way along the paddock and into the stand of trees, where I waited.

I could see Paul's bedroom window from where I was, so when I saw the light go out, I made my way back. I figured it was probably too late by then for Matthew to come back again."

Jess thought for a while before saying anything more.

"Would it be so bad if Matthew did know you worked here? He probably wouldn't want to bring his horse here if he knew, and the worst he could do would be to tell Paul. In fact, I think it would be a good idea for you to tell Paul yourself, before he finds out. He might be annoyed if he does, knowing you've kept it from him and he's lost a customer because of it."

Susan seemed to be near to tears again as she shook her head wildly, before looking at Jess with frightened eyes.

"The last thing Matthew said to me was that if we ever met up again, he'd finish me off for good, as Robert should have done in the first place.

He also said that Robert is no longer able to keep on a steady job, as he has frequent bouts of trouble with his lung, and the prison sentence wasn't long enough for the trouble I've caused the family."

Jess sympathised, but couldn't help feeling it was probably an empty threat, made on the spur of the moment, and not carrying any weight.

How wrong could she be!

CHAPTER 21

When Paul arrived at the farm, the owner wasn't available, having had a 'spot of business' elsewhere, but had asked his farm manager to speak to him.

He was a swarthy faced man, looking to be in his thirties, with an amiable air about him; his well tanned arms and weather beaten hands showing he was well used to outdoor work. He introduced himself as Des Shelbourne, and gave him a hearty handshake, expressing a genuine pleasure at meeting him.

He'd harnessed up a small cart, and whilst Krista was contentedly eating the grass alongside the farmyard, he proceeded to take him around the rest of the fields, showing him the type of crops they were growing, and the fields that would be producing hay for winter feeding.

Paul was pleased with everything he saw. The crops were well established, and the forthcoming fields of hay certainly looked to be lush and growing well, promising an early and very presentable crop.

When he left, the owner still wasn't back, but Des said that he was able to handle any sort of deal they came to, and would be only too happy to oblige with delivery.

Paul, explaining that this was a new venture and he didn't yet know how it would be accepted by his clientele, agreed a price with him for a small delivery, eliciting a promise from him that a better price would be given if the order increased significantly over time.

Knowing the price of commercial hay at present, he knew it only left a small margin of profit for him, but if the order increased, it could become more lucrative over time, and they agreed a delivery the following week.

He left the farm loaded up with items of salad crops, and a chicken for his meal that evening.

It seemed that their next venture would be into animals, already intending to build bigger pens to increase the flock of hens they already had. The next they hoped to follow with would be pig sties, for which they needed to source a local butcher to help with the slaughtering.

This, however, would be an expensive venture, necessitating the building of a packing room, and the purchase of refrigerators to hold the meat once slaughtered. At the moment that was still a pipe dream for the future.

Arriving back mid afternoon, Paul sought out Jess and Susan, who were having a well earned break before the customers started to trickle back to see to their horses.

"I'd like to talk to you both about what's happened today, so would you like to have a meal with me tonight up at the house? I've been given a large chicken and some salad, so I'll be only too happy to share it with you. It's far too much for me to eat on my own!"

They both agreed that would make a nice change, and they wouldn't need to cook themselves, so arrived at the house at seven o'clock after the stables had quietened down and most of the young people had left.

He talked animatedly over the meal about the days' events, describing the farm in detail and the type of crops they grew. He also told them about Des Shelbourne, whom he described as a 'decent sort', before they went back to the stables to do their evening round of the horses.

Several days later, a large cart drove into the stable yard, with Des driving. He'd decided to make the first delivery himself in order to check out the sort of business Paul was running, and whether the order might turn out to be a lucrative one or not.

Jess wasn't around and it was Susan who greeted him, showing him where to unload the hay and carrots he'd brought. He had a lad of around twenty or so with him and between them they made short work of the unloading, Susan going into the tack room and making them a drink before they left.

He seemed interested in the operation they were running, and she walked him around the stables, explaining how the business was run, and then they walked over to see the paddocks.

"How many acres do you have?" Des asked at length when she'd stopped talking.

"I really don't know," she answered truthfully, "it's not something I've ever asked, but there at least six more fields the size of this one."

He mulled it over in his mind. They weren't making the best of the land they had with the number of horses they were catering for. They could easily grow and provide their own hay. He couldn't understand why Paul wasn't doing that, but decided not to put it to him; after all, they'd been asked to supply the hay, so why do themselves out of a sale!

She walked him back to the house where Paul met them at the door and took him inside while Susan returned to work, where she found Jess already inspecting the delivery.

"It's nice stuff," she said when she heard Susan behind her. "I'm sure this will go down well with the customers."

Just before they finished that evening, Paul walked over and handed them a sheet of cardboard, on which he had painted the prices for bales of hay and sacks of carrots, which they pinned just inside the doorway.

Their customers seemed pleased with the idea of not having to bring their own feed with them, realising the excellence of that on offer, and the competitive price.

Just over a week later, all their purchases having been snapped up, they placed another order.

Des brought the delivery himself a couple of days later, Jess also being present this time, and they all helped with the unloading, Jess noticing that Des seemed to be paying a lot of attention to Susan.

Over the course of the next month, the order grew in size, and very soon a larger hay wagon began arriving on a weekly basis; the horse drawing it being replaced by a tractor, still being driven by Des, and now accompanied on a regular basis by the lad they'd seen before.

By now it was quite obvious that there was a growing affinity between Des and Susan, but in light of her previous disastrous relationship, Jess didn't question her about it, and it didn't seem to be about to progress at any time soon. Des seemed to sense that there was something about Susan that warned him not to cross the line.

One afternoon, the weather being fine, Jess decided that she'd take Nero out for a ride, and left Susan sitting on a seat in the sunshine reading a book.

Reading seemed to have become her latest passion, and she often walked into the village to exchange library books. She seemed to take a lot of pleasure in browsing through the books, often taking an hour or more to make her choices, before coming back with several, which she read avidly in her free time.

Paul too was out, although he said he'd be back before the stables became busy that afternoon.

Instead of hiring another man to help out, he'd now taken to helping them himself, deciding to save the extra money of another wage, as he was still paying back the loan from his father.

He, in turn, pleased with the way his son was making a go of things, brought a couple of his own mares to him for stud, and also sent a couple of new clients his way. They too were pleased when the mares produced excellent ginger foals with feathery white fetlocks, both looking exactly like Nero.

He was beginning to obtain a reputation, realising that if he was to continue, he'd definitely need another stallion in the near future. Nero was still performing excellently as yet, but time was not on his side as he was growing older.

Today, Jess was enjoying the sunshine, and Nero was prancing along, lifting his head and snorting every so often. He already knew where they were heading, and also knew that he'd be able to lift his heels and have a long canter on the bridle path, impatient to get there.

Unexpectedly, a motor car rounded the bend in front of them, and the driver slowed down as he noticed their presence ahead.

Nero, startled by the unexpected appearance, skittered around and she had to hold tight to his mane, soothing him gently, as he side-stepped all over the road.

Stabled as he was on the opposite side of Paul's house, he very rarely saw or heard motor vehicles, and he viewed them as a challenge.

As the car passed, she waved and shouted a thank you to the driver, who merely nodded his head and continued on his way. She didn't recognise him, but then, there were several more cottages and a farm further up the lane to the stables, and he could have been going to any one of them, so she didn't turn to look behind her.

If she had, she'd have seen him turn into the main entrance and stop in front of Paul's house, and she might have gone back, knowing that Paul was out and Susan was round the back of the stables, from where she was unlikely to hear his arrival.

Turning through the opening in the hedge and onto the bridle path, Jess tapped Nero with her heels. It was just the signal he'd been anticipating, and he broke into a steady trot for a while, before another tap was felt, and he broke into his long awaited canter.

Like the excellent horsewoman she was, Jess adjusted her weight into just the right place, and holding tight to his mane, prepared to enjoy the canter which would last for nearly two miles.

Mane and tail streaming, he took an easy stride forwards. Jess, having snatched the headscarf from her hair, also enjoyed the feel of her own long hair streaming out behind her, as with another tap of the heel, he broke into a full gallop, Jess whooping happily into the wind streaming towards her.

In the meantime, the driver, having stopped in front of Paul's house, got out of his car and knocked loudly on the front door. Receiving no reply after several tries, he went round to the back, wondering if he might be at the rear of the house, but he found nobody there either, and received no reply to numerous knocks on the back door.

Wondering if there might be anybody in the stables, he walked across and looked around there as well, but all he found were horses eyeing him up suspiciously as he looked into each loose box, idle chewing at their hay nets.

Not yet having realised there were more stables round the back, he walked into the barn, and looked around there, finally calling out to see if there might be anybody he couldn't see or hear.

Susan, at last hearing his call, put down her book, and shouted loudly, "I'm coming!"

She'd realised the shout had come from the barn, and approached it from the entrance at the side, nearest to where she was sitting.

As she made her way between the pallets and moved towards the front entrance, not seeing or hearing anyone, she called out loudly, her voice echoing back from the dim interior.

There was no reply, and thinking that whoever it was had walked out through the front entrance and back into the stable yard, she made her way towards there.

It was as she was making her way between two stacks of hay that a hand shot out and grabbed her wrist in a fierce grip. She stopped instantly and cried out in fright, shrinking backwards from the dim figure alongside her.

Suddenly the man stepped straight out of the shadows to stand right in front of her, a twisted and evil look on his face.

"It is you! I thought it was last time I was here! I recognised your voice, even though I couldn't see your face!"

She was transfixed with fear, as the light fell on his face, and she realised that it was Matthew – her husband Roberts' brother!

He started dragging her towards the back of the barn as she began to scream loudly, and fought back with all her strength – but he was too strong for her, and she was powerless to halt their progress.

Suddenly, he reached round and grabbed her by the hair, throwing her down on a pile of old sacks in the far corner.

"Now you're gonna' get your comeuppance!" he hissed at her. "I've waited a long time for this! And it's no use shouting or screaming – there's nobody here but us! I've already checked!"

He was slowly undoing the belt on his trousers as she made a wild attempt to get away, her heels scrabbling on the floor.

The walls of the barn were at the rear and the side of her, but there was an old farm cart on the other side. She tried wildly to scramble underneath it, but he grabbed her feet as she did so, and pulled her back out again, laughing now.

"Too late!" he shouted, as he straddled her and began to undo the straps of her dungarees before pulling them down.

She beat at his chest with her hands and tried vainly to push him off, but he was far too strong for her, and his weight was pinning her to the floor.

Soon her dungarees and panties were round her ankles, effectively stopping her from using her feet or her legs, as he stood up once more and looked down at her.

She was absolutely terrified!

She lay there, hands trying to cover herself, watching as he picked up the leather belt once more and wrapped it round his knuckles.

Reaching down, a leer of triumph on his face, he gripped her thin shirt and ripped it open from top to bottom, buttons popping off as he did so, finally ripping her bra' from her shoulders, and standing over her once more, breathing deeply.

"Now we're gonna' have some fun!" he said, eyes roving over her naked body and licking his lips in anticipation, before raising the hand holding the belt and bringing it down across her legs.

She screamed in pain and kept on screaming as he brought it down time and again on her naked body, covering her skin with raw bleeding welts, before standing back to regain his breath.

"That should teach you! That's payback for what you did to my brother!" he hissed between heaving breaths.

Slowly, be began to unbutton his trousers, and as they fell down around his ankles he threw himself on top of her, knocking all the breath from her already heaving lungs.

Putting all her last reserves of strength into it, she struggled against him, but he easily pinned her arms above her head with one hand, whilst forcing her legs apart with his knee. The other hand fumbled to drag his underpants down.

Suddenly, she felt his weight being bodily lifted from her, as he seemed to fly backwards away from her.

Opening her eyes, she saw him flying through the air, before she heard the thump and sudden exhalation of breath, as his body hit one of the wooden pillars holding up the roof. He slid down it, and landed in an untidy heap on the floor.

Peering into the gloom, the man now standing in front of her had his back to the light, and she couldn't make out who it was at first. He was standing staring down at her before he suddenly let out a mighty roar and turned on Matthew.

He gripped the front of his shirt and hauled him to his feet before landing a mighty blow straight into the middle of his face; Matthew hitting the pillar once more and falling back down to the floor. He was hauled up once more, and another blow hit the side of his jaw.

He seemed incensed by the sight of her body, but as he was about to lay into Matthew once again, another voice cut across the silence.

"That's enough man! You'll kill him! What's going on here?"

Turning her head to the left, the light caught the face coming towards them from the front of the barn, and she recognised it as Paul.

There were now three men in the barn, and her completely naked body was still prone on the floor for all eyes to see. She grabbed wildly at the empty sacks around her to cover her nakedness, as Paul came towards them: but she wasn't quick enough to stop Paul seeing the open and bleeding wounds across her entire body from a shaft of sunlight falling through a gap in the roof.

"What the hell's happened here?" Paul exploded as he reached them, moving his head around from her to the man standing alongside the almost unconscious figure, who was wiping the blood from his face with the back of his hand.

"Can't you see what's happened?" the other man spoke for the first time, his breathing hard and laboured still, his hands clenching and unclenching in fury.

Her hand flew to her mouth. She'd recognise that voice anywhere, and for the first time realised that the angry and incensed man standing before her was none other than Des.

During all that had happened, she'd forgotten that he was due to make a delivery that afternoon; it had gone clean out of her head!

He always tried to make his delivery in mid afternoon before clients started arriving to see to their horses, and he and Susan usually had a drink and a quiet chat together before he left. Seeing how well they were getting on, and knowing they only saw each other once a week, Jess always made herself scarce while they talked.

Engrossed in her book, she'd forgotten all about the delivery, although Jess hadn't. Knowing Paul was also out, she'd purposely chosen that afternoon as the perfect time to take Nero out for his exercise, and to give them time alone together.

Galvanised into action now, Paul knelt to look at the man sitting on the floor, his trousers still round his ankles; and a sorry sight he looked with blood pouring from his nose and staining the front of his shirt.

It was quite obvious what had happened, or was about to happen, here, but they needed to get a doctor to look at Susan, and while the doctor was looking at her, he would call the police. Let them figure out what to do with this piece of scum before him!

Susan, by this time sitting up with Des alongside her, had his arm around her shoulders and he was holding her against him while she sobbed uncontrollably, scared to hold her too tight for fear of hurting her with all the wounds she'd sustained.

"Have you any idea who he is?" Paul asked of them both.

Des shook his head. He'd never seen the man before, and as they both looked to Susan, she made no reply, but the look on her face gave them cause to wonder as they surreptitiously glanced at each other.

"You keep your eye on him, and I'll go and call a doctor to see to Susan," Paul said, and looking pointedly at the man, said, "and then I'll call the police!"

Susan knew the game was up. It was time to own up and tell the truth. She'd have to tell them about her past, knowing that Matthew might let the cat out of the bag if she didn't, as his final act of revenge.

She nodded her head.

"Yes, I know who he is," she admitted. "He's my brother-in-law."

Paul and Des exchanged glances once again. Neither of them knew Susan was married, and as far as Des was concerned, altered a lot of his thinking towards her.

Ever since they'd started supplying the stables, he'd been doing this particular delivery himself and not asking their usual driver to do it, making it quite obvious that there was some reason he wanted to visit the stables himself. He really liked Susan, and wanted to get to know her much better, but now that looked as if was a non-starter seeing as she was already married.

Susan piped up again in the silence that followed.

"Don't call the police, **please**! Just get him out of here and I'll explain everything, then I'll leave here and you'll have no more trouble from him."

Paul was dismayed.

"Why should you have to leave? Don't you realise the severity of what he's done to you? He could get a long prison sentence for what he's done!"

She nodded and huddled against Des, beginning to feel her whole body shaking.

"Yes, I know only too well!" she sighed. "This isn't the first time this has happened to me – but not at his hands – those of his brother!"

Paul and Des looked incredulously at her.

"Get rid of him and I'll explain everything – but first I need a warm bath to clean up these wounds. They'll heal in time!"

Helping her struggle to her feet, Des found an old piece of tarpaulin in the cart for her to cover herself, and helped her to Paul's house, where he'd said there was plenty of hot water for her to bathe in his full-size bath.

In the meantime, Paul had waited for Matthew to dress himself before showing him to the stone sink in the tack room, where he watched him wash his nose and face, and then followed him back to his car.

He made it clear that it was only by Susan's insistences that he was getting off so lightly, but if there were a next time, he wouldn't get off so easily – he would see to that himself! Before he called the police!

He watched Matthew stumble across the yard to his car and waited while he turned his car around and drove out of the yard, standing in the gateway watching until he was out of sight before retracing his steps to the house.

Under Susan's instruction, Des had gone to the loft flat and was just returning with some fresh clothes for her when they met at the door. He hesitated, but Paul invited him back inside, where, over a glass of well earned whisky, Des gave him a description of what he'd heard and seen when he drove into the yard. Just as he finished, Susan came down the stairs, looking embarrassed when she saw them both waiting for her.

They were obviously expecting some sort of explanation, and while she'd been soaking away the worst of the soreness in her wounds, she'd been thinking of how much, or how little, she could get away with telling them.

Paul made them all a cup of coffee, and solicitously invited her to sit in an armchair instead of a hard wooden one at the table, placing a small footstool in front for her to put her cup on.

Once seated, she began on her pre-rehearsed story. It would be just enough of the truth to satisfy their curiosity, but definitely didn't include her time in prison, or why she'd been sent there.

She told them about meeting Robert during the war and becoming pregnant when he was demobbed – how their parents had forced them into marriage, and how things had rapidly turned sour after she'd miscarried. She went on to say that they'd started rowing after that, and he'd started hitting her during the course of these rows, which eventually turned into regular beatings, until she'd decided she couldn't take any more and had eventually walked out and left him.

She'd stayed with a friend for some time after that, and worked on the land before coming to work for Paul.

There she left the story. There was just enough truth in it to assuage their curiosity, and hopefully for them to ask no more questions of her.

When she'd finished, Paul realised that Jess had been left to cope with the evening rush all on her own, and said he'd need to go and help out, but Susan, feeling a lot better now, said she'd be all right on her own.

"You two go, I'll be fine here on my own. Des has been away from work for far too long, he needs to get back as well. I'll go back to the flat soon and have a lie down on the bed until Jess comes back. She's bound to want to know the story too."

She had refused to let Paul call a doctor, saying she had a tub of Vaseline in her bedroom which she'd rub into the cuts.

She was also feeling a lot worse than she was letting on, and the soothing balm was just what she needed as well as a good long lie down without any more questions being asked. She knew the tears weren't far away either!

CHAPTER 22

Jess arrived back and settled Nero in his stall before making her way down to the stables. She'd enjoyed their afternoon gallop, and was a little late returning, but knew that Susan was eminently capable of coping until her arrival.

Usually the early arrivals were those returning after a day at school, and it wouldn't get busier until later, when those returning from work also joined the throng. It didn't begin to ease down until sometime after seven o'clock, when they could return to their own quarters for a meal and a well-earned rest.

When she walked into the yard, there were already several young girls seeing to their horses, having come straight from school, their well-heeled parents having brought them by car, but she was surprised to see there was no sign of Susan.

She was normally around when the evening rush started, but she was even more surprised to find the delivery cart and the tractor still in the yard. It was usually well gone by the time customers arrived, and she was even more surprised when Susan didn't show up at all.

People were already asking for horse feed, so she had to open the store and start bringing it out for them immediately, leaving her no time at present to go looking for Susan, or to wonder where she was.

It was quarter of an hour later that Paul arrived to help her out, accompanied by Des who, with only a hasty word to her, climbed into the tractor and drove away. Both their faces were sombre, as Paul told her that Susan had had an accident, but that she was all right, and she'd explain everything later.

She thought it must have occurred when the delivery was being unloaded, but as Paul assured her she was going to be all right, and was just a little shocked, she carried on working with his assistance.

It was when everything had quietened down and the last of the customers had departed, leaving just one or two clients still out exercising their horses, that Paul sat her down in the barn and explained what had happened that afternoon.

"I believe Susan has already told you the story of her background before she started here," he began.

She nodded without saying anything, not sure of what Paul might know, or what Susan might have told him.

"Well, her brother-in-law turned up here this afternoon while she was on her own!"

Jess looked at him wide-eyed, listening incredulously to the story he was now telling her.

"Luckily, Des turned up to make the delivery just in the nick of time, otherwise she would have been raped as well," he finished off.

"Oh my God!" Jess gasped. "Where is she now? Is she all right?"

"She had a hot bath at my house, where she bathed her wounds. She wouldn't let me call a doctor. She said she'd go back to her own room and bathe them with some ointment when she'd finished. I imagine that's where she'll be now."

Jess jumped up and ran to their quarters, almost falling up the stone steps in her hurry to get there, but when she opened the door, Susan was already sitting in one of the armchairs in a dressing gown and drinking a cup of tea. She smiled wanly.

"Did Paul come and give you a hand?" she asked, putting her mug down on the window ledge, seeing from Jess's agitation that she'd already heard what had happened.

Jess nodded as she shut the door after her.

"Are you all right?" she asked.

"Yes, I've nothing that won't mend – save for my pride! I'm only glad Des arrived when he did! Although I'm sorry he had to see me in such a state!"

Shrugging off her overalls, Jess poured herself a cup of tea from that left in the pot, and sat down opposite her, where Susan recounted the events of the afternoon from her own perspective, telling her also what bare facts she'd told to Paul and Des.

When she'd finished, Jess set to and made them something to eat. She was hungry and Susan declared she was too, but when she came to get out of the chair and move to the table, it was obvious that she was far from all right. Her wary movements and the grimaces of pain showing on her face didn't need any words, and Jess made her go straight to bed when they'd eaten.

When she'd washed the dishes and been down to settle the horses for the night, she put her head round Susan's door to say she'd bring her cocoa to the bedroom, but found her already asleep.

She drank hers alone before going to her own bed, wondering whether Susan would continue working here after this, or whether she'd feel it necessary to move on.

It was then that she vowed never to leave Susan alone at the stables again – she'd always stay close at hand in case her help was ever needed.

Susan had assured her that she didn't think Matthew would ever dare to show his face again after what Des had done to him, but she had no intention of ever taking that chance.

A week later, Susan was back at work again, and looking out for Des. It was his usual day to deliver the feed and she was looking forward to having a long chat with him. She wanted to thank him for coming to her rescue, and this time, she was going to invite him to have a meal with her at the local pub, as a way of thanking him properly.

When she heard the tractor coming along the lane, she coyly hid just inside the barn, intending to walk out and meet him as he stopped in the yard, but to her surprise, when she did, it wasn't Des driving. It was the lad who'd accompanied him on his first visit, Jimbob, as they all called him.

Disappointed at his non-appearance, but not wanting to seem too anxious to see him, she only asked where he was after they'd finished unloading.

"Must be busy," the lad offered. "I wuz asked to bring it today. I usually does the deliveries, but for some reason, Des likes to do this one on his own. Can't understand why, it's no different to the others," before swinging up onto the tractor and driving away.

After he'd gone, Susan sat down on a bale of hay and tried to think of an explanation as to why Des hadn't brought it. There could be so many possibilities, but perhaps he **was** just busy with something else that day, and he'd be there the following week as usual.

After another two weeks had passed and he still hadn't been back, she decided that she'd probably never see him again. Perhaps he'd been embarrassed by what had happened, and decided it was best not to go there again. Who knew what could be his reasons?

Des, thinking that Susan was still married, although separated, and probably not in contact with her husband any more, had decided it would be best not to try and continue with their relationship. He'd already been thinking of taking their friendship to a higher level and asking her to go out with him, but decided it would too painful to continue seeing her if it wasn't possible to progress that relationship any further. Who knew, she and her husband might eventually decide to get back together again. It was highly unlikely, but could still be a possibility, leaving him out in the cold once again.

He'd once been married himself in his early twenties, but that had failed within only four years. They'd both realised after a very short time that they'd made a mistake, and she'd eventually walked out on him.

Living in a rented property, there'd been very little to share, and they'd both just taken what they wanted, both wanting to just walk away from the situation.

Soon after, he heard that she was living with someone else, but he'd never seen her again, and had heard just two years ago that she'd drowned on a holiday in Devon.

As they'd never been divorced, he was still her next of kin, her belongings being returned to him. Most of it he donated to charity, but the more intimate items he'd returned to her parents. He left them on their doorstep late one evening, after the lights had gone out, together with a letter of explanation, but no return address.

Now another prospective relationship was over.

He'd rung Paul from the farm office to find out how she was, and finding that she was now back to her normal self and working again, decided it would be best to put her out of his head altogether. Better not to get in too deep knowing it couldn't come to anything.

Paul, for his own part, had taken down the registration number of Matthew's car. If the man ever came near the stables again, he would hand it to the police, and despite whatever Susan said, he would tell them what had happened and have Matthew arrested.

He wasn't happy with leaving two young girls alone at the stables anymore, so engaged another male worker to help out during the daytime. He would also be a help with the never ending maintenance jobs that needed doing, as he had all the accounts to maintain, and new clients to see whilst trying to increase the business.

Being mindful of the debt he owed his father, he had put off doing this previously, but now realised he'd have to stop worrying about that for the time being, knowing he'd already paid an appreciable amount back. His father wasn't pressing for its return, and provided he kept up with the regular payments being made, seemed quite happy with things as they were.

He soon found and engaged a middle-aged farm worker from the village. Nathan was a good worker but had lost his job after being laid up for six months with a badly broken leg. When he was ready to return to work, he found he'd already been replaced and no longer had a job.

He was pleased to have another so close to home, meaning only a ten minute walk to work and back, and he was a strong and willing worker.

Paul briefed Nathan that the girls had had trouble at the stables and didn't want them left alone for too long, but he didn't elaborate on what had happened, just giving him a brief outline of a man having caused them some trouble which had badly upset Susan. Nathan, having three daughters of his own, was very understanding of the situation, and promised to keep a wary eye on them.

They also now had a second stallion, Angelo by name, but not by nature. He was a beautiful black horse, with long black mane, tail and fetlocks, but a bit fiery in nature, especially when he got wind of a mare being brought to him. They weren't able to put him too close to Nero, but built another stable on the other end of the block to house him, leaving an empty one between them, and having his opening onto the other side of the yard so that they couldn't see each other at any time.

Everybody kept a wary eye out for Matthew, Susan never being left on her own at any time. They knew Nathan wouldn't recognise the man, but gave him details of his car and its colour, together with a brief description of the man himself. Nathan liked, and got on well with the girls, and promised he would keep an eye on them both, guessing it was to do with a relationship Susan had had with the man that had gone wrong, and nobody enlightened him any further on that thinking.

None of them were ever to know what happened after Matthew had left!

CHAPTER 23

The fortunes of Beech Tree Farm and those of Frank and Callum, now into his twenties, were going from strength to strength.

Orders for the following season were already coming in after Christmas that year, and they were now supplying many small shops; and quite a few larger ones as well, with their home-grown produce.

They had bought a motorised lorry a couple of years ago, and had purchased another the previous summer, both second-hand, which increased enormously the amount of goods they could carry in one journey.

They still used itinerant labour for the picking and packing, but instead of re-building the wooden shed in which they'd once lived, they'd built a block of brick accommodation units just behind the farmhouse, with kitchen and washroom facilities at one end. This was able to house five couples; but they still used daily workers from the local villages when needed.

They also had a farm manager and foreman who supervised the labour force, which took a lot of the day to day running out of their hands, and they were able to concentrate on increasing the sales side of things.

Maura, for her part, already had her flock of a hundred hens to see to, housed in a wooden shed with an outdoor run for daytime use. Every morning she sold her eggs and other produce from a small shed at the gate as Alison had once done, and it gave both Frank and Callum a pang of regret whenever they passed her and thought of Alison's bright and smiling face standing in the same place. Maura, although a conscientious and caring wife, could never take her place in their hearts, and she never tried to, still remembering the family of her own which she too had sadly lost.

It was one evening at the end of January and they were all sitting in the stone-flagged kitchen, enjoying the warmth generated by the large range, in front of which Frank and Callum sat, while Maura was contentedly writing a letter to a friend at the table in the corner, when Frank put down his paper and looked across at Callum.

"Something on your mind, lad?" he asked.

He'd been sitting there for some time, a far-away look on his face, and Frank, finally noticing how still he'd been sitting, and for how long, asked the question.

Pulled back from his thoughts, Callum looked across at his father; seeming to contemplate what he was about to say and how to begin.

Maura too looked up from her letter writing, and was now listening to the conversation.

"I've been thinking about something for a while now, and I'd like to run the idea past you," he finally burst out.

"Fire away lad!" Frank said, folding his paper and putting it to one side. "If it'll make us some money, I'm all ears. You know me; I'm always ready for listening to a new idea."

"I've been keeping a record of Maura's sales at the front gate and there isn't a day when she doesn't sell everything she takes down there within three hours."

Frank nodded, and Maura voiced her agreement.

Every morning they loaded her little cart with the produce they had to spare and one of the men drove it

222

down to the gate for her, where they unloaded it into the shed. There was a flap across the side facing the road which she could drop down and display a number of items at a time: heavier things like potatoes and carrots standing in a sack beneath it; a scale on a box alongside with which she could weigh them out.

The prefabricated buildings across the road had now been replaced by proper brick built family homes, on which they'd both worked, until first Frank and then Callum gave up their jobs in order to work full-time on the farm. It was from these that most of their custom came, although, as there were becoming an ever increasing number of motor vehicles on the road, they received a lot of passing custom, particularly at the weekends. People were now travelling for days out in Southport and the surrounding areas of Ainsdale and Formby.

They had removed a hedge and installed a gravelled stopping place for these vehicles only the previous summer.

"I've been thinking about sending out a lorry to sell our produce door to door around all the local villages. I'm sure there'd be a market for it," Callum continued, realising they were both ready to listen to his idea.

Frank's immediate thoughts were to reject the idea out of hand, but decided to think about it first, perhaps overnight, before making a decision.

"It would mean buying another lorry and hiring a driver for it. It might cost more than we'd make on the venture," he said, voicing his own thoughts on the idea.

"That's what I've been thinking about," Callum said. "What if we were to use a horse and cart for the time being – with me driving it? There's a large cart at the back of the bunkhouse doing nothing since we bought the motors, and we still have a couple of horses. They're not often used now. They spend most of their time grazing in a paddock."

Callum's idea was beginning to appeal to Frank. What harm could there be in giving it a try. They already had the cart, and he was right, their horses weren't earning their keep any more – in fact, he'd been thinking of selling one of them, keeping the other for a while longer until he could decide whether it was really needed any more.

He looked at Maura, and she nodded her head.

"I think it might definitely be worth giving it a go," she said, joining in the conversation for the first time. "We've nothing to lose, and everything to gain if it works."

Frank nodded in agreement.

"Anyway, we've plenty of time to think about it," Callum chipped in. "We won't be lifting the first of the early crops for some time yet, and all we have left is over-wintered apples and pears. They're way past their best, and only fit for stewing. They wouldn't present a good picture of our produce to the public!"

This lightened the atmosphere and they all laughed, whilst Maura left finishing her letter until the next day as she got up to make them a hot drink before bed.

Callum's idea, had however, gained Frank's attention, and he thought long and hard about it during the next few days. It was worth giving it a try, and there were quite a number of outlying villages around, populated by people who perhaps wouldn't have thought of coming to buy from them.

It might turn out to be a good idea, and there was nothing to lose by giving it a try.

A few months later, they started bringing in the spring crops and Maura opened her stall once more.

She was now selling the jams and chutneys she'd made during the winter, and after using up her collection of jam jars, she'd started asking her customers to return the empty jars. She was trying to negate the problem of buying more each winter, although she always did end up having to buy more, as the ones sold to the passing motorists were hardly ever returned.

Callum had also been busy painting up the old cart in bright and eye-catching colours, moving it into a corner of a barn so that he could work on it in all weathers. He also buffed up and polished the horses' harness, and by the time the first crops were brought in, he was ready to start the new venture.

His first day was tiring, travelling from village to village, often finding there weren't many people around and having to trudge from door to door offering people the produce he had for sale. Some were sceptical of the quality, and weren't even willing to look, but he did, however, sell everything by the time he returned home in mid afternoon, but he was somewhat disillusioned by the reception he'd received.

Frank assured him that things would get better when people got to know him, and eventually came up with an old hand bell he searched for at the back of the barn. It should be loud enough to attract their attention!

"Ring this when you get into the village. People will get to know it and come out when they hear it," he suggested to Callum. "When we lived in Liverpool, the coalman used to have one for the same purpose, and everyone used to go out to him when they heard him ring it. They'll soon get used to the sound of it and they'll come out to meet you."

225

Within another week, it was working a treat. Most villages had only one main street going straight through them, and all he had to do was move along it, ringing his bell when he reached certain points and waiting for them to come out to him.

By the second week, he'd sold everything he had by lunchtime, and had to return for more. By keeping to regular times in regular places, he found that they were often waiting for him when he arrived and rang his bell, and the money was beginning to roll in.

It was no longer hard work, but a pleasant way to spend the day, chatting to local villagers, and forming a strong bond with some of them – even being given drinks and often cakes or biscuits during his round.

Sometimes he received far too many of these gifts, and often brought home their offerings to share with Frank and Maura for their tea.

By the end of the summer, he had earned enough through this venture to put it to Frank that they buy a lorry for the following year. He had kept a meticulous record of his sales, and now laid them on the table before Frank and Maura, who were both impressed by the profits he'd made.

"The cart is far too small for the amount of produce I'm selling, and I usually have to come back to the farm two, or even three, times a day for more supplies.

There's also the problem of the weather. Sometimes the produce is spoiled by my having to keep pulling the tarpaulin on and off it each time I stop when it's raining, and customers can't really view the produce I have to sell unless I take it right off, which can cause more damage."

Frank took his point as Callum paused and looked at him before continuing.

"I've marked out the days when it was raining, and you can see the difference in the sales I've made, and the amount of unsaleable stock I've brought back."

Maura and Frank both leaned over and studied the figures for those days he'd marked, and noted that the end of the day sales were about a third down on those of good days.

"We're near the end of the season now. Winter's coming on fast, and we won't have much left to sell very soon. Let me think about it over the winter months, and we'll make a decision before the spring crops are ready for harvest," Frank said.

He wasn't ready to commit himself yet until he'd talked it over with Maura. She was a shrewd business woman, and sometimes thought of things he hadn't. Callum was young, and all fired up with his ideas, but perhaps he'd have time to calm down over the long winter months when he was needed for the outdoor work of getting the fields ready for the next growing season.

Even though it wasn't always possible to work the land during that time, there were always repairs and numerous other jobs to be carried out, and it might give them all time to think his ideas through more carefully before making the commitment.

As the summer months progressed, Jess had noticed that Susan was more subdued than she'd ever seen her, always being present when the supplies were delivered in the afternoon, and becoming more and more disappointed when she saw once more that it wasn't Des driving. She seemed to hope that it might one day be him again, but it never was.

One afternoon, finding the hosepipe left out in the yard, Jess went to pick it up and put it away before it either got damaged, or somebody caught their foot in it and had a nasty fall. She didn't realise that Nathan had just uncoiled it to swill down the stable yard, and was just picking it up when he turned on the tap.

Unfortunately, the nozzle was facing upwards in her hand at that precise moment, and she was drenched, water running from her face and hair down onto her clothes. In complete surprise she dropped it, whereupon it spun round with the pressure of the water and soaked the front of her trousers.

To make matters worse, Nathan appeared at that moment, full of solicitous apologies when he saw her, but then, unable to contain his feelings at the sight of her dripping form, he began to laugh. She was annoyed at first, but then she too saw the funny side, and began to laugh with him, realising what had just happened.

"I think I'd better go and change, don't you?" she said, when she finally managed to control her laughter and shook her dripping hair.

"I think that'd be best!" he answered, as his laughter abated. "Customers will be arriving soon, and they'll wonder what's been happening!"

Going back to the flat above the stables, she could still hear him chuckling as she climbed the steps and opened the door. To her surprise, she found Susan already there. She was sitting in her usual armchair, and had obviously been crying, as she dabbed at her eyes and blew her nose on hearing Jess's arrival.

"What's the matter?" she asked.

228

Susan looked at her dripping figure in surprise.

"What's the matter with **you**?" Susan countered. "How did you get so wet? You look like a drowned rat!"

Explanations over, she stripped off her overalls and towelled herself dry, going to her bedroom and putting on some dry clothes before turning to Susan once again.

"What were you crying for? Have you had bad news or something?" she asked.

"No, nothing like that – I'm just being silly," Susan said, looking morose and forlorn again.

Jess filled the kettle and put it on the gas ring to boil, before setting two cups of tea down in front of them.

"We've just time for this before we go down and open the feed store. In the meantime, you can tell me what's wrong."

Knowing that Jess wasn't going to let her get away without an explanation, she poured out her heart to her, tears running down her face once more.

"I like Des very much, but ever since that day in the barn," giving Jess a knowing look, "he hasn't been back here. I know he likes me too, because Paul told me he kept ringing him every so often to see how I was – but he's never been in touch with me again. I just can't understand why not. I miss him so much!"

Jess understood her feelings. She too very much regretted parting with Callum and would have tried to find him if she'd known where he might be. She still longed to be with him, even though so many years had gone by.

Would be have found somebody else by now and already be married? She would probably never know.

Knowing her own sense of loss, she decided she'd do her best to bring Susan and Des together, but how to go about it? She didn't even know where the farm was that

229

their supplies came from, and even then, Des might not live at the farm, but might have a home elsewhere.

Lying in bed that night she began to form a plan, and with Paul's help, she might just be able to pull it off.

With this in mind, she went over to the house to see Paul after their last customer of the morning had left, making an excuse to Susan as to why she needed to see him, but she needn't have bothered.

Susan explained that she was going to walk into the village to get some items herself that she needed from the small shop. It didn't stock a great many items, but they usually had all she needed, and she said she'd bring back some nice cakes for their tea. The delivery van should have been by now, so they should still have a good selection of bread and cakes on display.

Having already spoken to Paul that morning, he was waiting when Jess arrived and put her plan to him.

"Yes, I've noticed she's not been her usual self for some time. I put it down to the ordeal she's been through, but I'd no idea it was because of Des. I realised he wasn't delivering himself, but I just thought he was too busy."

When she explained what she intended to do, he frowned for a moment.

"You'll have to be careful how you go about it. You'll need to be pretty tactful in your approach."

"Oh, I will be. You don't need to worry about that. I've already thought it all through."

The next day, Susan was surprised to find Paul ready to help with the unloading when the feed arrived. Jess was nowhere in sight, but Paul explained that she had something she needed to do, and he'd be helping that day.

230

Surprised and puzzled that Jess hadn't said anything to her, she soon forgot all about it while she was helping with the unloading; Nathan as usual unloading a lot more quickly than anyone else.

When they'd finished, she went straight back up to the flat and put the kettle on. She had at least an hour before customers began to arrive, and she'd picked up some new library books while she was in the village; one of which was proving an extremely good read, and she was anxious to get back to it.

It was for that reason that she didn't see Jess, sitting astride Nero, following the feed vehicle a minute or so after it left the yard.

It wasn't a long journey to the farm, in fact not quite two miles in Jess's estimation, and it didn't take that long to reach it.

When the tractor turned into the driveway, she carried on past the entrance and stopped further along the road, assessing the farm and biding her time before trotting back and turning into the entrance herself.

She met a man coming down the track towards her, and gathering up all her courage, she asked where she might find Des.

"Could be anywhere!" he said, taking off his battered old cap and scratching his almost bald head, before retrieving a grubby handkerchief from his pocket and wiping the sweat from his forehead. "The farm office is at the top of 'ere - through gate on t'left – farmyard's on the right if you wants the missus though. Gaffer probably won't be around at this time."

She thanked him and continued on until she reached the branch in the track he'd indicated.

From her vantage point on top of Nero, she could see the roof of the building over the hedge to her left, and she wheeled him towards it, stopping just inside the gate. She still used no saddle, but had put a head rein on in case she needed to tie him up anywhere, which she proceeded to do by using the gatepost.

She could see through the window at the front that Des was inside, standing at a table and looking intently at something spread out in front of him, leaning forward, his weight resting on his knuckles.

He looked up as he saw her, and opened the door, a smile of greeting on his face.

"Come in," he said, standing to one side to usher her in.

At least he seemed pleased to see her – that was the first hurdle overcome.

"To what do we owe this pleasure?" he continued, indicating a straight backed chair at the side of the table for her to sit on.

This was where she had to tread carefully, and not give the game away!

"Oh, it was a nice day so I decided Nero could do with some exercise. Your tractor was just leaving the yard, and as we were both going the same way, I followed it to the main road, and then, when it turned right along the road, my usual ride took me in the same direction, so I kept on following.

I was surprised when he turned in here. I must have passed this place dozens of times, and I never knew we were getting our supplies from you, so I decided to come and have a nosy round.

I hope it's not inconvenient," she added coyly.

He grinned and sat down himself.

"Not much to see really; fields and fields of crops and pasture land, and not much else – apart from my ugly mug!"

She couldn't agree with that statement. He was far from ugly – and quite good looking – in a rugged sort of tanned and weather-beaten way!

"And what else do you grow – apart from what we buy from you?" she queried, trying to spin the conversation out and make an opening for the question she really wanted to ask.

"Fruit and vegetables mainly. Everything's very seasonal here, so there's different things at different times of the year. I'd show you around, but I haven't much time this afternoon. I'm expecting a rep from one of the fertiliser companies in about half an hour.

Boss man has decided on a glass house for next spring to grow tomatoes, so I need some advice about the sort of mediums and the best fertilisers for growing them."

For her, this was about to become boring, and she knew she didn't have much time left before his visitor arrived. She'd have to come to the point quickly or she'd miss her opportunity.

"That sounds great," she said, realising the time had come to dive in with both feet. "Susan and I have often wondered what else you might be able to bring with you on your delivery – perhaps some nice salad bits for our tea, but we haven't seen you for a while, and haven't had the chance to ask you."

His face clouded over and the smile left him.

"Is she all right?" he asked quietly, giving her just the opportunity she'd been waiting for.

"She's fine now," she said, knowing exactly what he was alluding to, "but she's missing your visits."

233

He became solemn as he looked at her.

"I've been missing them too," he replied.

"Then why don't you come to the stables anymore?" she asked rashly, realising this might possibly be the only opportunity she'd get.

He looked gravely into her face.

"There's no point really, is there? There's no point starting a relationship that can't come to anything!"

"Why not?" She was puzzled more than anything by his answer, wondering if he might already be married.

"Because she already has a husband, even though they're not together any more. He could still want her back at any time, and I couldn't bear to lose her if she decided to go back to him. I've already been married once, and she walked out on me without a word of warning."

She stared at him in surprise.

"What makes you think she's still married to Robert?" she asked.

"Isn't she?" he queried, his manner becoming eager.

"No, she's not," Jess laughed. "Robert was already seeing somebody else before the incident happened; that was the cause of their last argument – a really bad one, and their neighbours called the police. She was beaten up pretty badly and spent some time in hospital recovering. When she came out, he'd left the flat and never came back. He wrote and asked for a divorce and she was only too happy to agree. She's already heard that he's remarried the other woman – but God help the poor woman being married to somebody like that! I wouldn't want to be in her shoes!"

This was the story she and Susan had agreed on; one that they'd both stick to if they ever had to tell anybody,

Susan being particularly adamant that that's all that Des should ever know. They were both pretty word perfect when they'd talked it through and gone over the finer details in case of awkward questions being asked.

Jess could pretend that that's all she knew, but Susan would have to be more careful with her rendition.

Des had brightened up considerably, as a boyish grin spread across his face.

"Then can we expect you to bring the delivery yourself next week?" she asked now, eager for him to agree. She wouldn't tell Susan, but would make sure she was there when it arrived, and she'd warn Nathan to make himself scarce too, as she would, after they'd finished unloading.

"You try and keep me away!" he laughed as he stood up; realising that the rep he'd been expecting had just pulled up in front of the office.

Jess stood up too and he opened the door for her.

"Sorry we can't talk for longer," he said, "but I'll definitely be there next week – in person."

"So will Susan – I'll make sure of that," she said, as she untied Nero and used the rails of the gate to climb onto his back, waving to him as she trotted off down the track towards the road.

She certainly would make sure Susan was waiting, but until then, she'd say nothing, and leave it to be one big surprise for her.

The following week, Jess made sure they were both waiting in the yard when the delivery arrived, eager to see the look of surprise on Susan's face.

She was both puzzled and annoyed when she saw the tractor turn in, being driven by Jimbob, and not by Des.

Why had he broken his promise? He'd seemed so eager to see Susan again, so what had changed his mind?

She was glad now that she hadn't mentioned her meeting with Des and that Susan hadn't been expecting him.

Nathan, having also been put in the picture, looked at her in puzzlement and she gave him a wary look, shaking her head and shrugging her shoulders, warning him by her expression not to say anything.

They'd finished putting everything away and tidying up the yard after the tractor had left, when they heard the sound of a motor car turning in. It was a snazzy little green sports car that appeared, and who should climb out of it but Des, wearing a green jumper in exactly the same shade as the car, and a pair of tan slacks. His face was wreathed in smiles, and obviously very proud of his new vehicle.

"Well, what d'you think of her?" he smiled at them, standing back for them to admire it.

Jess glanced at Susan, whose face was registering a new radiance at his sudden appearance, tongue tied and not able to say anything for the moment.

"It's very nice," Jess said, trying to cover Susan's obvious lack of words.

"Just been to pick her up," he said, coming towards them. "I need somebody to go out for a spin to test her out. Would you like to come Susan? We could have a meal at a pub as well."

Susan just looked up at him, words failing her, until Jess stepped in.

"I'm sorry," she said, "but we're both working, and customers will be arriving soon. Maybe you could both go out when they've all gone; say around sevenish?

236

She'll need time to change, and then she'll be free for the rest of the day."

She turned to look at Susan for confirmation, who smiled and nodded her head mutely, still not finding any words.

He held up his hand.

"Problem solved. I've already spoken to Paul and he's going to help out tonight."

Turning to Susan he continued, "You have the rest of the day off, so go and get changed and then we'll get going."

Susan needed no second bidding, as she scampered off to the flat to get herself ready.

"Thanks, Des," Jess said. "I thought for a moment you were going to let her down when I saw Jimbob bringing the feed."

"I'd never do that when I'd given my word," he answered, as he sat back down in his car and began to read the Owners Manual while he waited for Susan to come back.

Jess was still brushing down the yard when Susan arrived back in a pretty yellow summer dress and a long sleeved cardigan in a slightly darker shade.

"Enjoy yourselves!" she shouted as Susan jumped into the passenger seat, and Des solicitously lifted out a warm blanket from the back seat to put over her legs in case she was cold.

It was shortly after ten o'clock when she heard them arrive back, having gone for a canter with Nero when all the customers had left, before making herself a meal and sitting down to read the book Susan had already enjoyed.

Susan bounded up the steps to the flat, and was obviously bursting with happiness when she bounced through the door.

"I take it you had a good time?" she smiled, looking up from her book and seeing the radiance on Susan's face.

"Oh, it was wonderful!" Susan enthused. "He's such a gentleman, and we got on ever so well – I could have gone on talking with him all night."

Jess got up to make their cocoa while she kept on talking – happy for Susan, but feeling a growing determination within her to try and find Callum. She knew his uncle's farm was in Lancashire – somewhere! Could it be so hard to find?

CHAPTER 24

True to his word, Frank had thought long and hard about the purchase of a new lorry to fulfil Callum's idea of a motorised delivery service.

Winter hadn't been kind to them that year, with a serious amount of frost and snow during December, January and February, putting their chances of early crops well back, and money was always tight during the winter months. The money they made during the summer had to carry them through the winter, and so a lot of the work force had had to be laid off for a considerable time that year.

He knew it was hard on them as well, not having any wages coming in, but if he had kept on paying them through the winter with no money coming in, he wouldn't have had a business left to run when spring finally arrived. He felt sorry for them, having found himself in the same position when the factory he worked in had burned down during the war, and knowing he'd lost his own home because of it. He just hoped they'd be able to find some occasional employment to see them through, although he did call on some of the workforce for help when the weather was fine and there were jobs that could be done, trying to give an equal share to each of them.

He'd put Callum's idea to the back of his mind, occasionally bringing it out and dusting it off when Callum brought it to mind once again, but wasn't yet ready to give it any serious consideration until the bad weather abated.

Who knew how long it was going to last for? When the snow did finally disappear, it would leave the ground too soggy to grow anything in for some considerable time. He could only hope for some drier months to give them a chance to get started on the planting.

Callum, knowing and believing in the efficacy of his idea, was still very keen to make it a reality, but he too knew that there must be produce for him to sell, otherwise his plan couldn't come to fruition, and the whole idea would fall flat.

Thankfully, the snow was all gone by the beginning of March, and the weather turned sunny and bright, with a light breeze blowing on most days, and very little rain during the month, giving the soil a chance to dry out. By the end of the month, they were able to begin planting again, and some of the workforce was re-employed during the next few weeks.

They all worked hard, and soon the green shoots began to show once more and the fields took on a greenish hue instead of being a dirty brown colour.

During this time the greenhouse was delivered and erected; only a small one at first, to see how they would be able to manage the tomato crop. Soon the first flowers were appearing on the plants, and in anticipation of an early season, Callum once more brought up the idea of the new lorry.

Over the coming week, Frank began to think seriously about the idea again, and finally decided that they might be able to buy a second-hand vehicle for the time being to see how things went. It was with great pride that Callum was able to take delivery of his new vehicle in mid May.

Mechanically it was in good condition, but the paintwork wasn't very good, and that too he took into the barn, giving it a bright coat of red and yellow paint to make it stand out. The side curtains were ripped in places, but as he wasn't able to do anything about that, he patched them up with some strong tape that they used around the farm, also giving the runners a thick coating of grease to make them easier to open and shut.

Soon he was ready to take it out on the road.

There were plenty of potatoes, carrots, cabbages, Brussels sprouts and lettuces, as well a few tomatoes, to load it up with, and his former customers were pleased to see him back again, when he climbed out of the lorry and rang his hand bell once again.

He had managed to take out plenty of stock without having to go back for a re-load, and began to think he would be able to widen his journeys further afield when more vegetables became available, thus increasing his customer base.

It was in July, with more stock having become available to him, that he decided on a new route, taking in other villages which he hadn't yet visited. Whilst making his way towards one of these, he suddenly rounded a bend and saw some gypsy caravans travelling along the road towards him.

At once he was wary, and pulled his cap down over his eyes as much as he could, hoping it wasn't Giovanni. He didn't want to have to meet them on a lonely road like this, especially after the way he and his father had taken off and left them without any warning. He didn't know what their reaction might be.

As the caravans were straggled all over the road, he pulled in to the side to let them pass, acknowledging their

241

cheery greetings and gestures of thanks by bringing his hand up in a gesture of his own, thus partially hiding his own face from view.

Some of them seemed familiar, but he wasn't quite sure if they were from Giovanni's band, and after they'd passed, he was just about to pull back out into the road again, when another rounded the bend further on, the horse at a trot and looking as if it was trying to catch up with the others.

He recognised the caravan immediately, and also the horse pulling it; it was Brendan, Jess's father, and he held his breath as it finally reached and passed him.

Brendan was sitting alone on the drivers' seat, and gave him a small salute as he passed, but didn't look at him and gave to sign of recognition, appearing in a hurry to catch up with the rest of the group.

After he'd passed, Callum craned out of the drivers' seat to see if there was any sign of Jess, but the rear door of the caravan was closed. If she was still with her father, he needed to find out where they were making for, so turned the motor round and followed as soon as they were out of sight, keeping a good distance behind.

After a short while, he began to realise the direction in which they were heading. It was towards the site in the woods where he and Frank had first met up with Giovanni's group. It was so close to the farm, he knew that if he kept an eye on them, sooner or later he'd see Jess if she were still with them, and might perhaps have the chance to talk to her.

Over the next couple of weeks, he went often to the site, watching through the trees when he found where Brendan's caravan was parked, and seeing no sign of Jess, he realised she was probably no longer with them.

He knew that she hadn't married Silas, so had she married somebody else? Perhaps she was still living within the group with her new husband, or perhaps she'd married into another group and may be travelling with them. Could he pluck up the courage and speak to Brendan and ask what had happened to her?

When he did finally pluck up the courage and returned to their camp a couple of days later, it was to find that they'd already gone.

He knew now that through his own stupid procrastination he could have missed any chance of ever finding Jess again.

CHAPTER 25

Fred and Doreen Manson, both teachers, but she working in the local primary school, and he as a games teacher in the secondary school, were enjoying the second week of the children's summer holiday.

They never saw much of each other during the week, as, although Doreen's day ended at four o'clock, and it was only a short walk to her own home, Fred's school was near Southport, necessitating a bus ride every day, and he had to leave home before eight o'clock every morning in order to catch it.

After school finished, cutting through local villages to drop people off, the ride usually took nearly an hour before reaching his own village. As he often stayed on after school to clean up kit, or to supervise practice games such as football or hockey in the winter, and tennis and netball in the summer, he frequently didn't arrive home until eight or even nine o'clock in the evening: hungry and only wanting food and sleep.

The weather had been very wet during the first week of the holiday, but this week had begun fine and warm, and Fred, always an active man and in his late thirties, was feeling the lack of activity.

Doreen, five years his junior was, however, content to sit in the garden of their little cottage and read a book, occasionally spending time weeding and hoeing the small flower beds around the edges of the lawn. They were producing an excellent show of flowers this year, and she enjoyed the scent assailing her nostrils as she sat and read.

His parents had both been killed during the war years when an unexploded bomb went off in a neighbours' garden. They were on a few days visit to her sister in the Aintree area, and all sitting enjoying the sunshine in her garden, when, without warning, the bomb exploded only six feet from the other side of the fence. Having landed in some rather overgrown bushes at the end of the garden some months previously, nobody had even known it was there. Both his parents, her sister and her husband were blown out of existence, and as he was their only child, Fred had inherited the cottage.

It was only small, but big enough for just the two of them, as they'd never been blessed with children so far during their twelve year marriage, and they were both contented with the life they were living.

Growing tired of sitting in the garden doing nothing, Fred went to the small shed at the side of the house and brought out his bicycle.

"Going to give it a birthday?" Doreen asked, looking up from her book to see what he was doing.

"I thought it probably might need it," Fred answered, "it wasn't cleaned after our last outing. I'll clean yours as well while I'm at it, shall I?"

"Thank you," she replied.

It was one of those jobs she knew needed doing, and was glad that Fred was going to do it for her.

He went back to the house for some hot soapy water and a cloth, while she turned and stretched luxuriously before becoming engrossed in her book once again.

After half an hour, he seemed to be finishing off the job, so she went back into the house to make some tea, and brought out some cakes and biscuits to go with it, noticing when she brought them out that although he was sitting in his chair once again, he hadn't put the bikes away.

"Leaving them to dry in the sun, are you?" she asked, nodding in their direction as she set the tray down on the small garden table.

"No," he answered, "I thought we'd go for a spin on them if you feel like it. I need to stretch my legs, and we could stop for a bite to eat at that pub you like."

She would have preferred to go to the pub by bus, but, on reflection, realised it would do her good to get some exercise as well. They'd spent nearly the whole day sitting in the garden yesterday, and it would do them both good.

Washing the dishes, she changed into a pair of shorts and a thin blouse, taking a warm jumper and a waterproof with her in case the weather should turn wet again. Unlikely, looking at the clear blue sky, but nobody knew how long it would stay that way with the vagaries of the British weather.

They reached the pub just before one o'clock and enjoyed an excellent ploughman's lunch, sitting outside under a thatched roof shelter in the garden, and decided to take a ride round the area before returning home.

Having roused herself from her state of lethargy, she found she was rather enjoying the pleasant ride through the country lanes.

It was as they were returning on the homeward journey, that they heard the sound of a car engine behind them, accompanied by the ever increasing sound of loud music as it came nearer. It appeared to be going quite fast; the roar of its engine growing louder as it drew nearer, and he could hear the sound of loud laughter as well.

Fred, who had been riding alongside Doreen, dropped back behind her, but worried by how fast the vehicle seemed to be going, called to her to pull into the side and wait for it to pass.

Following his example, she did so, and they both turned to look towards the approaching vehicle.

It was a large, red, Triumph Roadster, and Fred envied the man driving it. He would have loved to own a car like that, but unfortunately, it was way beyond his means.

As it drew nearer, he could see there were a man and a woman inside, and as it swept past he saw that the man was wearing a tweed jacket and cap, with a white silk scarf streaming out behind him in the wind.

The woman was wearing a fur jacket, despite the warmth of the day, and sunglasses shading her eyes; her head covered with a blue and white scarf.

They both seemed to be laughing as they passed by, without even noticing them, as the car rapidly sped on.

It was as he watched them speeding up the road that Fred noticed the girl on a horse some way up ahead.

The horse already appeared apprehensive; skittering and dancing about on the road, trying to turn its head to see what was behind it. The girl was leaning over, stroking its neck and trying to calm it down.

It seemed only seconds before the sports car reached them, and it was obvious it was very frightened by the noise, bucking and prancing around.

The road was quite narrow, never having been built for large cars like this, and although the man pulled to the far side, he still passed very close to them before roaring on up the road and disappearing round a bend without a backward glance.

The horse was now extremely frightened.

As the car passed, reared once in panic and bucked hard on the road, trying to get away from the monster terrifying it.

Fred and Doreen watched in horror as the girl flew into the air, and disappeared into the undergrowth beyond the side of the road with a loud scream, whereupon the horse reared once more and took off at a gallop.

Without a word to each other, they mounted their bikes and pedalled up to the scene as quickly as possible. Dropping them down at the side of the road, they made their way cautiously forward into the undergrowth as best they could; finding that it only went a short distance before a steep embankment dropped away beyond.

Below them was a fast flowing stream, and there, lying on the edge of the water, up against a large boulder, was the girl's body; prostrate and unmoving!

For the moment they were uncertain what to do, when they heard the sound of a vehicle coming towards them – wondering at first if it was the car returning. Making their way back to the road, they saw it was a large lorry, and they flagged it down.

The driver, an amiable lad in his twenties, stopped immediately he saw them.

"Something wrong?" he asked anxiously, having seen their bicycles lying at the side of the road, and them quickly making their way out of the undergrowth, both of them looking extremely agitated.

Fred took charge and explained the situation as the lad immediately jumped down from the cab, and went round to the back, where he produced a rope from the back of the vehicle.

He followed Fred back to the top of the embankment, where they looked down, and seeing where the body was placed, the lad looked round for a suitable tree to tie the rope round, before cautiously using it to steady his progress down to the bottom.

It wasn't particularly steep, but it was a bit slippery after the previous week's rain, and he was wary of that fact whilst making his way down.

Reaching the bottom, the girl was just beginning to stir as he leaned towards her over another large boulder.

"Are you all right?" he called.

"Mmm ..." was his only reply.

She seemed dazed.

"Are you hurt anywhere?"

"Mmm ..." was her next reply, as she raised an arm and lifted it across her eyes to keep out the sun.

Carefully making his way through the surrounding undergrowth, which was being splashed by water from the stream, at the base of which was a miasma of muddy ground and smaller rocks, he managed to make his way to her side.

He leaned over and looked down at her.

"Are you hurting anywhere?" he asked again.

His shadow now shading the sun from her eyes, she removed her arm from across her face and looked up at him.

"I think I'm okay," she answered, making an attempt to move her head from side to side before trying to sit up.

Suddenly, she heard him give a sharp intake of breath, and she looked up at him again. The sun was bright behind his head, and she couldn't make out his features.

"Jess?" he queried, an incredulous tone in his voice. "It is you, isn't it?"

She knew the voice, but it was a lot deeper than she remembered.

"Callum . . .?" she asked, uncertainly.

"Yes, it's me," he answered, squatting down alongside her.

"I can't believe it! After all these years, and we have to meet because I fell off my horse," she laughed, as she pulled herself into a sitting position, wincing as she did so, and trying to wipe the mud from her face.

"What hurts?" he asked solicitously.

"Nothing much!" she replied. "Mainly my pride!"

Just at that moment, they heard a call from above. Fred was asking if she was all right.

"I think so," Callum called back. "I'm just seeing if she's all right before she tries to get up."

Having sat up, she checked herself all over; making sure everything was working properly, before trying to get up. She had a lot of cuts and abrasions to her bare arms and a deep cut on her forehead, but everything seemed to be in working order as she tried to stand. Suddenly she gave a small cry as Callum helped her to her feet.

"It's my left wrist," she admitted. "It's very painful – I'm not sure if it's just a sprain, or whether it might be broken."

"Good job it's your left and not your right. We should be able to get you back up to the top all right."

It was much easier going back up than going down, Fred being able to tie the rope round a tree and help with pulling them up, and they were soon standing at the top once more; Fred pushing aside the brush to enable their progress as Callum helped her back to the road.

"Where's Nero?" she asked, her first concern for the horse as she looked around her.

"No idea," Callum replied, "I didn't see him on the road."

"He galloped off in the direction you were coming from. Didn't you see him?" Doreen said.

"He's probably gone back to the stables," Jess replied with relief before Callum could answer. "There's a turning just up ahead and it leads straight back there. He knows this route well – we often ride out this way."

"I'll take you back there then," Callum replied. "Then I'll go and get the Land Rover and take you up to the hospital."

When they arrived back at the stables, there had been anxiety and consternation all around when Nero had galloped into the yard on his own, but they were pleased when Jess finally turned up unharmed some time later. Even if it was in a gaudy coloured lorry carrying vegetables!

Paul, having been informed that Nero had arrived back without Jess, had already got out his new car. He'd bought it some weeks earlier; Krista now being too elderly to ride any more, and was just about to go out and look for her.

They were all pleased to see her arrive back safe and well, Paul telling Susan to take her up to the flat and make her a cup of tea: he would stay and help Nathan see to the customers who would begin arriving shortly.

Jess, proud of their accommodation, and anxious not to let Callum go so soon after they'd met once more, invited him back with them for tea.

Although their flat was on the small side, they'd made it bright and cheerful. They'd sanded and polished the floorboards, laying down bright and cheerful rugs, hung bright flowery curtains, and added colourful pictures to the newly painted walls. With windows on both sides, one side overlooking the stable yard and the other overlooking the paddocks, there was plenty of light flooding in, and Callum thought they'd made a real home from home out of it.

They drank their tea, while Jess gave them all the details of what had happened, before he left Susan to clean Jess up, while he took the lorry back and returned with the rather battered Land Rover. At least it was an improvement on arriving at the hospital in an elderly and rather gaudily painted lorry.

She waited anxiously. He'd disappeared from her life so suddenly once before, and she just hoped he wouldn't do that again this time; but she needn't have worried, he was back well within the hour, just giving her enough time to get cleaned up and changed.

Her arm was x-rayed at the hospital, and she was pleased to find it wasn't broken, just badly sprained, and keeping it in a sling for a few days should see it back to normal again.

Her first thought on arriving back was for Nero, and she took Callum round to his loose box while she checked him over.

"You were riding **him**?" he queried when he saw the size of Nero. "Rather big for you isn't he?"

She laughed.

"He may look big, but he's a real sweetheart when you get to know him!"

Nero was already nuzzling against her, whickering and snuffling as she put her good arm around his neck – or as far round as she could reach, before she opened the door to bring him out.

He trotted out quietly, and Callum reached a hand out, holding it just below his muzzle. Nero threw up his head and rolled his eyes warily.

"Now that's not very friendly," she chided him, taking Callum's hand in hers and holding it out to him.

This time he put his head down and snotted all over Callum's hand.

"I think he likes you!" she laughed, as Callum wiped his hand on the horse's neck.

This time he didn't object, and stood placidly while Jess ran her hand down his legs, checking that he wasn't hurt, before Callum walked him round the yard, while she checked for lameness, before returning him to his stall.

"You'll do!" she said, taking out a couple of carrots from the nearby sack and giving them to him, before she took Callum back to the flat.

Susan was going out with Des that evening, so was all ready to go when they arrived back, and Jess told Callum that she'd make them some food if he was able to stay.

"No problem!" he said.

Anxious to get her to the hospital, he hadn't thought to pick up any money when he'd returned home. The takings from the days' sales were still in the lorry, and all he had in his pocket wasn't even enough to buy one portion of fish and chips.

"Oh dear," she said as she looked through their cupboards. "I have some baked beans, some soup, and a bottle of salad cream – not a very inspiring menu, is it?"

Producing the paltry amount of coins from his pocket, he replied, "Afraid I can't be much help either! I didn't have time to pick up any money when I went back to the farm!"

When they'd finished laughing, she took down a tin of soup and some baked beans. Unable to manage on her own, she asked him to do the cooking and make the toast, while she helped with what she could manage. They

253

surprisingly enjoyed the makeshift meal, although they had so much to talk about that the dishes were inadvertently all but forgotten about and were still in the sink next morning.

When Susan arrived back shortly after ten o'clock, Callum had just left, and she was bursting with excitement.

"Des has asked me to marry him!" she crowed, as soon as she burst through the door. "He's taking me into town to choose an engagement ring on Saturday!"

"Oh, that's wonderful!" Jess cried, jumping up from her chair and flinging her arm around Susan.

"Have you set a date yet?" she continued, putting a pan of milk on for their cocoa.

"Early spring, we thought," was the answer, as she flopped into an armchair. "They should be able to spare him from the farm then for a weeks' honeymoon. His uncle has a farm in Scotland, and he lets out a holiday cottage near Loch Lomond. Des says that's the best time of year to go to Scotland as well, although it can still be a bit cold - but I don't think we'll have time to notice the weather, do you?" she blushed and giggled.

"Why are you blushing?" Jess retorted, amused by her coyness. "You've already been a married woman!"

A cloud seemed to come over Susan for a moment.

"What's the matter?" she asked. "Have I said something wrong?"

Susan was looking worried.

"I don't think I've anything to worry about from Robert now, he seems to be settled with his new wife, and I haven't heard anything about him for years, but what's going to happen if Matthew comes looking for me again? We both need to keep working after we're married, and he'll be two miles from here – Matthew may arrive at any time when I'm on my own.

"Don't worry about it; I don't think he'll come back again, especially after what Des did to him before."

Neither of them realised how prophetic her words were!

CHAPTER 26

Frank and Maura were delighted to hear that Callum had found Jess, and they talked until after midnight when he arrived home.

Next morning after breakfast, Frank asked him to delay going out on his rounds, as there was something they wanted to speak to him about.

"Maura's little farm shop is doing well, and she's selling everything in it within a few hours every day. We've decided to pull the old wooden shed down, and build a much larger and better shop on the site, and take on staff to help her run it."

Callum was enthusiastic.

"I've been thinking that myself for a while now. You can see how much my sales have increased since getting the lorry, so I'm sure we could make much more of the shop as well."

They both nodded before Frank continued.

"I've heard there's a new estate of private houses about to be built alongside the Council owned ones. The builder has already been given the go-ahead, and he'll be erecting about a hundred houses when he gets started."

"So many houses have been bombed out in Liverpool and the surrounding areas that the demand for new housing is becoming overwhelming," Maura chipped in. "We foresee many more new homes springing up around here before long, and there should be much more demand for our produce in the future.

Once we get it up and running, I intend to extend the produce we sell, buying in local cheeses, jams, cakes and pastries, as well as a range of different types of bread."

Enthusiastic now, Frank chipped in as she drew breath.

"I've already enquired about another ten acres our neighbour has for sale. He's getting older now and looking to scale down his own farm in the future, ready to retire."

Gripped by their enthusiasm Callum too had plans, and decided this was the perfect time to voice them.

"Great idea! I may have plans myself for the future, but I'll still be working here as long as you need me."

"I'll always need you!" Frank replied, looking directly into his face and clapping him on the shoulder. "You've always been my right-hand man, you know that."

"Thanks dad," he replied, "but one thing I do need from you is somewhere of my own to live. I know the house is big enough for all of us, but I would like somewhere to call my own – somewhere to entertain friends. I had thought of renting a small cottage in the village, but I wouldn't have anywhere to park the lorry, and I'd have to come back here every day to load it before I even start my rounds. We have plenty of room here, especially with the extra ten acres. Could you perhaps find me a small plot to build my own place."

Frank and Maura exchanged glances.

"We've already had thoughts along that line," Frank replied. "There's the remains of an old cottage alongside the woods. It's fallen into disrepair over the years – I believe it was once the home of a gamekeeper when the woods belonged to one of the local gentry – but Ben must have purchased it years ago, along with the cottage. He had no use for it, so it's much in need of restoration. Why don't you go and have a look at it when you've finished your deliveries today?"

Callum was already aware of the cottage and its location, having explored it a few times when he was younger, and had once made a den inside, before Uncle Ben had warned him off and said the roof was dangerous and could collapse at any time.

He was excited. It wasn't very big, but once renovated, and perhaps enlarged a bit in the process, it would make a perfect home.

After he'd finished his rounds that day, he'd purposely made his last call to the village near the stables, and called in to see Jess.

She was busy in the stable yard when he arrived, surrounded by young girls' clamouring for attention, wanting to buy feed, and also asking questions about their horses' care and condition, which they only saw once or twice a day until the weekends.

He waited for a lull before approaching her.

"Jess, there's something I'd like you to come and see with me tonight."

Flustered by all the activity around her, and unable to do much more than take their money and give them their change, she was a bit off-hand with him for a moment, until she realised how pleased she should be to find him back again so soon and obviously anxious to see her.

"Sorry," she said, when the last of the girls had gone back to their charges. "As you can see, I'm a little busy at the moment. Can you come back later when they've all gone?"

"I'll pick you up later. Would seven o'clock suit you?"

"That would be great. The adults should all have gone by then as well, but Nathan and Susan can see to the rest if there are any still here."

"I've something very exciting I want to show you!" he said mysteriously, fanning her curiosity, but when she questioned him, he merely tapped the side of his nose, and swung back into the driving seat, a wide grin spread across his face.

"I'll see you later," he called back as he drove out.

Susan was pleased to hear Jess was going out that evening. Des was calling for her and it meant that they could spend the whole evening in the flat together without interruption. She had plans for their wedding whirling round in her head, and she wanted to talk them over, not realising that they'd be of little interest to him.

After an hour of listening to her plans, Des suggested going for a drink and some fish and chips in the village – anything to get her off the subject for a while.

There were only a few people in the bar when they walked in, and they found a quiet table in the window overlooking a field of cows. Susan turned to look out of the window, and after a few minutes gazing at the creatures munching quietly, she turned back again as she saw Des walking towards her with their drinks.

There was a newspaper lying on the window seat alongside her, and she idly picked it up and put it on the table in front of her. It was already open at one of the inner pages, and there, looking up at her from a small box in the centre of the page, was a picture of Matthew.

She involuntarily gasped and drew back as if she'd been stung. Des, returning to the table with their drinks at that

259

moment, picked it up to look at what had so disturbed her, his face falling as he realised what the editorial was about.

"What's it saying about Matthew?" she asked after a few seconds hesitation.

Hoping to put the paper, and the matter, to one side without further discussion, he realised that wasn't going to happen.

"It seems he's gone missing, and nobody knows where he is," he answered.

She looked back at him suspiciously.

"You haven't had anything to do with it, have you?" she questioned.

Surprised, he put the paper down and looked at her.

"Me? No!" I haven't seen him since he left the stables, and that's the honest truth. I've no idea where he is," he answered truthfully, hoping she wouldn't question him too deeply.

She hadn't seen the mess he'd made of Matthew's face when he'd left the stables, which he felt might have been contributory to his disappearance. He couldn't help feeling that something had happened to him as a direct result of those injuries, but in all honesty, he'd answered her question truthfully, and didn't intend making any further enquiries into the matter. In fact, he'd hoped never to have to think about him again.

Trying to take her mind off the subject of Matthew, he surreptitiously slid the paper onto the seat alongside him, and brought the subject back to the wedding once more, this time talking about where they might live afterwards, rather than the tedious trivia of what she might wear and whether to have a matron of honour. She'd already decided it would be Jess if she felt the need to have one.

As farm manager, a larger room was afforded him at the end of the bunkhouse, where he'd lived since coming to work for Frank. As well as a bed and washing facilities, it contained a small kitchen area and a table with two chairs.

He knew that Susan couldn't be expected to share those quarters with him, so his mind had turned towards renting a cottage in the village, and he wanted them both to try and find one that might me suitable.

This was another topic close to her heart and she was delighted with the idea of a cottage in the village, although she'd already made it clear that she wanted to go on working at the stables, at least for the time being. She thought of adding the rider 'until we start a family' but thought that was better left for another time, and the picture in the paper went clean out of her head as they made plans to search for one.

Callum had picked Jess up in the Land Rover, dead on seven o'clock as he'd promised, and took her back to the farm.

The route was already familiar, and when they turned up the track towards the farm, she was more than a little surprised.

"Isn't this the farm where Des works? Is this where you live too?" she asked, incredulous that she'd already been here without ever knowing that he was also here. They must have been living so close to each other for so long without their paths ever having crossed.

"I didn't know you'd been here before!" he said, surprise registering on his face as he pulled into the yard and parked alongside the house. "I didn't see you, and dad never mentioned your visit."

Surprised that Frank was here too, she merely gaped at him in surprise.

"I didn't know either of you lived here! I saw Des in the farm office. I never came to the house, and I never saw your father," she clarified, and explained the reason for her visit to see Des, leaving out the finer details of the attack on Susan. She merely said Susan had had an unpleasant experience with a man at the stables and that Des had turned him off the premises.

When she'd finished, he didn't press her with any questions, realising that there was more to the story than she was willing to tell at present.

As a courtesy to Frank and Maura, he took her in to meet them first, and Frank greeted her like a long lost friend.

"Lovely to see you again, Jess," he said, giving her a hug, and then introducing her to Maura.

Maura, never having met her before, wasn't quite as effusive as her husband, but she too gave Jess a perfunctory hug and a friendly smile. Knowing her own daughter had been taken away from her by a gypsy, she couldn't help feeling a little animosity towards all of their kind.

After a long chat over tea and biscuits, accompanied by an explanation of how they'd come to be not only living at, but also owning, the farm, and a catch-up of events that had happened since they'd all last met, Callum took her along the footpath from the side of the farm towards the woods.

It was perhaps two hundred yards from the house, and some of the trees had already been cleared around it to allow for expansion of the field nearest to it, but that only enhanced its position.

It now received far more sunlight than it ever had in the past.

Unlike him, never having seen it before, she gazed on it with fresh eyes.

"It's a bit of a mess," she said, screwing up her face, before noticing his disappointed face, and continuing more brightly, "but I'm sure you could make something of it - given time. It'll mean a lot of work though."

"Oh, I've got it all worked out. I just needed to see it and work out what I could do with it to make it larger. With the trees being cleared, there may even be room for a small garden."

He walked round and round the exterior, making notes in a small notebook, leaving Jess to sit on the edge of a collapsed wall while he sketched and made notes, until he noticed she was looking bored.

"Sorry," he said, "let's go into Southport and get some fish and chips. Are you hungry?"

She nodded.

"I didn't finish 'til late, so I only had time for a quick sandwich before you arrived."

With that, he put away his sketches and they walked back to the yard, where he threw them onto the back seat, and prepared to drive out.

As they drove down the track towards the road, she suddenly noticed a gypsy caravan parked behind a hedge. It had been hidden from view when they'd first arrived by the overhanging branches of a large tree, but from this angle, it was now visible.

She put her hand on his arm, and he slowed to a stop.

"That looks like Kyla's caravan," she said, noting the distinctive pattern in which it was painted: green background, with a blue and yellow stripe along the sides.

He didn't see much of Kyla and Silas these days; being out on his delivery round all day, and they, along with the boys, working in the fields. In the evenings everybody seemed far too tired to socialise much, and he'd been so used to passing the caravan every day, that he no longer noticed it.

"Yes, it is Kyla's", he said. "She and Silas have been working here for some time now, and the two boys also work out in the fields with them."

She seemed delighted to find them, and told him he must tell them she was here so that she could visit with them.

"Your parents were here too, but it's a while ago now. I was told there were gypsies camped in the wood, and I went down to see who it was. When I saw it was your family, I came down numerous times to see if you were still with them. I watched them from the trees, but by the time I plucked up the courage to speak to them, they'd already left."

"No, I've never seen them since the day I left myself," she said sadly. "I've always hoped we could be reconciled at some point, but I didn't know where to find them. Maybe they'll come back again, but whether I'll have the courage to go and see them, I really don't know."

He realised now that they had a lot to catch up on. She had obviously never married Silas, something he'd known since Silas and Kyla had arrived together, but he didn't yet know how she'd managed to evade their marriage. As she was no longer with the gypsy group, he also needed to know how and why she'd left them, and what she'd been doing since.

They continued on their journey to Southport, where they ate their fish and chips on a seat overlooking fragrant floral gardens facing out towards the sea, and he finally managed to catch up on what had happened since he and Frank had left the camp.

She also wanted to know all the ins and outs of how he'd come to be driving a fruit and vegetable delivery lorry through the lanes of Lancashire, and his story became as long and convoluted as her own.

There was so much to tell that they talked for what seemed like hours, and when it became too cold to sit there any longer, they climbed back into the Land Rover and continued their conversation sitting inside it.

It was after midnight when they arrived back, and Jess tiptoed quietly to her own bedroom so as not to wake Susan.

What she didn't know was that Susan had only arrived back a few minutes before she did!

CHAPTER 27

It was during the following week that Aleisha came into Paul's life.

A retired army colonel had become obsessed with the beautiful Shire horses he'd admired for so many years, and after his retirement, had bought two mares of his own, installing them on his eighty acre property with 18th century manor house, near Lancaster.

Soon two became four, and a friend of his, a gentleman farmer from Yorkshire, also the owner of two Shires, persuaded him to put them to stud, and recommended Nero.

He himself had taken one of his own horses to him for stud two years ago, and asked Colonel Fitzpatrick and his wife over for the weekend to look at the progeny.

Struck by the beautiful markings and the admirable confirmation of the filly, he decided to ring Paul and book a stud when one of his mares was next due in season, which he did a fortnight later.

Paul consulted Jess after the call, not being sure whether Nero might be too old now, fertility usually waning with age, but she informed him that he'd covered the last mare they'd had with his usual vigour, and it had already been confirmed she was in foal. With that assurance, Paul rang the Colonel back and arranged for him to contact them when the mare was ready.

A month later, a very smart horsebox drove into the yard, with the Colonel's stable manager driving, and a young woman, perhaps in her late twenties or early thirties, at his side.

Paul couldn't help noticing her. Dressed in riding breeches, boots and plaid shirt, with a headscarf restraining her long brown hair, she wasn't exactly the picture of a glamorous woman, but there was something about her that drew Paul to her immediately.

Her smile, formed by an over-generously wide mouth, and long, tip-tilted nose, with large brown eyes, gave her face a character all its own, one that endeared her to him as soon as she stepped down from the lorry.

The man, clad in tweeds from head to toe, including his peaked cap, was also wearing riding boots as he climbed down and introduced himself to Paul. He didn't introduce the young woman, and Paul felt he looked on her as someone of no-consequence. Perhaps she was just one of the stable hands he'd brought along to oversee the horse.

The mare, when they brought her out of the lorry, was docile and amenable, seeming none the worse for her long journey, and walked quietly to the stable Jess had already prepared, where she settled in immediately.

They spoke for a few minutes, and he introduced Jess, who was looking the mare over and making sure she'd suffered no injuries, before offering her a bucket of water, and hanging up a hay net for her to munch on.

Once again, he only gave Jess a perfunctory glance, nodded his head, and then proceeded to ignore her, turning his attention once more to Paul.

The girl, standing at his side and looking at Jess, merely shrugged her shoulders, and joined her in the stable as the men walked back to the house.

267

"Charming, isn't he?" was her opening remark as she closed the stable door behind her.

Jess raised her eyebrows and smiled; it wasn't her place to criticise someone she didn't know.

"Treats all women like that," she said, picking up a brush and beginning on the long mane. "Don't let him get to you – he seems to enjoy antagonising women – think he must have had a bad experience with one at some time in his life. I just keep out of his way as much as I can. His name is Grimble, but everybody at home refers to him as Grumble, which he never stops doing."

Jess smiled again, and said nothing, whereupon the girl stopped what she was doing, and held out a hand towards her.

"I heard them say you were Jess – I'm Aleisha by the way. I notice he didn't have the good grace to introduce me. I guess he looks on me as just part of the furniture – necessary, but inconsequential."

Jess shook hands with her, and they resumed grooming the mare before leaving her to settle down, while Jess took her up to the flat for a cup of tea and some biscuits.

Susan was already there, her usual bubbly self, and the girls were soon chatting over the tea and biscuits, the ice well and truly broken.

She was staying for a few days to be on hand to see to their horse, so Paul had told them she'd have to bunk in with one of them. Neither of them minded which room she shared, as she seemed to be so friendly, but she eventually decided on Jess's room, as it overlooked the stable yard and was almost directly above where the mare was housed.

Paul in the meantime had taken Daniel Grimble back to the house, where he offered him a meal which the girls had prepared for them of salad, cold meats and cheeses, before his drive home.

His face, when he saw the food laid out on the table, was one of disdain, leaving Paul in some confusion.

"The girls prepared this for us. Don't you like salad?" he inquired solicitously of his guest.

"It'll do to be going on with," he replied unpleasantly, "I'll get cook to make me something more substantial when I get back."

Paul had already taken a distinct dislike to this man, and found his manner very unpalatable, particularly towards Aleisha and Jess. He decided he probably treated all women like that, and unpleasant though he undoubtedly was, Paul knew he wouldn't have to put up with his company for very long, and was anxious to be rid of him as soon as possible.

The man, however, had impeccable manners, and ate his food fastidiously, chewing each mouthful many times before swallowing it.

Finishing his own food well before Daniel, Paul made them both a cup of tea to pass the time, as conversation between them was very limited, and then offered to show him Nero before he left. He was anxious to get him out of the house, and to curtail his visit.

Nero was none to receptive when he saw Daniel looking through the stable door, and kept well back, but on seeing Paul, he came forward once more, knowing there was usually a tasty carrot or an apple to be had. He rolled a wary eye in Daniels' direction the whole time he was eating.

"I'd like to see the horse walk round," Daniel said, and then, almost like a command, he stood back and said, "Bring him out here for me!"

Paul was taken aback by his imperious tone, and he felt his hackles rise. Never one to be cowed by anybody, he stood his ground.

"Not without Jess present. She's the one who handles him. They both came here together, and I wouldn't bring him out in front of a stranger without her present."

"Scared of a bloody horse, are you?" Daniel's tone was half-joking, half-sneering.

"On the contrary! If you weren't here, I'd be only too happy to handle him, but I wouldn't bring him out in front of a stranger without her present – and he doesn't seem to have taken to you very well," he rejoined. Nero had now retreated to the back of the stall once more and was rolling his eyes, always a sign that he wasn't happy with a situation.

"Well then, if the Colonel's happy with his arrangements, I suppose I'll have to be too. I wouldn't hide behind any woman's skirts!" he sneered.

Paul was now becoming angry.

"I'll call Jess if you really need to see him, but if not, I'll see you on your way. The turn into the lane is difficult for a big vehicle like yours and we usually make sure it's clear for the driver first. You have a long drive ahead of you, and I'm sure you're anxious to be on your way."

Daniel looked at him for a moment, but then shrugged his shoulders, backing down under Paul's unwavering gaze. He was a bully, and as all bullies do, he backed down when confronted head on. He realised Paul wasn't someone to be cowed very easily, and marched back to his vehicle without a backward glance.

Paul waved him into the lane, and he drove off without so much as a gesture of thanks, his face impassive and intent on turning the vehicle into the narrow lane.

270

Paul heaved a sigh of relief when he'd gone, having realised by now that the man was obviously of military background and used to having his orders obeyed without question. Unfortunately, he would have to return to pick the mare up again once she'd been served; not a prospect Paul relished!

The mare stayed with them for a week, during which time Nero served her twice, and they all hoped that he'd been fertile enough to impregnate her.

Paul wondered what would happen when Nero was no longer able to perform, and wondered whether the Colonel would entertain selling the foal back to him if it was a colt, and then he could continue with the same successful blood line.

Angelo had long since been sold, proving more trouble that he was worth, often managing to escape, and causing them all some moments of alarm when Nero was also out of his stable. Luckily he'd always been recaptured before he could cause any trouble, but everybody was afraid that the inevitable might one day happen, and Nero would probably come off worse, considering his elderly years. Two powerful horses of that size would probably be almost impossible to control if a fight were to take place.

He spoke to Jess about this, and they both decided it would be best to let Angelo go, and she persuaded him gently, but firmly, to give up the idea of a Shire stud.

It had long been his ambition, as he loved the Shire horses with their usually placid and amenable nature, but realised the sense in what she was saying. They still only served four or five mares a year that were brought to them, and without the stallions, they would be able to offer another four stables for livery. A venture which brought in far more regular money than the occasional stud fees ever had, although it would never be what he really wanted to do.

The death of Krista some four weeks later reinforced her argument, and he brought Nero into the stable next to the house which she'd once occupied, allowing him to live out the rest of his days without hindrance.

He already had another two studs booked for him; which he fulfilled with his usual vigour, but the second one didn't produce a foal, and Paul, under Jess's guidance, declined any further applications for stud, explaining that the stallion was now elderly and losing his fertility.

With a little alteration to the stallions' stables, they were able to offer another four liveries, which, once advertised, were occupied within the first week, and Paul managed to pay the rest of the loan back to his father within just a few months.

CHAPTER 28

The following year was to prove a momentous one for all at the farm and the stables.

Des and Susan were married in the second week of April, on a gloriously warm, sunny Saturday.

Having already had the white wedding dress previously, she declared she didn't want to be married in white again. She felt it had been a bad omen on the first occasion, and didn't want a repetition of the disaster that had been.

Instead she wore a simple two piece suit in lilac silk with a tight little cinched-in waist, thanks to careful monitoring of her diet during the months since Christmas, and a wide brimmed hat in the same shade. She finished the whole outfit off with pale grey satins shoes and a grey fur stole around her shoulders.

Des was smart in a dark blue pin striped suit and white shirt, with a matching tie. Even though Susan wore high heels, he was still half a head taller than her.

Neither had any family attending, Susan still being adamant that she didn't want to see her parents ever again, and both Des's parents having been killed during the war.

His father, a tank gunner, was blown into oblivion by a land mine whilst travelling through France. His mother had been killed during the middle years of the war when the shelter she'd been inside had received a direct hit.

He and his brothers had been evacuated to Wales at the time and the couple they were staying with kept them on at the farm for the next few years until they were old enough to go out into the world and fend for themselves. Although they were happy to give them a home, they also expected them to help on the farm after school and in the holidays, which is where Des had gained his experience.

Communications had been so bad during the war years that neither of his parents knew of the others' death before being killed themselves.

The only close family he now had left were his two elder brothers, now running a chicken farm together.

They'd written a long letter wishing them well, and apologising for their non-appearance at the wedding. It seemed their small flock of chickens now amounted to over 1,000 birds, and they couldn't spare the time to come over. Not having seen them for over ten years, and having rarely heard from them, Des wasn't at all surprised.

The small congregation amounted to just a few friends and work colleagues, and Paul had offered to lay on a small celebration at the local pub as a wedding present, but they thanked him and declined. It seemed Des had already arranged to rent his uncle's cottage for a week, and they were anxious to be on their way to Scotland and settle in before it grew too dark.

Jess and Callum attended the service, and afterwards a very mysterious Callum said that he wanted to talk to her on the following day.

The next week was going to be busy with Susan missing, and Sunday was usually a busier day than most, as people spent more time with their horses at the weekend, but Paul and Nathan said they'd cover for her for a couple of hours in the afternoon.

Both seemed to know why he wanted to see her, but both were being very mysterious about it.

He picked her up at one o'clock and took her back to the farm, parking in the yard and walking her towards the cottage he'd been working on.

She was amazed when she saw how much work had been done to it. It even had a roof in place.

"Wherever did you get the time to do all this?" she asked, stepping inside and looking around.

"You forget that I finish my rounds most afternoons by three or four o'clock and I don't see you until after seven. That means I have several hours every day to work on it, and I've also had help from my father and others on the farm when they weren't too busy. Sometimes they've worked on it all day for me when the weather's been too bad to do anything in the fields."

She looked around with new eyes at the interior as he pointed out the layout.

"There'll be a small porch at the side with a stone flagged floor when we put it up, for coats and muddy boots," pointing to a marked out oblong in the dusty earth, "and that'll open straight into the living room. Look, you can see where the fireplace already is."

She went in through the opening; no door as yet in place. She could indeed see, as the chimney breast was already in place, disappearing through the ceiling and into the floor above.

"And that's where the stairs will be," he continued, pointing to a hole in the ceiling.

"There'll be two bedrooms above, and there's just enough room to squeeze in a small bathroom as well. All the latest mod cons for us!" he announced proudly.

There was a door at the side of the fireplace, and he took her hand and led her through, into another room of equal size to the first.

"This is the kitchen," he continued.

A sink had already been installed against the front wall, looking back down the track towards the farm, with two small brick walls on which it stood.

"There'll be a cupboard fitted into there for all the cleaning materials, and others alongside for dishes and food.

"The range is due to be delivered any day now, and that'll go against that wall," he said, indicating a brick plinth that had already been fitted into the floor to hold its weight, with a hole in the ceiling above for the flue.

"What's that door for?" she asked, indicating an opening between the sink and that where the range was to stand.

"That has yet to be built," he answered, "but when it is, it'll be a little sunroom, rather like a small greenhouse, for us to sit in on sunny days."

"Us?" she queried, turning back towards him. "Where do I figure in all this? It's your cottage!"

"Not for long I hope," he said, smiling, as he produced a box from his pocket. "Will you marry me Jess?"

Inside was a sapphire ring and he held the box out towards her.

"It was my mother's and I'd very much like you to have it."

She stood and stared, not knowing what to say.

"Don't you like it?" he asked, looking crestfallen. "I'll get you another if you don't."

"I think it's beautiful," she answered quietly.

"Won't your father be annoyed about you giving it to me?" she asked warily.

He smiled and shook his head.

"Dad knows that I wanted to ask you to marry me, and he's let me give it to you with his blessing."

She stood and stared.

"You still haven't answered me," he said, looking crestfallen. "I'd very much like an answer – one way or another!"

She took the box and looked at it for a few seconds before removing the ring from it and slipping it onto the third finger of her left hand.

"Is that enough answer for you?" she said, smiling.

"Thank you, Jess, I've wanted to ask you for so long, but until I knew I could give you the home you deserve, I didn't dare say anything."

Putting his arm around her, he swept his other hand around the room.

"I hope my wife-to-be approves of her new home-to-be."

"She very much does," she laughed, looking down at her ring and touching it reverently. "And she very much approves of the beautiful ring as well."

Suddenly they heard the sound of clapping outside, and looking through the window frame, which as yet contained no glass, she saw Frank and Maura standing there, having just walked up from the house.

"I take it she said yes," Frank asked, grinning from ear to ear, to which they both added a resounding "yes".

"Come down to the house when you've finished here. We have a bottle of Champagne on ice to celebrate your engagement. It'll be wonderful having you both living so close," Frank said.

He was so glad Callum was going to stay on the farm. Having lost Alison, he was the one thing left in his life that he didn't want to lose, and hoped one day to be able to leave the farm to him.

A week later, when Des and Susan returned, they moved straight into their new cottage.

Des had found it for rent over a month ago, having previously looked at a couple which neither of them liked very much, or which weren't suitable. Suddenly, out of the blue, he'd received a letter from the letting agent they'd previously consulted. It said that this one was about to become vacant, and they viewed it straight away, both declaring it was absolutely perfect.

It was partly furnished and they spent time browsing the second hand shops for pieces with which to continue furnishing it, both insisting it had to be a brand new bed. Neither of them could countenance sleeping in somebody else's bed, especially when they found out the previous tenant had just died. That was why the cottage had suddenly become vacant, after he and his deceased wife had lived there for over twenty years. They were pleased to hear he'd died in hospital and not in the cottage.

It had a tiny little garden at the front, and a better sized one at the back, both very neglected; but it gave a nice aspect out over farm fields at the back. They both decided it could quickly be whipped back into shape with a bit of hard work.

Although Des had his car, work was within walking distance for him, so he didn't need to use it for that, but Susan still had to get to work over two miles away, insisting on staying on at work for the time being as she enjoyed it so much. She nearly added, 'until the babies come along', but decided that was better left unsaid so soon after their marriage. It was something neither of them had ever discussed, and she wondered if it wasn't high on Des's agenda, but then, she wasn't sure if she wanted children herself at this moment in time.

Des bought her a bicycle, which she enjoyed riding, so was easily able to get to work and back, although it was a bit tedious when it was raining.

She and Jess both shared the flat during the daytime, eating their meals together, but Jess found herself missing her company in the evenings, and especially the times when they'd shared their cocoa and a heart to heart before bedtime.

Callum often worked until late on the cottage on the long, light, summer evenings that followed. She knew the work he put in was bringing their wedding closer, and often went over to help him where she could, but there wasn't often a lot for her to do, and there were always others around helping him out. She found just sitting and watching could be boring, and sometimes chilly, so often took to staying in the flat and waiting for him in the evenings. He always came over and spent some time with her after the light began to fade and he could no longer work, but didn't stay for very long. He was always tired these days, and the work of loading his lorry for deliveries called for an early start.

"How about a spring wedding, like Des and Susan had?" he mused one day towards the end of the summer. "The cottage should be well finished by then."

She agreed. It was a perfect time for a wedding, and would give them plenty of time to paint and furnish it during the winter months.

Susan had already agreed to make all the curtains for her.

They approached the minister in the little parish church, and a date was set for the second week in April, the same week that Des and Susan had married, which spurred Callum on even more with his efforts to finish the cottage well in advance. He managed it just before Christmas, and they all celebrated together in the big farmhouse with Frank and Maura.

The new shop they were building near the gate gave much more access for the parking of cars in the front and side of it, and would help passing trade enormously.

Maura had been visiting local bakeries and dairies to ask them to supply their goods, and had had some very favourable answers, although the financial side of the deals would be left until after the shop was finished and she could see how much room needed to be allocated for each product. She wanted to be able to display a good range of everything without the shop appearing too crammed, and she wanted an assurance of a continuation of supply within a reasonable time.

Several women came forward to say they made their own jams and chutneys, and would be only too happy to supply her, but she had to be careful. Regulations had to be adhered to when it came to selling products from the shop to the general public, and she had to decline their offers.

She'd decided she would run the shop herself, with just one assistant, taking on more in the future if necessary, and Callum had begun to make it clear to Jess that he hoped she might become Maura's first assistant.

She wasn't opposed to the idea; in fact, she quite liked the prospect of working there with regular hours and not having her work spread out at irregular intervals throughout the whole day.

She would also be only a short walk from her new home, but she worried about how Paul would cope without her, and Nero was also a big consideration for her.

He wasn't her horse, even though she felt he was, and as he was now in his twenties, she was loathe to leave him for anybody else to look after. She wondered whether he'd feel abandoned, and would pine to death because of it, not realising that events were about to take another unexpected turn.

CHAPTER 29

It was just before Jess's wedding that Paul had an unexpected telephone call from Colonel Fitzpatrick. It seemed his mare had been delivered of a beautiful filly foal, ginger with white feathering, exactly like her sire. He invited him up to see her.

"Couldn't be more pleased with her!" he enthused. "Beautiful little filly! Haven't seen your stallion myself, but my daughter says she's the image of him. You must come and see her – come and stay for the weekend and we'll show you our setup. You and my daughter could ride the fields together and she'll show you around!"

Wanting to see and become reacquainted with Aleisha once again, Paul agreed at once. He looked forward to being in her company much of the time and getting to know her properly.

Knowing his staff were capable of looking after the stables over a weekend, and could always telephone him if anything untoward happened, he entrusted the keys of his house to Jess. It was only a couple of hours drive back if anything should happen, and he had no qualms about leaving her in charge.

He left on Friday afternoon, but it wasn't a pleasant drive, as the day was cold and overcast, with a blustery wind blowing, and he was glad when he found 'The Manor', as the embellished name on either side of the high stone gateposts proclaimed. The tall wrought iron gates stood open, and he drove through into a tree lined drive turning away to his right, his view obscured by rhododendron bushes for most of the way.

After a couple of hundred yards, the rhododendrons petered out and gave way to a vision of rolling countryside on his left, looking down into a lush green valley, through which a wide river meandered. To his right, and facing out across the valley, stood the impressive manor house, stone built and undoubtedly a good few hundred years old. It was almost exactly what he'd pictured in his minds' eye.

As he stopped, taking in its facade, and wondering where to park, a figure pushing a wheelbarrow full of dead leaves and other long dead plant life appeared from the opposite side of the house and walked across the manicured front lawn towards him.

"You come to see the Colonel?" he inquired, taking a red and blue checked handkerchief from his pocket and removing an aged looked cap in order to mop his forehead and practically bald head.

"Yes, I have," he replied. "Where shall I park?"

"You'll find a covered shelter round back," he answered, indicating the nearest side of the house. "There should be plenty of room for you there, but don't park too near the Colonel's Bentley. He don't like nobody parking near it! Knock at the back door when you're ready and one of the servants will let you in."

There was room under the roofed area to park several cars, but as the Colonel's Bentley was the only one present at the time, he parked right at the far end, so as not to fall foul of anybody else who might need a parking space.

Removing his suitcase, he walked across the gravelled yard and rapped on the back door.

He heard footsteps within, loud on what sounded like a stone flagged floor, before the door was opened by a woman of indeterminate age, but definitely not elderly.

She wore a plain black skirt and a black polo necked jumper, and her smile was friendly as she opened the door.

"You must be Paul!" she said, as he nodded, and she stood back to allow him entry. "Do come in. We've been expecting you."

Once he stepped inside, she extended her hand and introduced herself.

"I believe you've already met Aleisha. I'm her elder sister, Annabelle, but everybody calls me Belle. Please feel free to do so yourself."

He followed her along the stone flagged passage and through a door at the end, on the way passing a kitchen to the right where three people were working busily inside.

The door led into a wood panelled hallway, with a solid looking carved wooden staircase against the opposite wall. Double lead lighted doors to their left looked out onto the lawn at the front.

"That's daddy's study," she said, pointing to a door on their right, but I'll take you to your room first and you can unpack and settle yourself in before dinner. I'll call back in about half an hour and take you to him. He'll probably offer you a drink before dinner."

The room to which she showed him was on the second floor, and its wide dormer window looked out onto the front lawn, across which the gardener was now returning with his wheelbarrow.

Beyond the lawn was a lovely view across the valley and into the far distance, until the land became just a distant blur with the sky.

It wasn't a big room, but big enough for his needs, with a large four poster bed against the wall opposite the window, a chest of drawers for his clothes, and a small wardrobe, with two comfortable armchairs facing out through the window.

He quickly unpacked his clothes and went into the small bathroom adjacent where he had a quick wash and brush up. He'd only just finished before there was a light tap on the door.

"Are you ready?" Belle's voice called.

He opened the door immediately and followed her down the stairs, where she showed him into the Colonel's study and, after introducing him, left them alone.

The Colonel rose from his desk and came to greet him, shaking hands vigorously.

He wasn't a be-whiskered elderly gentleman as Paul had pictured him, but a tall and erect man, clean-shaven and with thick salt and pepper coloured hair. He couldn't have been much more than sixty.

"Nice to meet you in the flesh, so to speak," he said, smiling surreptitiously. "Can I get you a brandy? Or perhaps a whisky if you prefer?"

"A small brandy will do me fine," Paul answered.

The Colonel opened a drinks cupboard against a side wall and poured him a generous measure. Never very much of a drinker, Paul wasn't sure he'd be able to manage it all, but out of politeness felt he had to.

He decided to refuse if it was offered again over the weekend.

They exchanged pleasantries before a gong sounded in the hall, and the Colonel ushered him into the dining room through a door below the stairs, where be found Belle and her husband, whom he was introduced to as Andrew, already seated at the table.

After a few moments conversation, the Colonel started looking towards the door.

"Where's Aleisha? She should be here by now. Didn't she hear the gong?" he asked irritably.

Paul turned and also looked hopefully towards the door. He was surprised how anxious he was to see her again.

"She won't be long," Belle informed him. "She was out on one of the horses and it threw a shoe, so she had to walk him back. She said if she didn't show for dinner, she'd get something later in the kitchen."

Paul hid his disappointment and ate the three course meal with relish. Surprising how hungry he was, even though he'd stopped and bought a sandwich at a pub on the way up!

After the meal, Belle and Andrew said they were going to see friends that evening and gave their apologies, leaving him alone with the Colonel. They talked for a while, but he found the conversation quite boring, as he spoke a lot about his army life, and kept trying to ply him with more drink, downing another three large brandies by himself when Paul refused.

Feigning tiredness, Paul asked to be excused at nine o'clock and went back to his room, disappointed that he hadn't yet seen Aleisha. Maybe she wasn't as anxious to see him as he was to see her!

He was sitting in bed reading about half an hour later when there was a light tap on his door.

"Are you decent?" a voice called, and without waiting for an answer it was opened to admit Aleisha.

She came and sat on the edge of the bed and quickly gave her apologies for not being there to greet him. It seemed she'd had to wait for the farrier before she was able to bed the horse down for the night, and he had already been out on another call.

"Anyway, I'm all yours for the rest of the weekend. I've not made any other plans at all," she informed him. "I'll take you to see the foal straight after breakfast, and then we'll saddle up a couple of horses and spend the day out riding. I know a nice little pub where we can get a decent lunch."

The Colonel walked over to the stables with them the next morning, eager to show off the foal, which turned out to be as good as he'd had intimated, and did indeed look very like Nero. She was a stocky little thing, and even though the mare tried to shield her from them, she still by-passed her and came over to greet them in a very friendly and inquisitive way.

"I've already had two offers to buy her," he crowed, "but she's going to head my next generation of breeding stock. No way am I selling this little beauty!"

When he'd left them, they tacked up, Aleisha saddling a quiet bay gelding for him, and her own grey mare for herself, before they set off to explore the property. When they'd covered the full eighty acres, she turned their path along a bridleway skirting the fields and they followed it down into the valley, where the village nestled alongside the river, and they enjoyed an excellent lunch.

The afternoon they spent on a quiet walk alongside the river, and finally turned back uphill, returning to the Manor by a circuitous route; entering through the front gates this time.

The day had gone so quickly as they talked incessantly, and he knew by the end of it that he couldn't part from her after the weekend without seeing her again, and he knew instinctively that she felt the same.

The next morning, she said that they'd rest the horses that day and go for a long walk after lunch, but first her father wanted to see him in his study.

He knocked at the door before entering, expecting another boring chat with him, but what the Colonel had to say was something he'd never expected, and something that would change the course of his life.

The Colonel was sitting by the fireplace with a glass of brandy alongside, and the Sunday newspaper on his lap. He folded and put it down on a side table when Paul entered, and indicated for him to sit in the chair opposite, starting into what he had to say immediately.

"That horse of yours has produced such a lovely filly – she'll do me proud in a few years, and I'd like to keep using that blood line."

Paul, thinking he was about to propose another stud for Nero, began to explain that he was no longer using the stallion, but the Colonel interrupted him immediately.

"Goddam it man," he stated, "it's not the horse I want – it's you! I want you to come and be my stable manager and oversee the breeding programme!"

Paul stopped in mid-sentence and stared at him, at a loss for words.

"But what about Mr. Grimble?" he finally said.

"Sacked him ages ago! Heard rumours from the stable lads about him being none too kind to the horses and caught him myself whipping one of the mares with a crop. Sacked him on the spot!"

He didn't know what to say. It was certainly an exciting prospect, and one that he very much relished. He still held the ambition to breed the beautiful Shires and knew that the livery yard would only ever be a second best option, something to earn a profit and give him a living, but not what he really wanted to do.

Before he'd really had time to think about it, the Colonel started speaking again.

"If you're thinking about your livery yard, I already know somebody who'd be quite happy to buy it from you. He's been looking for one for years, but never found one suitable enough. My daughter assures me yours is the perfect prospect for him, and he doesn't live very far from where you are at the moment; in fact, his daughter already has a horse stabled with you. I haven't spoken to him yet, but as soon as you make up your mind, I'll get in touch with him straight away.

I'll leave it for you to think over, but don't leave it too long. I could do with someone pretty sharpish. There's only my daughter and the two stable lads looking after the horses at the moment."

With that, he picked up his paper and took a swig of his drink.

"Well, go on man, what are you waiting for! I thought you and my daughter were going out. She'll be waiting for you!" he said, before opening the newspaper and burying his head in it once more.

Paul's head was spinning as he left the study. It was what he'd always dreamed of.

A breeding programme left solely for him to run, with four mares already in their prime, and another young up and coming filly for the future. There'd be no overheads for him to worry about. The Colonel would be footing all the bills, and he'd be able to see Aleisha all the time. What more could he want?

During the following week he thought long and hard about the offer. He was excited by the idea, but worried as to what would happen to Jess and Susan, who would possibly lose their jobs. Susan wasn't so bad, as she already had a husband to support her, but what would happen to Jess?

She hadn't yet told him about her engagement to Callum, Susan being the only one she'd told, and hadn't been wearing her ring at work, keeping it on a silver chain around her neck whilst working.

Knowing the Colonel was anxious for an answer; he called both girls and Nathan into the office on Friday afternoon, and explained the position to them, and the dilemma it had left him in. He told them he very much wanted to take up the offer, as it was something he'd always wanted to do, but he was worried about whether they'd have a job under the new ownership.

Instead of being anxious, he was surprised when the two girls looked at each other and grinned, Jess being the first to speak.

"That's solved everybody's problems then," she explained. "I've become engaged to Callum and he's renovated a cottage on the farm for us to live in after the wedding. Frank is also building a new and bigger farm shop by the main road, and I've been asked to help run it with Maura, but I've been worried about leaving you in the lurch."

When she'd finished, she turned to Susan, an expectant look on her face, who excitedly broke in with her own news.

"I've just discovered I'm pregnant, so I won't be able to work for you much longer either," eliciting enthusiastic congratulations from them all, although Jess had already known since the beginning of the week.

Nathan was the only one with no prospects and looked a bit crestfallen.

"Things is easing up a bit with jobs these days. If they don't keep me on, I reckon I'll find another job in time," then a bit more brightly, "but good workers are hard to come by, so if you write me a good reference, happen they might keep me on here. New boss is gonna' need a good worker anyway with the girls gone."

Another problem came into Jess's mind at that moment.

"What's to happen to Nero? You're not going to sell him, are you? He's far too old to go to a new home now."

"I've already been worrying about that," Paul replied. "He's too old for stud any more, and the Colonel probably won't want a horse that can't be of any use. He's always been your horse more than he's ever been mine anyway, so if you've room for him at the farm he can go with you. He's yours from now on."

Jess was overjoyed, and asked Callum if he could leave work on the cottage that evening as she wanted to talk to Frank and Maura, and wanted to include him in what she had to say.

When she'd finished telling them all that had gone on that day at the stables, and that Paul wanted her to have Nero, Frank answered without hesitation.

"Of course you can bring Nero here. There's a small paddock alongside the new shop. I was going to leave it fallow for the time being in case passing trade increased and we needed to enlarge the parking area. It'd be the perfect place to keep him where you could keep an eye on him during the day, and Callum could build a small loose box for him in a corner where it's sheltered by the trees."

She was overjoyed by his reaction and hugged him; thanking him for his understanding.

"Nero and I have been together for so long now. We have a special bond between us and I really didn't want him to have to go to anybody else at his advanced age. Now I'll be on hand to see him through his last years."

Her face told its own story, and Frank was really glad that he'd been able to grant her wish.

Paul's problems now at an end, there was nothing to stop him fulfilling his lifelong ambition and taking up the Colonel's job offer. He 'phoned him the very next day and accepted, whilst the Colonel said he'd get in touch with his friend and make sure he was still interested in buying the stables.

An hour later, the Colonel 'phoned him back and said his friend was delighted, and would come over the next day to see him and go over the details; also giving him his 'phone number so they could make their arrangements.

Paul 'phoned him immediately, and it seemed the man, Jacob Braithwaite, lived less than twenty minutes drive away, on the outskirts of Southport, and he agreed that Sunday was also a good day for him to discuss the details.

Jacob, a florid faced Yorkshire man, appearing to be in his late forties, and looking well used to the outdoor life, arrived with his two teenage daughters to find the yard buzzing with activity.

He seemed impressed with the setup and the amount of customers coming and going all the time, and also with the amount of feed being sold. Paul showed him around while the girls attended to the clientele, pleased that he'd seen it during one of the busiest periods they'd ever had.

Eventually, Paul took him back to look around the house, where Jess and Susan had set up sandwiches, cake and biscuits for them before they left. Afterwards, the girls went back out to the yard while Paul and Jacob talked figures, and Paul was surprised how much he was willing to pay for the property. It was way in excess of what he'd expected, and they shook hands on the deal before he collected the girls and they eventually left late in the afternoon.

Having already cleared the debt to his father, he was left with just a small mortgage, which was less than half the price he was to receive for the property, and would leave him comfortably off for the future.

He rang the Colonel that night to tell him of the deal and everything seemed set for a bright future for all involved. Aleisha was also delighted when he spoke to her after finishing his conversation with her father.

A couple of months later he was on his way to the little cottage in the grounds of The Manor which had once been occupied by Robert Grimble. He was looking forward to a future with his beloved horses, and also with Aleisha.

He was now going to be able to do what he'd always wanted to do, and he'd no longer have to worry about money ever again.

CHAPTER 30

The new farm shop was opened on a Saturday morning, both that and Sunday being the days they found busiest for sales, especially with the passing trade going for days out around Southport.

Maura and Jess had checked it over and over the previous day, making sure everything was in order, and laid out just as they'd envisaged it. They arrived at 8a.m. to watch Frank and Callum pinning up a banner above the entrance:

LACEY'S FARM SHOP
NEW SHOP NOW OPEN

It wasn't large or ostentatious, but prominent enough to catch the attention of passing traffic, and could also be seen by anyone entering or leaving the new estate opposite, nearly all the houses being occupied by now.

Standing back and admiring their handiwork, Frank felt a pang of sadness that it wasn't Alison here to see the success of the business she'd been instrumental in getting started. Tears sprang to his eyes, but were quickly dashed away before anyone should notice.

Maura, perhaps sensing his emotional state, came over and linked arms with him, as they looked up at the sign; at the same time as their first customer pulled into the new parking area.

Signalling to Jess, they went inside and prepared to serve their first customer, and after that the day flew by. They'd had a telephone extension linked to the 'phone in the house, and had to ring back occasionally for more stock to be brought down during the day, Callum on one occasion staying to help out as they seemed so busy.

As it was a fine and very warm weekend, it was mainly salad items they were selling out of, although there were plenty of tomatoes, lettuce and cucumbers in the new greenhouse to keep up with demand, and by the end of the weekend, Frank decided that they may need to either extend the old one, or buy a much larger one and keep both going. However, before he decided on such an expense, it would be better to see how things went during the rest of the year.

There wouldn't be so much fresh produce to sell during the winter time, mainly just root vegetables and a few brassicas. Sales then would mostly be based on bread and cakes, plus tinned items and jars of jams and chutneys, but they didn't envisage too much drop in trade.

Several weeks later, Jess was sitting on a seat at the side of the shop eating her lunch, sharing tasty bits of apple and carrot with Nero, who was leaning over the fence and watching her expectantly, when she heard a shout from inside.

"Can you come and help please Jess? It's starting to get busy here."

Handing Nero the remains of the carrot, she put her own dish down on the seat and covered it with a plate whilst she went inside. With a bit of luck she'd be able to finish it later when the rush was over.

Once it quietened down, Maura went into the small office cum storeroom at the back to have her own lunch, and Jess finished hers off sitting at the counter, after which she walked round and began to tidy shelves. It was surprising how untidy things became when customers were rooting through them, never thinking to put them back as they'd found them.

As she was finishing off, she heard the shop bell jangle and returned to the counter, to find a young woman standing there.

"Hello," she greeted Jess, extending a hand to shake hers, "my name's Gaynor Roberts, and I represent Roberts' Bakery. I saw your new shop was open, and I thought you might be interested in trying out our bread and cakes."

"I'm afraid that's not my decision to make, but I'll go and fetch the owner if she's finished her lunch. Would you wait a moment please."

Going into the office, she found Maura had finished and was just drinking a cup of tea whilst leafing through a newspaper.

"There's a lady here to see you from Roberts's Bakery. She wondered if you'd like to try their products."

She knew Maura wasn't that pleased with the products they were already having delivered from a bakery in Southport, some customers having commented that the bread was often dry and tasteless, as was the pastry, and knew she'd be pleased to try out another supplier. Maura put her cup in the sink and followed Jess back to the shop.

The young woman was browsing the shelves, particularly round the bread and cakes section when they returned, and had her back to them, as Maura walked across to speak to her.

"Hello," she said, "I'm Maura Lacey, and I'm the owner here."

The young woman swivelled round instantly, stepping backwards as she did so, and almost knocking over a stand full of biscuits.

The two women stared at each other, before Jess heard her gasp, "Mum?"

Maura too was staring, her mouth agape.

"Gaynor?" she exclaimed in a hoarse whisper. "Gaynor? It is you, isn't it?"

The young woman nodded, and suddenly they were in each others' arms, hugging, laughing and crying all at the same time.

"Oh mum," Gaynor cried, "I've been trying to find you for so long, I thought you must have been killed when I went back to the house and found it had been bombed."

Just then, more customers started coming into the shop, and Maura ushered her daughter into the office where they could talk without interruption.

Sitting her down and making some more tea, Maura explained how she'd been bombed out, and how she'd been re-housed in a pre-fab across the road. She also explained, trying to be as gentle as she could, that her father had been killed by the bomb whilst she was visiting a friend.

This didn't hit Gaynor quite so hard as she thought it might.

It seemed she'd visited the local police station, who had a list of the dead, but her mothers' name wasn't on it. They told her the list wasn't always complete, but she'd gone on hoping to find her mother still alive.

Maura explained cautiously about meeting Frank and marrying him, skimming over the details for the time being, not knowing how she'd react, but Gaynor seemed to be pleased that she'd found someone else.

Further explanations could wait until the evening.

"And what about you?" Maura finally asked, as she poured them both more tea. "I thought you were with that gypsy?"

"I was for a few years, but then I found the constant wandering around and never having a permanent home was becoming too much, so that's when I came home and found the house had been bombed out."

Maura nodded, anxious to hear more.

"What happened after that?"

"I had nowhere to go; no money; no home; nothing; so I decided to join the Land Army, and I worked on a farm in Shropshire for most of the war.

When it was disbanded, I came back to Liverpool. I'd still had no confirmation that you were dead, so I wanted to keep looking.

I got a job delivering milk at first, but I had to be up at 5a.m., and you know me, I never liked getting up early, so that didn't last long. Then I found a job in a bakery – Roberts's Bakery. I worked in the shop for a year, and it was a job I really liked.

The owner's son, Michael, was away at Agricultural College when I started there, but when he finished, he came to help out with the bakery while he was looking for a job, and that's when we first started seeing each other.

To cut a very long story short, Michael and I finally got married, and his father decided to open another bakery near Southport, offering Michael the job of running it. While he's doing all the baking, I'm visiting local shops and trying to drum up trade for the new outlet, and it seems to be going very well so far."

Ever the saleswoman, she continued enthusiastically, before Maura could speak. "I hope you're going to give us a try; I'm sure you'll find the bread and cakes are excellent. Michael's a really good baker!"

"Of course I will. I'm not too happy with my present supplier anyway," Maura laughed, and then continued, more seriously this time. "And what about children? Do I have any grandchildren?"

"Not yet. We've only been married a short while, and I want to help Michael get things up and running before we even think about kids."

"And do you live near here then?" Maura asked hopefully.

"You won't believe this," she laughed, "but we live this side of Southport. We have done for the last eighteen months – right on each others' doorsteps without even knowing it. It's only four or five miles from here. I was just on my way back to the shop to drop off the few samples I still have left before going home, when I spotted your sign outside. I've passed here so many times, but I thought you only sold fruit and veg. I can leave leave all my samples with you now. See if you can sell them this afternoon, and do try them yourselves. I'm sure you'll enjoy them."

Just then the door opened and Jess's head popped round.

"Sorry to have to break this up, but there's a lot of people in the shop and I can't manage on my own."

Maura didn't want to leave things as they were, with so much as yet unsaid, but Gaynor jumped up immediately.

"I'll go and bring the samples in for you, and then I'll head off. I've another call to make anyway, but I'll come back to your home tonight and we can talk more freely."

"That would be lovely. I'm sure my husband Frank would be pleased to meet you. He has a son too, Callum, and he's engaged to Jess, the girl you met in the shop.

If you follow the track up past the shop, we live in the farmhouse at the end."

Maura was bursting with joy all afternoon, and when they broke for a tea break in a quiet moment, she said to Jess, "Did you like Gaynor?"

"I didn't really have time to get to know her, but she seemed nice enough," Jess replied.

"I've been thinking while we've been working. She'll be Callum's step sister; which also makes her your step-sister-in-law," at which they both laughed, suddenly being brought back to earth by a loud whinny from Nero.

"I guess he wants a carrot for his tea break too. He can't abide missing out on the action!"

Jess, too, had a reunion in her own life a few weeks later, when, returning from the shop after work, she saw a car parked in the farmyard; Callum and Frank leaning on the roof and talking to someone inside.

He looked a little embarrassed when he saw Jess approaching, but it was too late to avoid the inevitable introduction.

"Hi Jess," he said, "this is an . . . a friend of mine. She was just passing and she thought she'd call in to see how we're all doing."

Jess herself felt none too pleased, guessing he'd been going to say 'an old girlfriend', and prepared to give her the cold shoulder, say a peremptory 'hello' and keep on walking, but just as she reached them, the car door opened and the girl stepped out.

300

Jess was a little taken aback at how forward she appeared, and perhaps a little tarty, until she suddenly realised the girl seemed very familiar, and she took a closer look.

"Gina?" she queried.

Her sister looked very different from when she'd last seen her. She used to be skinny with long black hair; now she was a head taller and she'd filled out, with curves in all the right places, and short cropped hair with ear piercings, sporting long dangling hoops from them.

"Jess?"

They stood looking at one another for some time before Frank suddenly declared, "I knew she looked familiar. From the day I first met her on our wedding day I knew there was something about her I recognised. I said so to Maura, but I couldn't place her. Now I know why!"

And so there were two reunions at the farm; one at the farmhouse with Maura and her daughter, who brought her husband Michael along with her to meet them, and another at the cottage, between Jess and Gina; Callum sitting in the background and listening to their girlie chatter until he became bored and took himself off to bed.

CHAPTER 31

Susan had left the stables on the same day as the new owner arrived. He and his daughter had spent a couple of days going over the routine with both her and Nathan during her last week, and she was sad to leave; but even more pleased when she heard they'd decided to keep Nathan on.

It was now four months since leaving the stables and she was walking home from the village shop in the rain. Heavily pregnant, her mackintosh no longer fitted her very well and she had to grip it together at the front, only having one hand to hold it. In the other she held a whicker basket, heavy with the items she'd just bought, and her skirt was becoming very wet and heavy against her legs.

Putting her basket down at the side of the road, already covered by a piece of plastic, she felt she had to sit down for a while, rain or no rain, and she hitched herself up onto a low stone wall under a tree and enjoyed the rest. After a while, the rain began to ease off and she decided to continue back home and enjoy a nice hot bath before changing her, by now, very wet clothes.

Once she and Des had got over the shock of her unexpected pregnancy, they were both overjoyed by it, and Des told her to stay at home from now on and rest.

He was very concerned for her welfare, and wanted to give her and the baby the best care he was able to.

The cottage only had two bedrooms, but the second one was big enough for a child, although they already knew that if any more came along, they'd have to find somewhere bigger.

Susan spent quite a bit of time at the farm shop now that it was up and running, buying her fresh produce and having long chats with Jess, who now lived in the farmhouse with Frank and Maura until after her wedding. Callum, the cottage now finished, was already living in it, where he and Jess spent most of their free time, the two couples often socialising together of an evening or at weekends.

Heaving her bulky figure down from the wall, and getting her balance before picking the basket up, she heard a speeding car coming up the road from behind her. Moving into the hedge as close as she could, and out of the roadway, the car swept past, throwing a great deal of water over her as it ploughed through a deep puddle.

Angrily, she stared after it. Not only was she wet from the rain, she was now literally dripping from head to toe, water running from her hair and down into her eyes.

Her glare suddenly turned to fear as she looked after the receding vehicle.

The car was exactly the same make and colour as Matthew's! Was it him? Had he recognised her?

Going through the puddle like that would be just his way of getting his own back on her!

She was just about to turn into the lane where they lived, but she stood on the corner, waiting to see if the car returned. It was unlikely he knew exactly where she was living, but as the lane was only short, and there were only three cottages along it, it wouldn't take much effort to find out which one was theirs.

She waited five minutes, but the car didn't return, and she quickly made her way back to the cottage, standing for a further few minutes in the cover of a holly bush by the gate to make sure there was nobody watching from the end of the lane.

Once inside, she changed her clothes, and spent most of the day brooding whether Matthew had found her again.

Had he been passing by chance? Had he recognised her? She hoped that if it was him, he mightn't have recognised her, trussed up as she was in the heavy black cape – one of Des's, as she hadn't been able to fit into her own any more. Did he know she was living here, and was he about to reap his vengeance on her once more?

But she need have no further worries on that score!

After the incident at the stables with Susan, Matthew had realised that either Des or Paul would only need the slightest excuse to lay into him again, and he had left as soon as he was able. He'd seen Paul standing by the gate watching his departure until the car was out of sight.

However, it wasn't only his nose that had been broken when Des had hit him. As he drove along the road, dabbing frequently at it with his handkerchief, he began to find the sight in his right eye becoming fuzzy and blurred. Blinking rapidly to try and clear it didn't seem to help, and it began to get worse, until he could hardly see out of that eye at all.

Already deciding to pull over and check it when he had a straight stretch of road ahead, he failed to see the tractor coming round the sharp right hand bend ahead until it was almost on top of him.

Veering wildly to the left he missed it by inches, expecting to be struck any minute by one of its overhanging pieces of equipment. He closed his eyes in anticipation, only opening them again when he realised it had passed him by unscathed. He'd heard angry words shouted at him by the driver, but in his wild panic to get out of the way, they were unintelligible to him.

Heaving a sigh of relief and opening his eyes once more, it was only at the last minute that he realised he was on the grass verge, and careering into the bend far too fast.

A large oak tree stood at the side of the road, only coming into his line of vision as he slalomed into the bend, tyres squealing wildly as they vainly tried to grip the road, but far too late for him to avoid it.

The steering wheel already hard over to the right, he hit it a glancing blow with the left hand side of the car, and fractions of a second later, he felt himself flying through the air. The car tumbled turned over as it ploughed through the hedge ahead and rolled over and over down an embankment, finally dropping many feet into the river below and landing on its roof.

Being thrown around the interior of the car during the descent, he was disorientated, and before he could come to his senses and make any attempt to scramble out, the car had sunk below the surface, disappearing into the murky depths below.

When he didn't return home either that day or the next, his wife became worried and asked the police for help to find him, but as he hadn't told her or anyone else where he was going, they had no idea where to start looking for him.

There was an appeal put out in the papers for any information as to his whereabouts, which Des and Paul both saw, but after a hurried 'phone call between them, they both decided not to say anything.

"It's best we say nothing about his visit. If anything has happened to him, there could a lot of awkward questions asked. Best let things lie and say nothing!" was Paul's adamant reply.

They both knew that Susan and Jess would never say what had happened on that day either.

It was many years later, when the rapidly silting river was dredged in a routine operation, that his car was found – with the gruesome skeletal remains still inside.

Any injuries they found on his body were put down to the crash, and no further inquiries were made; the police closing their already dormant files on the matter.

It was put down to a lapse of concentration by the driver, resulting in an accidental death, and the truth of what had happened leading up to his death lay buried forever.

Printed in Great Britain
by Amazon

80146768R00180